LASSITER WILLIAMS

THE RAGE

REGENT STREET PRESS
Philadelphia, Pennsylvania

FOR ANNY AND KIM

First paperback edition 2019

Cover and interior design by TLC Book Design
TLCBookDesign.com
Cover: Tamara Dever, Interior: Erin Stark

ISBN: 978-1-7337386-1-3 Paperback
ISBN: 978-1-7337386 Ebook

REGENT STREET PRESS
Philadelphia
RegentStreetPress.com

Character List

NEW MURIANS:

Tribulation, also known as Trib, Flame Hair

Cuss, apprentice warrior

Heresy, warrior officer

Scath, also known as Bear Woman, head warrior, sister to Aoifa

Aoifa, also known as Crow Woman, Head Priestess

Jezebel, warrior

Morrigan, priestess, survivor

TRIB'S FAMILY:

Sarah, mother

Mary, sister

Crucible, sister

Sorrow, sister

Calvary, sister

THE ORIGINAL PEOPLE:

Peyewik, 12-year-old seer

Chingwe, Peyewik's best friend

Muhkrentharne, healer, Peyewik's grandfather

Menukan, wise elder woman

Okahoki, chief

Manichikum, old man of village

THE AWAY PEOPLE:

Kwineechka, storyteller

Nitis, Kwineechka's father

Shikiwi, Kwineechka's mother

Mikwin, chief

Nichan, Kwineechka's aunt

Hinutet, Kwineechka's wife

NIshingi and Nikismus, brother hunters

Kinteka, young fighter

PURITANICS:

Sky Eyes, Peyewik's attacker

Reverend Edward Wilson

John Green, also known as Jongren

Josiah, young fighter

CHAPTER ONE

Trib

Stinking marsh mud dripped down the collar of Trib's waist-coat. The back of her head stung where the stone embedded in the glob of mud had struck. She pushed a strand of sodden red hair out of her eyes and turned around.

Eight mud-splattered figures moved into a semi-circle around her. All were armed with rough-hewn swords on their backs.

"Who threw the mudball?" Trib snarled.

A huge, barrel-shaped young woman stepped forward. "I did," she said, pulling her sword off her back. "What do you mean to do about it?"

Trib assessed her challenger. She had coarse black hair that stuck out in intimidating spikes all over her head. She wasn't much taller than Trib but looked at least 50 pounds heavier. Her wrists, where they extended beyond the threadbare cuffs of her waistcoat, were as thick as Trib's ankles, and she held the heavy sword as if it weighed nothing.

Sweat prickled under Trib's arms and slid down her back. The marsh air was hot and heavy, like breathing through wet wool. "I mean to do nothing," she said, turning away. "Ain't worth the effort."

There were grunts of disapproval from the semi-circle as it drew in tighter, blocking Trib's retreat.

"Coward," the huge girl muttered.

Trib spun around. "I ain't a coward!"

"Can't tell by looking at you," the girl taunted.

Trib locked eyes with her challenger and broke into a slow, gleeful grin. "Reckon I'll have to prove it to you then," she said, reaching back for her own sword.

The two blades met with a clash of metal that made Trib giddy. "What took you so long, Cuss?" she asked, stepping back for another swing. "I've been itching for a fight all day. I thought you'd never get around to starting something."

"Sorry, Trib," the other girl grunted, parrying the blow. "The master-warriors have been keeping too close an eye on us apprentices."

"Don't worry, Cuss," a voice called from the semi-circle. "The masters ain't paying us any mind right now. Kick Trib's ass!"

"Reckon we could switch to grappling, Trib?" Sweat poured down Cuss's face as she strained to fend off a series of blows.

"No way in hell," Trib replied. It was an accepted fact among the apprentices that Cuss was the best grappler. "Fisticuffs would suit, though," she said, tossing aside her sword and starting to bob and weave.

Cuss, whose feet were planted up to the ankles in the mud, raised her fists and laughed. "You dancing a jig or fighting?"

The other apprentices laughed with her.

Trib grimaced at her friend's idea of fisticuffs, which was to stand still and trade heavy blows until someone fell over. Cuss had the ideal warrior's frame, towering and bulky with thickly padded arms and haunches, just like the Scath, the head warrior of the New Murian settlement. Trib, in contrast, was lean and narrow with long, ropey muscles and often had to rely on speed and agility to make up for her lack of bulk in a fight. She ducked under one of Cuss's jaw-shattering swings and aimed a hook at her friend's kidneys.

"Tribulation!"

Distracted by the sound of her own name, Trib stopped weaving, allowing Cuss to sink a fist into her belly.

"Oof." Trib doubled over as the semi-circle of apprentices made way for one of the master-warriors, a young woman named Heresy.

"Tribulation! Cuss!" Heresy shouted. "What in the Goddess's Name do you think you're doing?!"

Trib and Cuss blinked at each other.

"Uh...fisticuffs?" Cuss guessed.

"Brawling like a couple of farmboys in a manure pile!" the warrior corrected her.

"We're just sparring," Trib mumbled. "It ain't like we're using the Rage on each other."

"Aye," Cuss chimed in. "There's nothing else to do in this 'Dess-damned place, and we warriors have to stay in shape, don't we?"

There was a rumble of agreement from the other apprentices.

"You ain't warriors yet," Heresy pointed out. "You may have passed your initiations, but just because you can summon a Rage doesn't mean you're ready to be a warrior. I know you're a favorite of the Scaths, Trib, but even you need some real battle experience before the Scath makes you a warrior."

"How are we supposed to get real battle experience down here, hauling gear for the priestesses, when all the fighting is back home in New Murias, against the Puritanics?" Cuss asked.

Heresy glanced towards the edge of the marsh, where five black-robed figures were clustered around a small table.

"The priestesses are doing something important, otherwise the Scath wouldn't have sent us here," she said.

"Crows give me the shivers," Cuss said, irreverently naming the priest-esses after the birds they resembled in their flapping black robes.

"Aye," Heresy agreed. "There's something unnatural about them. But it was their Goddess who gave us the Rage, and it was the Rage that gave us the strength to beat the Puritanics out of the settlement. Every New Murian owes them her freedom."

"I heard the crows are making a map," one of the apprentices spoke up.

Trib snorted. "Why would they want a map of this place? There are no people here, nothing but rivers and trees and animals."

"And bugs," Cuss said, slapping the back of her neck and flicking away the tiny carcass of whatever had bitten her.

"You ain't the only ones who'd rather be up north defending the settlement against Puritanic raiders," Heresy said, jerking a thumb over her shoulder at her fellow master-warriors. There were eight of them sprawled here and there on hummocks of grass, pipes lit to keep the bugs away. They all looked as hot and restless as Trib felt.

"But it ain't a warrior's place to question orders," Heresy continued. "And I'm ordering you to quit brawling like farmboys." She turned and rejoined the other masters.

"'Dess damn it," Trib muttered.

"Heresy got me thinking about farmboys," Cuss said, picking her sword up off the ground and strapping it onto her back. "It wouldn't be so bad down here if we had some of those around to sport with, eh, Trib?"

Trib, who was far more comfortable with brawling than with boys, gave a non-committal grunt in reply. "I need to piss," she said. She started towards a stand of reeds, stepping carefully as she crossed the marshy ground.

Cuss followed along. "If you could have any lad you wanted right now, what would it be? Farmhand, manservant...?"

Trib stopped, the hair on her neck suddenly standing up. She had seen something move among the reeds.

"Well?" Cuss asked, oblivious. "What would it be? I'm partial to farmhands myself. They're brawnier..."

"Shh!" Trib hissed. The reeds were still now, but she started turning in a slow circle, taking in as much information as she could. The closest warrior was over 200 yards away, lying with her head on her pack and the hood of her cloak pulled over her eyes. The rest were even farther away, in various attitudes of repose, with curls of dark smoke marking their positions. The marsh was oddly quiet. No birdsong, no buzzing insects. The surface of the standing water was perfectly still.

Then she heard it, a breezeless rustling, followed by the sound of squelching mud. She turned back to the reeds and discovered the source of the sound.

"Summon your Rage!" she shouted, leaping forward and plunging up to her knees in a bog pit. For a moment she felt nothing but foolish. Then the foolishness turned to fear as the dark mass she had seen among the reeds erupted with the sparks and reports of rifle-fire.

"Protect the priestesses!" she cried, clawing her way to solid ground. She could see the warriors already on their feet, swords drawn. Heresy was loading powder and shot into a pistol as fast as she could, but there was nothing to aim at but shadows. Nor was there anything to take cover behind.

A bloodcurdling shriek pierced Trib's eardrum and she saw that Cuss's face was crimson, her eyes bulging. The first Rage had been summoned.

"Watch the bog!" she warned.

But Cuss didn't hear her as she roared and lunged towards the attackers in the reeds. Trib watched helplessly as her friend, whose mind had taken on a singular focus, became mired in the mud. The superhuman strength of the Rage propelled her forward, but her movement was slowed, and she became an easy target at such close range. Trib could hear the musket balls thudding into her body. She didn't stop, but it was clear that when the Rage died so would Cuss. Ignoring the urge to throw up, Trib turned her attention to the attackers who were gaining confidence and leaving their hiding place.

There was no question, they were Puritanic. There were fifteen or twenty of them, malnourished, scarecrow figures in dark, tattered clothing. Trib had no time to stop and think. They were less than ten yards away. She yanked her sword from her back and fixed in her mind the steps it would take to get close enough without sinking. Then she closed her eyes and summoned her own Rage. The vibration started deep in her chest and raced like fire through her body, bursting from her throat in a hurricane roar. She opened her eyes on a blood-red world, the destructive power of nature singing in her veins.

The Puritanics didn't know what hit them. She tore into them like an animal. She had never used the Rage on humans before, only straw dummies and wild pigs, but it felt natural. The men around her moved slowly, ponderously, and she hacked away at them with ease. Their bodies seemed to present themselves for the slaughter, their throats exposed, their vitals unguarded. She heard other battle cries in the distance, and her Rage burned hotter. The warriors were coming and their combined fury would be crushing.

But then a ball of fire erupted before her eyes. She stopped, momentarily blinded. The ground beneath her feet heaved and she was thrown into the air before crashing back to earth and darkness.

CHAPTER TWO

Peyewik

*V*ulture circled on an updraft. The marsh below smelled of its
usual decay, but also of blood, and it made him hungry. He
swooped in low and saw human bodies. One was still alive.
It rose to its feet and staggered through the mud. Vulture had
never seen a human like this. Its face was pale, and its hair bright
like fire. It shouted and threw a rock at Vulture. Vulture wheeled
away. He would come back when he could feast in peace.

Peyewik awoke with the smell of death in his nose. He took a
breath of morning air, and the smell faded. He wanted to wake his
grandfather and tell him about the bad dream, but he knew Muhkrentharne would say it was a message from the spirits. Peyewik
didn't want to know what the spirit of carrion-eating Vulture was
trying to tell him, so he climbed out from under his bearskin quilt,
pulled on his leggings and shoes, and tiptoed across the cabin without disturbing the old man's snoring. He pushed through the doorflap and into the first light of day. Raising his arms, he began to sing
his morning prayer.

Manito, spirit of the sun, I thank you,
For chasing away the darkness once more,
and blessing your children with the light and warmth of day...

He felt better when his prayer was done. Normally he bathed in the river after praying, but today he was going fishing with his best friend Chingwe, and there would be lots of time for swimming later. He went back inside to put a pot of beans in the coals to warm for his grandfather's breakfast. Then he grabbed his fishing basket and set out to meet Chingwe in the woods on the other side of the village.

No one was stirring as Peyewik passed through the cluster of bark-covered houses that was the village of the Original People. He stifled a giggle when he came to the house of Old Man Chikinum. The old man was known for farting in his sleep loud enough to wake the neighbors. The game was to hold one's breath when passing his house, and keep holding it as long as possible. Peyewik held his all the way to the woods, where he let it out with a triumphant whoosh.

Chingwe was waiting for him among the trees. His hair was still messy from sleep, and he was fidgeting impatiently.

"Hurry," he said, taking Peyewik's arm and pulling him towards the river.

"Why?" Peyewik struggled to keep up with his friend's long strides. Chingwe was twelve, only a year older than Peyewik, but he was already close to the height of a man. His skinny arms and legs seemed too long for his body until he started running. He was the fastest boy in the village, and people said he would make a great hunter someday soon.

Chingwe glanced over his shoulder. "My mother tans skins today. She wants me to help her."

"Tanning is women's work," Peyewik pointed out.

"I know this," Chingwe grimaced. "But since my sister got married my mother complains that there is too much work for her to do alone. I asked my father to take me hunting with him today, but he says I don't know how to stand still yet, that I will scare the animals away. I told him it does not matter. If the animals run away, I will run after them. But my father said no. So we must get away before my mother wakes up and starts looking for me!"

He was hurrying along at such a nervous pace that Peyewik had to laugh. "You look like a squirrel stealing nuts!"

"It's not funny," Chingwe said miserably. "Your grandfather would never ask you to tan hides like a girl."

"No, but my grandfather asks me to cook like a girl," Peyewik replied.

"That is different. He has no wife or daughter. The other boys do not laugh at you for that, but they will laugh if they see me making the curing soup with my mother and aunties."

"You are right," Peyewik said seriously. "We must get away. But first I need to fix my shoe. Hold this for me." He held out his fishing basket and bent down as though to retie the leather lacings of his shoe. As soon as the basket was in Chingwe's hand he straightened up and started running.

"A race to the river!" he called. "Last one there hooks the worms!"

Chingwe took off after him, the fishing basket banging against his knees. They left the woods behind and charged across the floodplain. Pushing through cattails and leaping over debris left by the spring floods, they reached the river path at the same time.

"You cheat!" Chingwe gasped.

"You are too fast," Peyewik laughed. "If I do not cheat, I will lose."

"This is true," Chingwe said, sticking his skinny chest out and striding down the path. "People say I am the fastest boy the People have ever seen. When my Blessing comes Manito will send a deer or a panther spirit to me. They will tell me I am to be a great hunter and there will be many stories about me."

"Yes," Peyewik said slyly. "There will be many stories told about the boy who runs away fast when his mother needs help."

"You are jealous because Manito will send a timid little mouse with your Blessing," Chingwe teased back.

Peyewik's face fell at the mention of his own Blessing.

Chingwe saw this and said, "I am sorry." After a pause he asked, "You have had another dream?"

Peyewik nodded.

"People talk about your dreams," Chingwe said matter-of-factly. "I think it's good when the spirits tell you when it will rain or where the next hunt should be."

"My grandfather says it is a gift," Peyewik mumbled.

"Your grandfather is a wise healer. You should listen to him."

"I know what people say about my dreams," Peyewik argued. "They say normal boys receive one Blessing when they are twelve years old, after many days of fasting and praying. I was seven years old when the first spirit came to me, and I did nothing to bring it."

"I remember!" Chingwe laughed. "You fell asleep in the middle of a game, and when you woke up you said Chipmunk told you there would be lots of rain to make the strawberries fat and sweet."

"It makes people afraid, even when the spirits tell helpful things," Peyewik said sadly.

Chingwe shrugged. "My mother makes shoes for you. My father teaches you how to hunt. You are like my brother. I don't care what people say. I am not afraid."

Peyewik thought about telling him what Vulture had shown him the night before. He didn't think his friend would be so brave then. But Chingwe had suddenly disappeared. He reappeared just as suddenly, hanging upside down from the branches of a mulberry tree. He gave Peyewik a purple grin and a handful of berries. Peyewik stuffed the berries into his mouth, trying to forget Vulture once more.

Chins sticky with purple juice, the boys continued along the river path, passing into a thick growth of sycamore and jewel weed. The sun was two hand spans above the horizon by the time they arrived at their favorite fishing spot. A huge sycamore had fallen into the river, creating a jetty perfect for dangling lines and catching shad before they swam upstream and got stuck in the nets near the village. The boys dug for grubs under the exposed roots of the trees, and then climbed up onto the trunk. They sang a prayer of thanks to the river spirit—and to any fish willing to be their breakfast—and plunked their deer-bone hooks into the water.

Peyewik leaned against the stump of a branch and yawned. The sun was warm on his bare shoulders, and the quiet chuckle of the river was soothing. He yawned, his eyelids growing heavy...

Fox was awakened from her daytime sleep by the smell of humans. She had smelled humans before, but these were different. They stank of rotting things. Fox peered out of her den and saw them moving in a pack towards the river. She gave a loud yip of warning.

Peyewik came awake with a start.

"There is a fox in the woods," Chingwe grinned at him. "I almost didn't hear it. You snore like Old Man Chikinum."

"Fox should not be awake during the day!" Peyewik said. A faint smell of rot reached his nostrils, and his whole body tensed. "Something is coming. We must hide!"

Chingwe thought he was joking and kept smiling.

Peyewik grabbed his friend's arm and yanked him towards the riverbank. Startled, Chingwe lost his balance. Peyewik caught him and pulled him down among the roots of the fallen tree. Crouching there he put a hand over his friend's mouth as the smell of rot grew stronger. Chingwe's face crinkled in confusion and disgust.

Peyewik tried to quiet his breathing and listen. There was nothing but the sound of the water moving at their feet. Then he heard voices, soft at first, growing louder as they drew closer. They were men's voices and Peyewik did not recognize the harsh, guttural language they spoke. The stench was overwhelming now, like the village waste heap on a hot day.

Peyewik watched Chingwe's expression change from confusion to fear, and he remembered their fishing gear sitting out in plain view.

A shadow fell across their hiding place.

Peyewik looked up and saw a monster standing on the tree trunk above them. Its face was the color of a plucked bird and half covered with hair like dried corn silk sticking out all over. Ragged clothing hung from its pale, bony body. The monster looked down, and Peyewik saw shards of blue sky where its eyes should have been.

The monster howled when it saw him. It bent forward and seized him by the hair, dragging him from his hiding place. Peyewik was too terrified to scream, but he heard Chingwe cry out. There was a second monster on the fallen tree, and two more on the riverbank.

"Chingwe, run!" Peyewik found his voice at last and saw his friend scramble out from under the tree roots. The monster on the log and the two on the ground moved to catch him, but Chingwe ran fast, faster than Peyewik had ever seen him run before. He darted among the trees like a deer, flashing in and out of sight. The monsters stumbled after him, but he had already disappeared around a bend in the river. Peyewik started flailing, kicking, and punching until a fist crashed into the side of his head and he went limp, the ground spinning beneath him. His captor made a rough sound, and he looked up dizzily. The monster's face swam before him, its eyes cold as a winter sky. The monster shook him and repeated the rough sounds. Peyewik tried to struggle again, and then to shout, but the monster put a hand over his mouth.

One of Chingwe's pursuers returned from the forest. It sounded angry when it spoke, and he hoped it was because Chingwe had escaped. The hand over his mouth relaxed a little, and he sank his teeth into it, snarling like a dog with a deer bone. The sky-eyed monster yelled and shook him off. Peyewik tasted blood as he tumbled to the ground and wondered if the monster was human after all. He tried to scramble to his feet and run, but Sky Eyes, sucking on his injured finger, kicked his feet out from under him. Sky Eyes barked at the other monster, and it turned and jogged back in the direction Chingwe had run, towards the village.

"Manito, be with me, be with Chingwe, protect us..." Peyewik sang a prayer under his breath.

Sky Eyes grabbed Peyewik again and tucked him under one arm. He jumped down from the log and started walking. Peyewik saw that he was being carried in the wrong direction, away from home and all that he knew, and he put all his strength into fighting. Sky Eyes lost his grip, and Peyewik tumbled down the riverbank onto the rocks at the edge of the water. Sky Eyes skidded down after him and splashed into the shallows.

"River spirit, help me!" Peyewik cried, trying to push himself into the current to be carried away. But Sky Eyes caught his ankle and dragged him back. Peyewik could hear him muttering under his breath. Without warning he pushed Peyewik's head under. Peyewik gasped reflexively and inhaled water. He panicked and thrashed as water choked his lungs. He thought of his grandfather and longed for home...Then darkness seeped in behind his eyes and his arms and legs grew heavy. Panic ebbed, and the river pulled him gently towards deep, quiet waters.

Then the river pushed him back, rejecting him from its peaceful flow. A heavy weight bore down on his chest, pressing him into solid ground and squeezing the river out of him. He coughed through a mouthful of warm water, and the weight lifted, allowing his lungs to fill with air. He opened his eyes and saw a pale face staring down at him.

Peyewik rolled into a defensive crouch, but it wasn't Sky Eyes above him. It was a boy, older and taller than himself. He wore a brown cloak pulled low over his face, but Peyewik could see his eyes.

They were the color of new leaves, not blue. Peyewik watched the boy and waited for him to move.

But the boy didn't move. He sat on his knees, his chest rising and falling with wheezing gasps. He gazed back at Peyewik, his green eyes fever-bright. Peyewik began to edge away. The boy stayed where he was.

Suddenly Sky Eyes reared up behind the boy. Rivulets of blood and water ran down his face, and he lurched forward with a roar. The boy answered with a terrifying shriek and exploded into motion, rising and spinning around so fast Peyewik saw only a blur. Then Sky Eyes was hunched over, clutching a knife handle protruding from his belly. The boy's green eyes burned with hatred as he kicked Sky Eyes to the ground. The man fell on his side, eyes bulging. He groaned, and blood came out of his mouth.

Peyewik stared at Sky Eyes, his breath coming in shallow gasps. He could feel Sky Eyes' spirit struggle as it was pulled away from his body, drawn towards the spirit world. Peyewik knew he needed to sing to it, to help it across the river of death, but he couldn't remember the right song. The spirit struggled harder and grasped at him, a cold clutching at his heart. Peyewik tried to back away from the now empty body. His own body felt empty too, as if his spirit had fled far away. He wanted to run, but his legs were shaking too hard. The green-eyed boy bent over and pulled his knife from Sky Eyes' body. Then he collapsed, the hood of his cloak falling back to reveal hair the color of flames.

With a shock that consumed the last of his strength, Peyewik realized that the boy who had saved his life was actually a young woman. And he had seen her before, through the eyes of Vulture, standing in a marsh, surrounded by death.

CHAPTER THREE

Trib

Tribulation felt as though she was burning from the inside out, choking on flames. She writhed in torment until a cooling liquid was poured down her throat. She heard someone singing, an unfamiliar voice, and words she didn't understand. The sound soothed her and the heat abated. She could breathe again and she opened her eyes.

A scarred face loomed over her.

"Scath," Trib croaked, relief flooding through her. Everything would be all right now that her master, the head warrior of New Murias, was there. "Was that you singing?" she asked.

The Scath made a sound halfway between a laugh and a growl. "Ye know I don't sing, girl."

"What's happened? Where is everyone?" Trib asked.

"By 'Dess, I'm expecting ye to tell me."

Terrible images flooded Trib's mind, and she shook her head to be rid of them.

"No!" she said. "I don't know what happened."

"Ye do know," the old warrior said calmly. "And ye will tell me."

Trib closed her eyes and saw the destroyed bodies of warriors and priestesses sinking into the marsh. She started to shake and pain flared all over her body.

"They're all dead," she whispered.

"How'd they die?" The Scath's voice was flat, unemotional.

Trib saw again the sparks of rifle fire, the dark figures emerging from the reeds.

"Ambushed by Puritanics," she said.

"No warriors of mine would be taken unawares," the Scath replied.

"It was hot," Trib said meekly. "We were bored. There was nothing to do, no one to fight. We wanted to be up north with you..."

"Ye were lazy and careless," the Scath interrupted. "The Puritanics took advantage."

"'Dess, forgive me," Trib said, trying to rise. A searing pain in her shoulder caused her to cry out.

"Lie back," the Scath ordered. "There's nothing ye can do now but tell me the rest."

"There was an explosion," Trib replied. "I was knocked out. They left me for dead."

"But ye weren't dead. Ye lived, while yer comrades died."

Shame washed over Trib, and she felt suddenly grateful for the pain and heat that punished her.

"Ye said ye were knocked out by some kind of explosion," the Scath continued. "Reckon the Puritanics got new weaponry. What did ye do after ye found 'em all dead?"

"It's hard to recall. Reckon I was fevered."

"As ye are now," the Scath pointed out.

"Explains why I'm hotter than hell," Trib said.

"Aye. Think hard, girl. What did ye do next?"

Trib fought her way through the heat and the fog in her brain. "I chased the vultures away and started following the Puritanics' trail out of the marsh. I don't know how long I followed it. Sometimes it was day, sometimes it was night. I was in pain but I couldn't stop. Those bastards had to die. And then I saw a man..."

"Puritanic?" the Scath asked.

"I ain't sure. There was something strange about him. He disappeared before I could catch up with him. I heard a shout, followed the sound to a river, and there was another man kneeling in the water. This one was definitely Puritanic."

"What was he doing in the water?"

"'Dess, damn him, he was drowning a kid," Trib remembered. "Rage came then. Don't recall any more. Where am I, Master Scath? How'd you find me?"

The Scath gave her growling laugh again. "I didn't find ye girl. I ain't here, and yer as lost as can be."

At that, the old warrior vanished.

"Scath!"

Trib tried to sit up only to have the right side of her body explode in pain. She fell back, breathing through her teeth until the pain subsided. She was soaked in sweat and knew that her fever had just broken, taking with it the hallucination of the Scath. She blinked the shadows from her eyes and mind, trying to sort the real from the dream without panicking. She turned her head carefully, taking in her actual surroundings for the first time.

The sole source of light was a partially blocked hole in the roof. She could just make out the interior of some kind of hut. She was lying on a low, narrow platform against one wall. Similar platforms piled with animal skins ran along the two walls she could see. Dried plants hung from the walls and roof.

There was a rustling beyond Trib's field of vision, and she tensed, sending another pulse of pain through her body. A figure wrapped in animal skins came into view. It was an old man, his brown face deeply lined, and long, gray hair hung over his shoulders. She realized with shock that he was a Native. She had never seen one up close.

The old man leaned forward and slid a hand under her neck. His grip was strong but gentle as he lifted her head and held a steaming bowl to her lips. There was no malice in his face, but Trib hesitated. She was in pain, weak and helpless. The old man could do anything to her. Instead, he continued to hold her head gently, the bowl at her lips while she decided whether or not to drink. The tea smelled good, and Trib was thirsty. She drank until the bowl was empty, then lay back on the pile of skins, exhausted.

"Who are you? Where am I?" Trib asked the old man. He looked at her without answering.

"What happened to the boy? Is he all right?" she tried again, though she wasn't sure her memories of the boy in the river were real and not another fever hallucination. The shadows were closing in once more. She struggled to keep her eyes open as the old man began to sing again. She couldn't understand the words, but his voice was soft and steady. The sound washed over and through her. Her breath slowed and her eyes closed. Pain and fear disintegrated as she slid into a dreamless sleep.

CHAPTER FOUR

Peyewik

"You are well, little one?"

Peyewik peered out from under the fur quilt at Old Woman Menukan, a tiny, wrinkled woman with a carefully arranged knot of gray hair at the nape of her neck.

"I am well," he said, though he didn't feel well. "Chingwe is all right?"

"Your friend is fine. He is not so bashed up as you," she replied.

"How long have I been sleeping?" he asked.

"A day and a night. Were your dreams easy? I burned cedar to keep away nightmares."

"I did not dream," Peyewik said warily, wondering if she was one of the people who talked about his dreams.

"I am glad." The old woman smiled, revealing her nearly toothless gums. "If you have slept enough, Muhkrentharne wants you to come home. He gave the flame-haired one gravelroot, and her fever has broken."

Peyewik burrowed deeper into the furs. After outrunning the pale-skinned men, Chingwe had returned to the river with seven of the village's strongest hunters and Muhkrentharne. They had found no trace of the pale men, except for Sky Eyes' body, which they had refused to touch because they thought his angry spirit might linger nearby. The flame-haired girl was still alive, but the hunters hadn't wanted to touch her either. They were going to leave her to die until

19

Peyewik, bruised and shaking, told his grandfather that the flame-haired girl had saved his life. He also told him that he had seen her in a dream the night before. To Peyewik's dismay, Muhkrentharne had then asked the hunters to carry Flame Hair to his house. The hunters were uneasy, but they did as he asked because he was an elder and the village healer.

Once back in the village, Peyewik had wanted to be near his grandfather, but Flame Hair smelled terrible and was delirious with fever. She kept crying out in the same ugly language Sky Eyes had spoken. The smell and the sound made Peyewik sick to his stomach, and he could not sleep. So Muhkrentharne had carried him like a baby, in arms like gnarled tree roots, to Old Woman Menukan's house.

Old Woman Menukan's husband had died years ago and her house was very clean and quiet. Peyewik did not want to go back to the smell and noise of Flame Hair.

"Get up, child," Old Woman Menukan encouraged him. "I have a salve for your bruises." She knew almost as much about plant medicine as Muhkrentharne and often helped him with his healing work.

Peyewik climbed gingerly off the sleeping platform, his whole body stiff and painful. The salve stank, but it eased some of the ache.

"The bruises won't look so ugly tomorrow," Old Woman Menukan said. Then she handed him a loaf of cornbread, still warm from the ashes of her cooking fire. "Take this and share it with your grandfather. Both of you need to eat."

Peyewik felt queasy and couldn't imagine ever being hungry again, but he was grateful for her kindness and thanked her.

As he pushed open the doorflap to leave, she said, "Little one, you know the People love to gossip. But you must not pay attention to what they say about your dreams or anything else." She smiled her toothless smile, and Peyewik wished again he did not have to leave her house. However, he missed his grandfather, so he set out for home despite the knot in his stomach.

He saw no one as he passed through the village. It was midmorning, and everyone was in the garden or working on the fishing nets by the river. He wondered where Chingwe was but was glad he didn't have to speak to anyone. For the first time in his life the familiar surroundings of the village felt strange to him, fragile, as though they might vanish on a gust of wind. He felt a sudden, cold ache in his chest and remembered Sky Eyes' spirit clutching at his heart. There was movement in the nearby underbrush, and he jumped. It was only a startled groundhog, but his heart pounded.

Then he smelled a good smell, a whiff of clean pipe smoke, and his heartbeat slowed. Muhkrentharne was sitting on the ground outside his house, smoking his pipe in the sunshine. Peyewik ran forward and crashed onto his knees in front of his grandfather, throwing his arms around his neck and burying his face in his chest.

Muhkrentharne patted his hair, and the cold grip on Peyewik's heart released. He was home, and the world was safe again.

"Come inside," Muhkrentharne said. "I gave the flame-haired one willow bark tea to ease the pain, hops to make her sleep. She is quiet."

Peyewik didn't want to go anywhere near Flame Hair, but he let Muhkrentharne take his hand and lead him inside. The house still smelled of her, but not as strongly. When his eyes adjusted to the dim light, he could see a figure on one of the sleeping platforms. He took a step forward and stared down at it. He couldn't believe this was the same creature he had seen at the river. She had been towering and fierce when she attacked Sky Eyes. Now, wrapped in mud poultices and sleeping quietly, she looked barely more than a child.

"She is a shapeshifter?" he whispered. "Or a demon?"

"She is of the race of men, like the People," Muhkrentharne said. "But there are strange spirits around her, and she is not of this place."

"She will go away soon?" Peyewik asked hopefully.

"She cannot go too soon," the old man said. "Her spirit has only just decided to stay with her body. She must heal first."

"But she does not belong here!"

"This is for a boy like you to decide?" Muhkrentharne asked sternly.

Peyewik dropped his eyes to the floor. "No."

Muhkrentharne put a hand on his shoulder. "The council of elders meets tonight to decide whether Flame Hair will be allowed to stay. Chief Okahoki has asked you to join us."

"Children never go to the council of elders," Peyewik said.

"The chief wants to know what you have seen with your eyes and in your dreams," Muhkrentharne replied.

"Chingwe will come with me? He also saw the pale men."

"Only you."

Peyewik didn't know why, but the thought of going before the council of elders made the cold creep back into his chest.

"You have bathed today?" Muhkrentharne asked. "Cleaned your body and sung your prayers?"

"I am afraid of the river," Peyewik said, remembering the water filling his lungs.

"I will go with you. We will sing to the river spirit and wash away all of the bad spirits. You will feel better."

Later that evening Peyewik did feel better as he followed his grand-father to the house of the chief of the Original People. He had never been inside the chief's house, which was the biggest in the village besides the Ceremony House, and he felt very important as he pushed through the doorflap.

But then the thirteen elders seated around the fire in the center of the house all turned to look at him, and all he wanted to do was hide. As Muhkrentharne guided him to their place in the circle, he caught sight of Old Woman Menukan, who gave him a reassuring smile. They sat just to the right of the chief, and Peyewik couldn't help peering curiously around his grandfather at the man the people said was the greatest hunter they had ever known.

Chief Okahoki's hair stood in a fierce crest on top of his head, and the bones of animals he had killed hung from the skinny braids at the nape of his neck. It was said his hunting skills were so great that animal spirits considered it an honor to have him wear their bones.

With a small shock, Peyewik realized that the chief was looking back at him. To his even greater shock, the chief gave him a wink and a small smile. Then the elders began to sing their opening prayer.

Manito, we the elders of the Original People thank you for the many years of our lives, and all that we have learned,

Though our knowledge of this world and the others is small compared to yours,

Tonight we ask you for wisdom, and that we may recognize it when it comes.

"Honored Elders," Okahoki said when the prayer ended, "since the time of my grandfathers, there have been stories from the north of a pale-skinned people who sailed across the Great Water. I had seen no proof of these stories until yesterday when some of the Pale Ones came close to our village and tried to harm two of our children. When they went away they left one behind, a girl with hair the color of flames. This girl is a man-killer. We are here tonight to decide what to do about her and about the other Pale Ones who may return," Okahoki said.

Without waiting to be sure the chief had finished, Old Man Chikinum spoke up. "If she is a man-killer, she has been corrupted by Snakebrother, and we must send her away!"

Some of the elders shifted nervously at the mention of Snakebrother. Peyewik had never heard him spoken of except in stories.

Snake was Manito's brother, and he was jealous of Manito's love for his children, the People. In the stories, Snake was always trying to make trouble for the People. There had been no new stories of Snake-brother for many generations.

After a polite pause, Muhkrentharne said, "If we send her away now, she will die."

"This does not trouble me," Old Man Chikinum snapped.

"Manito does not want us to harm any of his children—plant, animal, or human—without good reason," Muhkrentharne said.

"We have a good reason!" Old Man Chikinum declared. "She brings Snakebrother among the People. She is dangerous."

"We do not know for certain that she is dangerous," Muhkrentharne said. "My grandson saw her in a dream, and she saved his life."

Peyewik could feel everyone looking at him again and stared down at the earthen floor.

"You were there?" Old Man Chikinum asked Muhkrentharne. "You saw her save his life? Why should we listen to the stories of a boy? Especially this boy, who is visited by too many spirits. Maybe he is visited by bad spirits who spread Snakebrother's lies."

Peyewik wished he could sink into the ground. Beside him, Muhkrentharne grew very still. There was a beat of silence, and then his grandfather spoke, slowly and calmly.

"The spirits bring my grandson guidance that the People need. We must listen to him."

A murmur went around the room. Now the elders were not only staring at him, but talking about him as well, and Peyewik felt the cold ache in his chest again.

"You must tell us your dream, little one," the chief said.

Peyewik's tongue felt frozen in his mouth.

"Do not be afraid," the chief said. "Some of those here have not treated you with the respect due to one who brings a dream before the council." He gave Old Man Chikinum a hard look. "Dreams often contain messages from the spirits. It is the duty of the council of elders to help the dreamer understand these messages."

Peyewik suddenly became aware of many presences around the chief. They were the animal spirits who honored him. Old Man Chikinum and the elders faded away and Peyewik spoke only to Okahoki and his spirits.

"I have dreamed about the Pale Ones twice. The first time, I saw them through the eyes of Vulture," Peyewik said, remembering the feel of the wind in his wings, the smell of the rotten marsh and the blood below. "I saw the flame-haired girl surrounded by the bodies of other Pale Ones. She was the only one left alive, and she was hurt. The second time I saw through the eyes of Fox, and I saw other Pale Ones." He remembered Fox's sense of urgency and danger. "Fox was trying to warn me that these men were coming and that they were dangerous. These were the men who attacked me and Chingwe. I think Flame Hair chased these men away and saved me from Sky Eyes...from the one who tried to drown me."

He stopped talking and looked around nervously. When it was clear he had nothing more to say, the chief addressed the elders. "You have heard what I have heard. You are the elders. What do you advise?"

"I dreamed I was eating fish stew last night," Old Man Chikinum grumbled. "Maybe this is a message from the spirits, and I should tell it to the council..."

"Be quiet, you old turkey!" Old Woman Menukan cut him short. "I cannot tell whether you are talking or farting. They are the same with you. Too loud, too much gas."

Peyewik stifled a giggle and felt a wave of affection for the tiny, old lady.

The chief's mouth twitched towards a grin, and he said, "Tell us what you think, Grandmother."

"We must pay attention to the boy's dreams," she said. "I sing to the spirits often, and while I do not hear their reply as loudly as this boy does, my old bones have felt a change coming. The spirits showed Peyewik this girl, and she saved him. She is now part of the story of the Original People."

Peyewik didn't know how to feel about this. Some of the elders were nodding in agreement, while others had concerns that they voiced until Chief Okahoki held up a hand for silence.

"Flame Hair has done the People a service by rescuing one of our children from the men who attacked him. We must return that service by allowing her to heal. I propose that when she is strong enough, we send her back to her people with a message never to come here again. That will be her part in our story. She will heal among us, and then she will go and keep the Pale Ones and Snakebrother from us."

"She does not speak our language," an elder pointed out.

"People say there are some among the Away People, our brothers and sisters to the south, who speak the language of the Pale Ones," the chief said. "I will send a message to the chief of the Away People and ask him to send one of them to us. Does the council agree?" He turned to Muhkrentharne on his right.

"Let it be done," Muhkrentharne replied.

"Let it be done," said the elder next to him.

Peyewik watched the vote go around the circle. When it got to Old Man Chikinum, he scowled but mumbled his assent. When all had voted in favor of Okahoki's plan, the council sang prayers of thanks for Manito's guidance. Peyewik could tell the elders were relieved. He knew that all they wanted was to get back to life as it had been before Flame Hair and the Pale Ones appeared. He knew this because it was what he wanted as well. Unlike the elders, though, he felt no sense of relief. All he felt was the cold clutching at his heart.

CHAPTER FIVE

Trib

rib leaned against the outer wall of the old man's hut to catch her breath. The bullet wound in her shoulder and the sword cut on her leg were both throbbing, and where she wasn't in pain, she was shaking with exhaustion.

The old man was sitting in his usual place beside the flap that served as a door to the hut. He puffed on his pipe and watched her placidly, offering no help as she struggled to lower herself to the ground beside him, which was fine with Trib.

"I may not be able to swing a sword or even take a few steps without getting winded," she muttered. "But by 'Dess, I can sit on my own ass without help." She dropped the last few inches onto her backside, groaning at the jolt.

"'Dess-damned bag of bones," she said, thumping her uninjured leg impatiently. "I need to be getting stronger faster. I've been here too long."

She turned to the old man and said, "I reckon it's been what? Three weeks, maybe four?"

The old man gave her the same response he gave her every time she spoke to him, gazing at her calmly and saying nothing. Trib knew he didn't speak her language, but she found it helped her work out her thoughts, as well as pass the time, if she talked to him anyway.

"I have to get back to my people," she explained. "I need to get word to the Scath about that ambush I told you about, the one that gave me these injuries. She doesn't know there are Puritanics here in the south."

The old man exhaled a puff of smoke and looked away from Trib to the large, fenced-in garden nearby.

"When we sailed down here from the north, we left some people on the bay where our ship landed. Warriors, manservants, and some priestesses. They were supposed to be building an encampment while we were gone on the mapmaking expedition. If I could get back to them, they could get word to the Scath, and help me track down the bastards that killed my friends."

The old man was watching some women and children harvest beans.

Trib waved a dismissive hand at the garden. "Where I come from men do all that kind of thing," she said. "Leave the important work to the women..."

A woman carrying a basket of vegetables left the garden and headed for the center of the village. As she passed the old man's hut, the old man raised a hand in greeting. The woman looked at Trib nervously and hurried by without returning the wave.

"Not very friendly, is she?" Trib observed. She turned once more to the old man. "Reckon you could give me back my clothes and sword soon?"

She had been provided with a robe and leggings made of animal skins. While she was glad that it covered her completely, since many of the Natives, women included, went around bare-chested, she would've preferred her waistcoat and breeches.

"Just so you know," she added, "I ain't leaving here without that sword. It goes against the Scath's warrior code to lose a weapon. I'll tear this place apart to find it, if I have to."

Unperturbed, the old man took the pipe out of his mouth, knocked the ashes from the bowl, and stood up far more nimbly than Trib could've managed.

She squinted up at him. "I reckon you did a good job of patching me up," she said, "but you got no talent for conversation."

The old man headed for the garden without a word or a backward glance.

Trib watched him go and half-wished her hallucination of the Scath would come back, just so she'd have someone to talk to. She sighed and leaned back against the hut. From where she sat she had an unobstructed view of the garden and the outer edge of the village. She watched the Natives going about their daily business and wondered what the Scath would make of them. There were Natives in the north, but Trib had never seen them up close. There had been rumors about the Puritanics forming alliances with the northern Natives, but no one took them seriously. The northern Natives were too peaceful and few in numbers to be a threat to the New Murians. These southern Natives didn't appear any different.

Trib thought there were about a hundred of them, living in thirty or so huts of various shapes and sizes. She wasn't certain about the number because the Natives all looked the same to her—coppery skin, dark hair and eyes, minimal clothing—and she wasn't sure which ones she had already counted. That, and she wasn't good with numbers over twenty.

The huts were surrounded on three sides by trees, but the concealing underbrush had been cleared away. There were no fences or palisades, and the lack of defenses made Trib nervous, her palm itching for her missing weapon. The Natives, whose only weapons appeared to be hunting bows and tools, appeared to feel perfectly safe as they moved to and fro with children or baskets on their hips. The only thing that seemed to bother them at all was Trib herself. She had gotten the sense that they were avoiding the old man's hut. Even his grandson, whom Trib had recognized as the boy she fished from the river, only turned up every now and then to cook meals and to sleep.

When he had first appeared in the hut, she had been relieved to see that he was alive and well, but despite the fact that she had saved his life, he never seemed very glad to see her in return.

Trib's thoughts were interrupted by the sound of whispers and giggling. Three plump, naked children were peering around the corner of the hut at her.

"Where'd you come from?" she asked gruffly.

One of the kids pointed at Trib's head and laughed out loud. Trib reached up and patted her hair self-consciously. It was turning into a rat's nest at the back of her head.

"I lost my comb," she said defensively. She tried to frown and look scary, but this just made the kids laugh more. She was about to try growling at them when she noticed a fierce-looking man striding towards her.

The man's hair stood up in a spiky tuft on the top of his head and he wore nothing but a flap of animal skin. He looked angry, causing Trib's palm to itch for her sword again. She was still too weak to summon a rage, and she was calculating how much damage she could do without a weapon when the man's face suddenly broke into a smile. He scooped up a round-bellied little girl and tossed her gently into the air. The girl shrieked with glee until he set her down again. With a wary glance at Trib, he began herding the children away.

Trib stared after them, stunned by the children's adoring clamor, and by the fierce-looking man's obvious delight as he laughed and tossed each one in turn. Interactions like this never happened in New Murias. The men of the settlement—houseboys, manservants, and farmhands—weren't allowed to interact with kids, especially their own. Like all other New Murian children, Trib had been raised not knowing or caring who her father was.

A woman approached the fierce-looking man, and Trib watched curiously to see how they would interact. The woman embraced the man and then bent down to tickle and tease the children. Unlike most New Murian children, Trib hadn't known her mother either. Or at least not very well. She had a few vivid memories of her mother, before she died, but for the most part her childhood memories were of the warriors' barracks and of the Scath. With a twinge of longing, Trib realized how much she missed the Scath and her fellow apprentice-warriors. The twinge turned into a stab of grief when she remembered that she would never see many of the apprentice-warriors again.

Replacing her grief with the thoughts of revenge, she climbed to her feet, ready to force her body through more exercise. Just then another group of children caught her attention. This time it was some older boys playing a game at the edge of the forest. Two boys were squaring off, right arms clasped. It looked like a grappling game Trib had often played with Cuss. The image of Cuss's bullet-riddled body sinking into the marsh flashed through her mind, and she pushed it away by focusing on the boys.

She recognized the smaller boy as the one she'd pulled from the river, and watched him face off against a much taller opponent. The contest was over quickly, the smaller boy landing on his back in the dirt while the other boys cheered.

"Get up," she muttered.

The boy stayed down. Trib had spent years getting knocked on her ass by Cuss, until one day she figured out how to unbalance her taller, heavier opponent.

"Get up," she said again, willing the boy to stand up and keep fighting. She had failed Cuss when she let her friend die in the marsh. But she had saved this boy. Cuss and the other apprentice-warriors would never stand and fight again, but the boy still had a chance.

CHAPTER SIX

Peyewik

Peyewik picked himself up and held a hand out to Chingwe. His former friend's hesitation hurt him much more than the taunts of the other boys. Finally Chingwe grasped his forearm and mumbled, "Good match."

They both knew it hadn't been a good match; Chingwe was too much taller for it to have been fair. When they were still friends, Chingwe had always let Peyewik win. But the other boys had put Chingwe up to the wrestling match, challenging him to prove that Peyewik wasn't anything special or dangerous.

"See?" One boy thumped Chingwe on the back. "You are the one the chief should have asked to the council, not him. You are the one who is strong and fast. You are the one who ran to the village for help."

Chingwe dropped Peyewik's arm, and Peyewik turned away.

"Yes," another boy said. "If you had gone to the council, the man-killer would have been sent away. She does not belong here. Peyewik and his moth-eaten grandfather have been contaminated by bad spirits."

Peyewik paused, ready to turn and fight the boy. But it was Chingwe who came to his grandfather's defense. "Be quiet!" he barked. "You would have died, Pukwes, if Muhkrentharne had not cared for you when you were sick last winter. And you, Asxuktet, your arm would be crooked if Muhkrentharne had not set it for you when you fell out of the tree. You should not be so disrespectful."

A stunned silence followed, but Peyewik didn't turn around. He hadn't been included in Chingwe's defense. He walked away from the boys and the village, into the forest. Once among the cool shadows he climbed a fir tree and waited for the ache in his chest to subside. He had been coming into the forest a lot lately. It was the only place he felt safe and welcome anymore.

Things had been hard since the council. Although the elders had agreed on what to do, many of the villagers, including Chingwe and his parents, were uncomfortable with the presence of Flame Hair. What Chingwe didn't know, because he no longer spoke to Peyewik, was that Peyewik didn't want Flame Hair in the village any more than he did. Peyewik had taken to sleeping in trees in good weather rather than sleep in the same house with her. She continued to stink despite Muhkrentharne's attempts to disinfect her. He had even burned her filthy clothes, but the house still smelled. Muhkrentharne never complained though Peyewik had noticed that he spent more time in the garden when he wasn't tending to her.

Peyewik listened to the wind swish through the branches of the fir. The tree swayed soothingly, and eventually his chest no longer felt so tight and cold. He sang a little prayer of thanks to the spirit of the fir and climbed down. He walked along the edge of the forest, looking for a sassafras shrub. He had told Muhkrentharne about the coldness in his chest, and his grandfather decided he still had some water in his lungs. The sassafras was meant to dry up the water, and cure the coldness.

Peyewik found the shrub and took a pinch of tobacco from a pouch around his neck. He sprinkled it at the base of the plant and sang another prayer of thanks before digging out a few roots. Deep down, he knew that the coldness wasn't water in his lungs. It was Sky Eye's spirit clinging to him.

Wishing the sweet smelling roots really could cure him, Peyewik started for home. When he came to the garden, he paused to make sure Chingwe and the other boys weren't still hanging around. They were gone, but as he drew close to Muhkrentharne's house, Flame Hair came lurching around the corner and barred his way.

Peyewik froze, dropping the sassafras. He hadn't realized she could get around so easily yet. In the light of day she was grotesque, her scars livid against her glaringly white skin, her orange hair matted like ropes of poison ivy. She came close, dropped her hands onto his shoulders, and suddenly he was on the ground looking up into her awful face. She grimaced at him, and he squeezed his eyes shut in anticipation of the next blow. When nothing happened Peyewik opened his eyes and saw that Flame Hair was offering him a hand. He hesitated before taking it, then allowed her to pull him to his feet. Once he was upright again, she grasped his right arm with her right arm, and set her right foot against his. Peyewik had time to recognize the wrestling stance before he landed on the ground a second time.

The fall didn't hurt. Flame Hair was knocking him down gently, though Peyewik couldn't imagine why. He wondered if she was delirious again, if he should run for Muhkrentharne. Flame Hair hauled him to his feet and stepped back to catch her breath. She was sweating, and her legs were shaking, but she didn't seem delirious or threatening. Peyewik turned to go, but she grunted and resumed the wrestling stance. She was taller than Peyewik, taller even than Chingwe. Earlier, Chingwe had used his greater strength and reach to win the match. But Flame Hair hadn't seemed to exert any force at all when she knocked Peyewik over. It was as if she simply willed him off his feet.

Peyewik's curiosity got the better of him. He replaced his right foot against hers and took her arm. This time she went through the movement very slowly, showing him how she leaned into him with her knees, then shifted her weight onto her back foot. She didn't use her upper body until the very last second and then only for a quick shove to complete the unbalancing.

Peyewik picked himself up yet again, and Flame Hair showed him how to lock his knees in place and then pull her forward.

Peyewik blinked in surprise. Flame Hair was on the ground. He had knocked over the man-killer! She had landed lightly enough, but he could see that the fall hurt her injured leg. He was afraid she would be angry, but she gave him the grimace that he now understood to be a smile. He relaxed and realized how good it felt to knock Flame Hair down. She was, after all, the cause of all his problems. If she hadn't come to the village, Chingwe would still be his friend, and the villagers would not be whispering about him as much. He wanted to knock her down again. And then go knock down Chingwe and the other boys and any villager who looked at him funny. The thought made him smile, and he was a little too enthusiastic when Flame Hair gave him another chance to push her off balance. She hit the ground hard, and he saw her green eyes flash. He jumped back, ready to run. But Flame Hair broke into an undeniable grin and held out her hand. When she was on her feet she clapped him on the back, still grinning. He had impressed her.

Peyewik wasn't sure it was such a good thing to impress the man-killer, but at the same time, he felt better than he had in a long while. And Flame Hair, with her odd grin and clumsy movements, didn't look like a man-killer at the moment. In fact, as Peyewik looked at her, he felt the sudden presence of her spirit animal. It was something lithe and joyful, untouched by darkness or shadow. It was gone again before he could figure out what it was, as though it was shy of being seen.

For a moment Peyewik was too surprised to move. He hadn't thought about Flame Hair or any of the Pale Ones having spirit animals. They were too strange and separate. Or so he had thought.

"Peyewik!"

Peyewik, still in awe of his discovery, looked up to see his grandfather coming towards him.

"The chief asks for Flame Hair," Muhkrentharne said. "She must come now."

Peyewik turned to Flame Hair and saw that her face had gone hard and intimidating again. The playful spirit animal was long gone.

"Why does the chief want her?" he asked.

"One who speaks her language has come from the Away People. We must speak with Flame Hair now."

CHAPTER SEVEN

Trib

Trib was so surprised to hear English being spoken that she didn't immediately understand what the Native had said to her. "You will answer questions?" the Native repeated. "I will translate."

Trib stood before three men, as she leaned on a makeshift crutch. The men were seated on a platform against one wall of a large hut. The translator, a young man with long, black hair and strangely colored eyes, sat on one side of the platform. On the other side was the old man. And in the center sat a powerful-looking man introduced by the translator as the chief of the village. This was his hut. It was much bigger than the old man's, but it still seemed rough and unimpressive to Trib. The chief himself, however, had an entirely different effect on her. The Scath had drilled it into her apprentices never to back down in front of a man. One show of weakness and the bastards would stomp all over you, she'd said. But Trib had looked away from the chief's unwavering gaze almost immediately. There was no challenge or aggression in his black eyes, just an attention that made her feel as if the flesh had been stripped from her bones, and there was nowhere left to hide.

So she looked at the old man instead. She could see neither welcome nor hostility in his face, but she was used to that. His hands had been gentle on her wounds, and his balms had eased her pain. But she knew better than to let this lull her into a sense of safety and calm. She had been taught to be on her guard at all times, and the truth was that she didn't know how the old man actually felt about her, or what the other Natives' intentions towards her might be.

"Depends on the question," she answered the translator warily.

To her dismay she felt a flutter in her stomach as she looked at him. He was long-limbed and lean, and his hair hung loose down his back like a girl's. Adding to the effect were loops of colored beads in his ears and a thick fringe of lashes around gold-colored eyes. He had the kind of prettiness some of the apprentice warriors liked in a man. Trib didn't know what to do with attractive young men. They made her nervous and distracted her from her duties, so she left them to Cuss. She was sure Cuss would've fancied the translator. His meager clothing didn't leave much to the imagination—he was naked from the waist up. Cuss wouldn't have minded at all, but it made Trib blush, defeating her efforts to appear strong and aloof.

The translator looked back at her impassively.

"You are from the north?" he asked.

"Aye," Trib replied, wondering how much she should tell him. She wished for the thousandth time that the Scath were there. Answering questions was beyond her training. She decided that since the Natives had treated her well enough so far, she might as well tell them the truth. It wasn't as though these unarmed primitives could ever pose a threat to the New Murians, no matter what she told them.

"I'm from the settlement of New Murias, a week's travel to the north," she said. "Sailed down here along the coast a month past, maybe more."

"Why did you come here?"

Trib thought back to the black-robed figures standing at the edge of the marsh.

"No good reason I can see," she muttered to herself. More loudly, she said, "To make a map."

The chief looked concerned at this.

"How many more of you are there?" the translator asked.

Trib had to think. The map-making expedition was dead. She tried to remember how many people had been left on the bay with the ship.

"I reckon twenty or so."

"They are mankillers, like you?" the translator asked.

It took Trib a moment to figure out what he meant. "You're asking about warriors? No, only five or six of them. The rest are priestesses and manservants."

She expected to be asked to explain what priestesses and manservants were, but the translator had another question in mind.

"Your women fight alongside your men?"

Trib snorted. "No. Only women are allowed to be warriors where I come from. Men ain't trustworthy enough to carry weapons."

The next question came out sounding like an accusation.

"You kill one of your own?" he asked.

"One of my own...?" Trib was confused.

"The man by the river."

Trib's vision went red around the edges.

"Puritanics ain't my own," she spat.

She was still too weak to bring on a full Rage, but the flickers of red let her know that some of her strength was returning.

"Puritanics are liars, wife-beaters, and child-killers," she said. She pointed at the old man. "You need proof, ask your grandson. The Puritanic you're asking about, he was drowning that boy, and I stopped him."

To Trib's surprise, the old man spoke up.

"Muhkrentharne thanks you for saving his grandson," the translator told her.

"Aye, well, I thank him for saving me," Trib said gruffly, unaccustomed to politeness.

The old man nodded once in acknowledgment.

"These Pure Men are your enemies?" the translator asked, keeping the questioning on track. "How many of them are there?"

"There's more up north. But down here there can't be more than ten, after the one I killed at the river and the ones killed during the ambush."

"What do your people want from us?"

Trib stared at the pretty young man, bemused.

"We don't want anything from you," she said. "We didn't even know you were here."

She wondered what he thought his backwards people could have that the New Murians would want.

"And the Pure Men?"

"I reckon they're only here because of us, followed us down here to do us harm any way they can," Trib said wearily.

She was getting tired of the conversation. Talking was for priest-esses, not warriors. And her legs had started to tremble with fatigue, worn out by her grappling lesson with the boy. She had been offered a seat on the ground when she entered the hut but she had refused it, thinking she would be more impressive on her feet.

Trib looked up then, straight into the translator's eyes. They shone gold in the dim light of the hut and in them she saw an odd mix-ture of distaste and fascination. It was almost as disconcerting as the chief's gaze, and it made her legs tremble even harder. Finally, the translator turned back to the chief and her legs grew a little more solid beneath her. She cursed under her breath at the treachery of her own body.

After a brief consultation the chief spoke, and Trib could hear the authority in his voice even though she couldn't understand his words.

"You will carry a message from Chief Okahoki to your people, the Pale Ones," the translator said. "You will tell them this is the home of the People for many generations. It is protected by Manito.

Snakebrother and his violence cannot come here. You must go and tell your people never to return here."

Trib didn't know what it all meant, but she bristled anyway. The Natives were unarmed and powerless. They had no right to make demands, especially when they couldn't even tell the difference between a New Murian and a Puritanic. She was sore and tired, and her mind felt muddled. She wished the Scath were there to tell her what to do. All she wanted was to get back to her people, warn them about the Puritanics, and hunt down the men who killed her friends. She forced herself to think. The chief had asked her to deliver a message, nothing more. She could do that, and it might even help her get on her way faster.

"If you can point me in the direction of the bay, where my people are waiting, I'll deliver your message." She still had no idea where she was and could only assume that the bay was a large enough landmark that the Natives would know it.

The translator looked at her like she was an idiot and nodded.

"Then I'll leave today," Trib said.

The old man spoke then.

"Muhkrentharne says you are still weak," the translator explained. "You must rest before you go. Sleep tonight, leave in the morning."

"I ain't weak!" Trib blustered, just before her wounded leg gave out and she dropped onto one knee.

The translator looked down at her, his dark brows arched gracefully over golden eyes filled with sparks of mocking laughter.

"Dess damn it!" Trib cursed her body out loud this time as her stomach did a traitorous somersault. She had to admit that the old man was right. She needed to rest. "Fine," she grumbled. "I'll leave at first light tomorrow."

CHAPTER EIGHT

Peyewik

Peyewik was awakened by cries of alarm and fear.

Muhkrentharne was already out of his bed. "Stay here!" he commanded before rushing from the house.

Peyewik slipped out of bed and tried to run after Muhkrentharne, but came up against Flame Hair in the darkness. She grabbed him by the shoulders and shook him, shouting in her ugly language.

Somehow Peyewik knew exactly what she wanted. Without thinking, he knelt down and pulled a bundle out from under Muhkrentharne's bed. The edge of the longknife gleamed in the light of the banked fire. Flame Hair snatched the weapon greedily and ran from the house with a blood-chilling shriek. The sound reminded Peyewik of what he'd seen Flame Hair do to Sky Eyes and he suddenly gasped in horror at the thought of the demon he'd set loose in the village.

Just then Muhkrentharne returned, bringing with him the smell of smoke. "More Pale Ones have come," he said. "They have set fire to some of the houses on the eastern side of the village."

"I gave Flame Hair her longknife," Peyewik whispered. "I did not think about what she might do..."

"I saw her," Muhkrentharne said, "She is like a monster, but she is not harming the People, only the attackers. Even though she is injured, she fights with the strength of many men. It is a terrible thing to see."

Peyewik shivered.

His grandfather began pulling dried plants down from the rafters. "Some of the People will need medicine."

When he'd gathered enough supplies he said, "Stay here, Little One. I will come back as soon as I can."

Peyewik stood in the dark and listened to the sounds of chaos outside. His chest felt tight and his body cold. He thought of Sky Eyes and felt the angry spirit clinging to him. Suddenly Peyewik understood that the Pale Ones had come to the village in search of revenge for their dead friend. Fear rushed through him, but he was frozen to the spot. All he could do was shiver and imagine the terrible things that were happening outside.

He didn't know how long he stood this way before Muhkrentharne reappeared. The old man's eyes were bloodshot and his face was smudged with smoke, but he was whole and safe and his hands were full of freshly picked herbs.

"The Pale Ones are gone," Muhkrentharne told him. "Flame Hair killed some, the others ran."

He set about crushing the herbs with his wooden mortar. Their astringent smell filled the house, and Peyewik blinked as if waking up. There was no more shouting. He could hear birdsong. A sliver of light showed under the doorflap. Morning had come. He wanted to tell Muhkrentharne about Sky Eyes' spirit, how it must have brought the Pale Ones to the village, but his tongue felt cold and slow.

Muhkrentharne put the crushed herbs into a basket along with some soft skins cut into bandages. "Take these to Old Woman Menukan," he said. "She is tending the wounded in the Ceremony House."

Peyewik took the basket but hesitated at the door, afraid of what he would find outside.

"I cannot go with you," Muhkrentharne said gently. "The Chief has called the elders together."

Peyewik finally found his voice. "Was anyone killed?"

Muhkrentharne put an herb-scented hand against his cheek. "Manito protected us from Snakebrother last night. None of the People were killed."

Relief swept through Peyewik.

"Some lost their homes and others were hurt, so you must go. They need the medicine you bring."

Peyewik did as he was told. Outside, the fires still smoldered, filling the village with an acrid haze. People were clearing away the debris of ruined houses and hauling saplings from the forest. They were already rebuilding, but everything looked different, strange and alien. The village's appearance had finally caught up with how Peyewik had been feeling about it for weeks. For a moment he was disoriented and didn't know which way to go. Then a stiff breeze cleared the smoke and he could see the Ceremony House, undamaged, at the center of the village. As he started towards it, he saw a flicker of movement in the corner of his eye. He turned, thinking he'd seen a large, dark cat prowling the tree-line, but there was nothing.

Then a woman started wailing.

The sound made Peyewik's blood run cold. He ran to the Ceremony House and found Chingwe's mother on the ground, cradling her son in her arms. His long limbs sprawled about her awkwardly as she rocked back and forth, a wild song of grief pouring out of her.

Peyewik saw Chingwe's staring eyes and the blood pooled beneath him and knew his friend was dead. Chingwe's mother looked up and saw him.

"This is your fault!" she cried. "There are evil spirits about you. You brought the Pale Ones here, you brought Snakebrother's evil upon the People!"

Peyewik was shaking and couldn't answer through his chattering teeth. But he knew she was right. It was his fault. He had seen the

Pale Ones in his dreams and they had come to him. He had brought Flame Hair's and Sky Eyes' spirits back to the village, and the others had followed. Now Chingwe was dead.

Peyewik turned and ran blindly into the forest. He ran until he could no longer smell the smoke of the People's destroyed homes or hear the cries of their grief.

CHAPTER NINE

Trib

Trib leaned her sword against a tree and noticed that her hands were shaking. It was some time after dawn, and she was standing in the forest not far from the Native village. She had been chasing Puritanics, but they escaped when the Rage began to fade, taking her strength with it. She'd thought she was still too weak from her injuries to summon a Rage, but it had come easily when she heard the screaming in the night. Apparently it had served her well. A few paces to her left lay a dead Puritanic. She had the vaguest memory of swinging her sword at him but couldn't remember the actual killing.

Suddenly her right leg gave out and she sat down hard on the ground. A red stain was soaking through her robe. The sword wound in her leg had reopened, but she felt no pain. She patted herself down clumsily and didn't find any new injuries.

From where she sat she could see the village and the smoking remains of a few huts. She was calculating how long it would take her to crawl back to the old man's hut, if it was still standing, when she saw a tall figure coming towards her through the smoke. It was the translator. She wondered vaguely what he was doing out in the forest, and if he was all right.

The translator stopped when he saw the dead Puritanic.

"Don't worry," Trib croaked. "It's dead."

The translator kept his eyes on the body and started humming under his breath.

"What are you doing?" Trib asked, noticing that the translator wasn't making her feel nervous, that in fact she felt nothing at all. She was completely numb as the after effects of the Rage took over.

The translator stopped humming, but kept watching the body uneasily. "A prayer to help him cross the River of Death, or else his angry spirit will stay and haunt this place."

"It ain't angry," Trib said wearily. "Just dead, like I told you. Are there other dead Puritanics back there?" She nodded towards the village.

His expression was a mix of bafflement and horror. "You do not know how many you killed?" he asked.

Trib shrugged. "It's always hazy when the Rage takes over."

The storyteller took a step away from her. "Four," he said in a low voice. "There are four angry spirits in our village now."

"Four," Trib repeated. It was a good number. The dead men had probably taken part in the attack on the marsh. The Scath would've been proud of her, taking on all those Puritanics by herself. Trib thought she should feel something, victorious maybe. But she continued to feel nothing.

"I came to find you," the translator said. "Chief Okahoki asks for you."

"As well he should," Trib said without moving. "Now that the Puritanics know where your village is, you people are in trouble."

She expected a fear reaction from the storyteller, but he just stared at her.

"You must come," he insisted.

Sudden anger pierced through Trib's numbness, and she would've hit him if she'd had the strength. "In my own good time," she snapped. "I jump at no man's command."

The translator made a noise of disgust in the back of his throat and turned to leave.

Just then a terrible wail rose up from the center of the village.

"What is that Dess-damned noise?" Trib gasped, putting her hands over her ears.

The translator had stopped to listen. He looked back at her. "A mother weeps for her child."

"Why?" Trib asked.

"He is dead."

"No." Trib shook her head slowly. "That ain't right. I got to them first. They didn't have a chance to kill anyone. Not this time."

She was still numb, but she was seeing the bodies of her friends sinking into the marsh.

"Not the old man's grandson?" she asked in a small voice.

"No," the translator replied.

Trib was glad of this but still had the feeling that something very wrong had happened.

"You will come now?" the translator asked.

"Aye," Trib agreed distractedly, wishing the wailing would stop.

"You are shaking," the translator said.

"Just my hands," Trib replied before realizing that in fact her whole body was shaking. Even her teeth were chattering.

The translator moved reluctantly to her side. "I will help you. Chief Okahoki is waiting."

"Don't need help," Trib muttered. However, when the translator knelt down and pulled her arm across his shoulders, she let him. She saw him turn his head away in distaste, but she was too numb and tired to care.

<hr />

A short while later Trib found herself in the chief's hut again, sitting on the ground with a new bandage on her leg. The shaking had stopped, and the numbness was wearing off. She was exhausted and in pain. The wailing outside continued and grew louder as other voices joined in. It made Trib's head hurt.

"Why are there so many old people in here?" she growled at the translator, who stood nearby with his arms crossed. Ten or twelve old men and women were sitting in a circle that filled up most of the house.

"Elders," the translator said without looking at her. "The wise ones of the village will decide what the People should do next."

"Old folks ain't going to help against the Puritanics," she said. "Your chief needs fighters now."

The translator didn't reply, but she saw the muscle in his jaw tighten. The old people started singing.

"Why in Dess's name do you people sing so much?" Trib muttered.

The translator turned his back on her.

When the singing was done, the old people began a conversation that seemed to circle around the room endlessly, moving from one old person to the next and back again. Trib sat back tiredly and was half asleep when the translator spoke to her again.

"Chief and elders decide you must leave now," he said, sounding relieved.

"I thought they decided that last time I was here," she yawned.

"You go *now*," the translator emphasized.

"I got no problem leaving now," Trib said, suddenly awake and angry. "I was ready to go yesterday. Then Puritanics attacked your village in the middle of the night, and I risked my life to defend it. Don't I get a word of thanks?"

"You were like a demon when you fought the Pure Men last night. You brought Snakebrother to the village. Now you will take him away."

"I ain't a demon. It was the Rage. And what in Dess's name does Snakebrother mean?"

"Snakebrother is the god of chaos and violence. He brings grief and destruction to the People."

"You think *I* brought this Snakebrother on you?" Trib said. Not only was this not thanks, it was blame.

"With your...Rage...you killed five men. And you feel nothing about it. This is the influence of Snakebrother."

"Grief and destruction were brought to you by Puritanics, not me," Trib said, struggling to control herself. "Twice now they would've done much worse if I hadn't been here to protect you with my Rage. The Rage ain't demonic. It's a gift given to the warriors of my people by the Goddess, to give us the strength to fight the Puritanics."

"You must go," the translator repeated, a look of revulsion on his face.

"By Dess, I will!" she shouted. "I'm sick of you primitives and your backward ways. I got duties elsewhere. See if I care what the Puritanics do to you."

She hauled herself off the platform and limped through the circle of old people toward the doorflap. Halfway across she stopped, arrested by the continued sound of wailing outside. She caught sight of the old man and thought of all the ways he had cared for her. She thought of his grandson, and how he had looked when she first pulled him from the river. He had seemed dead, but he had come back to life. She had been able to save him. Unlike the others. For some reason she remembered that the boy needed more help with his grappling skills, and then she was overwhelmed by a terrible feeling of regret. She couldn't leave them to die the way Cuss and the others had died, at the hands of the Puritanics.

She turned slowly back to the translator.

"I'm sorry," she said through gritted teeth. She wasn't in the habit of apologizing and found it difficult. "You don't understand. You send me away for good, they'll come back with worse. There won't be anyone to protect you. More children will die."

"Why would they come back once you are gone? You said the People have nothing the Pale Ones want," the translator said.

Trib stared at the translator for a moment before turning to address the chief directly. "The Puritanics have taken everything from me," she said. "They've killed my friends and my family, all of them. They'll come back and do the same to you because they're evil. Maybe they are this Snakebrother of yours. But I ain't. The Rage makes my people strong enough to protect you, and we're the only ones who can."

"The chaos of Snakebrother feeds on itself," the translator replied before turning to the chief.

Trib nearly yelled in frustration. She was sick of hearing about this Snakebrother. She struggled to maintain her composure as the translator conveyed what she'd said to the chief. She could tell by the translator's face that he was against her, but the chief seemed to be listening carefully.

Trib knew it wouldn't be easy if the Natives accepted her offer of help. She would have to find the Scath first, before the Puritanics attacked again, and then convince her to protect the Natives. But the Scath had raised her to believe that it was the duty of the strong to protect those weaker. Surely she would see that helping the Natives was the right thing to do, especially after they'd saved Trib's life.

When the translator was done, the chief did not immediately dismiss her. He and the elders debated for a long time before the chief held up his hand and made a pronouncement that was followed by silence.

Trib could see that not everyone was pleased by what he said, especially the translator.

"Use this Rage of your Goddess to protect us from Snakebrother and the Pure Ones," the translator said without looking at her.

"Tell your chief and the old folks they are wise," Trib said. "It's the only choice you have."

"I do not think you can help us," the translator said quietly. "You are strange, angry, and violent. In the stories of my people, these are Snakebrother's qualities, and they have only ever harmed us."

"I reckon it doesn't matter what you think," Trib replied. "Tell your chief I'll leave now and return with reinforcements as quickly as I can. It will take some time, and the Puritanics could return any moment. You'll need to have an escape plan, a place to hide in case..."

"I will go with you," the translator interrupted. Everything about him conveyed misery at the prospect.

"Like Hell!" Trib exclaimed, wondering how she could have ever thought him attractive. Not even Cuss would like a man this irritating, regardless of how pretty he was. "You just said you think I'm this Snake-brother devil. Why would you go with me?" Trib asked.

"I do not want to go with you, but Chief Okahoki asked me to."

"What in Dess's Name for?"

"I am Kwineechka," he said simply. "Storyteller of the People."

Trib stared at him blankly.

"I must tell your people the story of the People. This is the tradition when the People meet other tribes. Our stories become one and create friendship and peace."

"I don't know what you're talking about," Trib said impatiently. "But standing here trying to figure it out is a waste of time I don't have. You'll come. Gather provisions and be ready to leave before noon."

"You are injured." He pointed at her bloodstained robe.

"I'm fine," she snapped. "You need to worry about keeping up."

As she limped her way out of the hut, she saw the storyteller give the chief a beseeching look. But the chief had spoken with finality. The storyteller was coming with her.

CHAPTER TEN

Peyewik

eyewik ran until his breath gave out, then he walked. He stumbled through the forest with the image of Chingwe's body before him, and the sound of his mother's cries in his ears.

There are evil spirits about you! You have brought Snakebrother's evil upon the People!

Peyewik knew it was true. He had dreamed of the Pale Ones, and they had come to him with all their anger and violence. Now, Chingwe was dead. Peyewik felt Sky Eyes' cold grip on his heart and knew he could never go home. He had to take his dreams and the bad spirits far away from the People so that no one else would be hurt.

He tripped over a root. The forest was growing dark. He had been running and walking all day with no idea where he was or how far he had come. He was tired enough to sleep, but too afraid of what might come to him in his dreams. The iciness in his chest was spreading, seeping into his muscles and bones. His arms and legs grew slow and heavy, and his chin dropped to his chest. He fell to his knees and could not rise. The cold had taken over; Sky Eyes' spirit had won. Then Peyewik heard something, a faint rumbling. With a tremendous effort he lifted his head.

A pair of yellow eyes stared at him from the gathering darkness. A feline body slipped like smoke from the shadows and came to stand before him, its purr a deep rumble in its chest. Peyewik looked into the eyes of the panther and felt no fear.

"Chingwe," he whispered, certain this was the spirit animal of his friend.

The cat turned and began to walk away, then stopped and looked back at Peyewik. Peyewik climbed to his feet and when the cat moved again, he followed. Soon he heard rough voices in the distance and caught a whiff of something rotten.

"I understand," he whispered to the cat, who gazed up at him for a moment then slunk back into the shadows, silent as a ghost. Chingwe's spirit had brought him to the Pale Ones. Peyewik was sure it meant that if he turned himself over to them, Sky Eyes' spirit would be appeased and the Pale Ones would leave the People alone. Resolve swept over him, and he walked towards the fire. The Pale Ones didn't see him coming so he opened his mouth to call out. Before he could make a sound a hand was clamped over his mouth and he was yanked off his feet by an arm around his waist. His first thought was that the Pale Ones had found him, but his captor moved away from the fire, deeper into the shadows. Peyewik tried to twist around to see who held him.

"It is better not to see me," came a harsh whisper from behind. It was a man's voice. The accent was strange, but Peyewik understood. "You have wandered far from home, little one, and the forest is not safe."

Through the trees Peyewik could see the Pale Ones getting to their feet and kicking out their fire. They were going away, and Chingwe's plan would be ruined. He tried to free himself so he could run to them, but the arm around his waist held fast. He was not released until the Pale Ones had moved off, stomping loudly through the trees.

"I will take you to your friends now," the stranger said.

"My friends?" Peyewik's heart jumped.

"They will take care of you," was the reply. "We must go quickly and warn them. Can you run?"

Peyewik was exhausted but he nodded. The next thing he knew the stranger had a tight grip on his hand and was pulling him through the forest at a fast pace. They didn't run away from the Pale Ones, as Peyewik expected, but in the same direction. He could hear them crashing through the underbrush somewhere to his left, until he and the stranger passed them by and the noise fell behind. Despite the growing darkness, the stranger ran easily and quietly, like a hunter. Peyewik tried to catch a glimpse of his face, but he wore a hooded robe.

Just when Peyewik thought his lungs would burst, another fire appeared through the trees and they slowed down. The stranger crept closer, still leading Peyewik by the hand. When Peyewik saw who sat beside the fire, he tried to break away.

"Do not fear the fighting woman. Go to the storyteller. His name is Kwineechka. He will take care of you. Warn him that there are Pale Ones nearby, approaching fast."

"You can tell him yourself?" Peyewik asked pleadingly.

"The fighting woman would kill me on sight," he said, his voice diminishing as he backed away. "I am sorry about your village, little one. I could not get there in time."

"Who *are* you?" Peyewik turned, but the stranger was gone. He turned back to the fire. He didn't want to go to it, but he had to warn the storyteller about the Pale Ones.

Kwineechka heard him before he saw him and alerted Flame Hair. She was on her feet with her longknife in her hand when Peyewik stepped into the ring of firelight. At the sight of him she lowered her weapon and turned to Kwineechka in confusion. She said something in her ugly language, but the storyteller didn't respond. He was staring at Peyewik in surprise.

"You are from the village of the Original People," he said. "The healer's grandson. Why are you here? Someone is with you?" He peered into the darkness behind Peyewik.

"I am alone..." Peyewik panted, still out of breath from his run with the stranger. "I..."

Flame Hair interrupted angrily, moving towards Peyewik with her longknife raised. Kwineechka stepped between them and said something loud and abrupt. Flame Hair glared at him, but lowered her weapon.

"Do not pay attention to her," the storyteller said, squatting down beside Peyewik. "Tell me what is wrong, little brother. Why are you out here alone?"

"No time," Peyewik said. "Pale Ones come this way."

The storyteller sprang up. "How many? From which direction?"

"Six," Peyewik said and pointed back the way he had just come.

Kwineechka told Flame Hair and she kicked out the fire. She hissed something at him as he helped her bury the embers.

"She says we must find a place to hide," the storyteller told Peyewik. "She will stay here, to draw them away if they smell the smoke and come too close."

Peyewik followed Kwineechka into the trees, and they knelt down behind a large rock.

"Keep your head down," Kwineechka whispered. Peyewik took one last look back towards the place where the fire had been. It was full dark now and he could barely make out Flame Hair's crouching shadow. She remained completely still as the Pale Ones drew closer. Peyewik could hear the leaves and twigs crunching under their feet now. He remembered the last time he had hidden from the Pale Ones, with Chingwe beside the river, and felt Sky Eyes' spirit tighten its grip on his heart until he was sure it would kill him.

CHAPTER ELEVEN

Trib

Trib crouched next to the smoldering remains of the fire, sword across her thighs, and listened for the approaching enemy. The Natives had disappeared into the dark trees behind her without a sound. She had been angry when the boy first appeared, taken off guard and suspicious, but the storyteller had insisted that the boy was alone. There hadn't been time to explain further. If the boy hadn't shown up when he did, she and the storyteller might have been taken unaware by the approaching Puritanics.

She could hear the Puritanics coming now. They were talking and laughing and making no effort to hide their presence. Trib's heart started to pound in anticipation of a fight.

Then she heard the Puritanics change direction, veering away from her hiding place and the Natives. She felt disappointed, but also relieved. In truth, she wasn't sure her tired, wounded body could manage another Rage so soon.

She was getting ready to go find the Natives when she heard one of the Puritanics shout about needing to take a piss. She heard him break away from the others and move back towards her. She debated summoning a Rage but decided she could handle one Puritanic without it. It never occurred to her that she could let him go, that she might steal away, and he would never know she had been there. She couldn't give up the opportunity to punish any Puritanic that came within arm's reach.

She could see the Puritanic now, a black shape moving against gray tree trunks. He came to a stop no more than fifteen paces away from her. She knew she would have to subdue him quickly before he could call for help. She rose and moved towards him as quietly as possible. He sighed contentedly as he relieved himself, completely unaware of her presence. He was tall, and she had to reach to get an arm around his throat. He yelled, but she stifled the sound in the folds of her robe and dragged him to the ground. She was surprised by how big he was, by the bulk of his body in her arms, and the strength of him. These were things she was never aware of when she was in a Rage. She held him down by wrapping her legs around his torso and brought her blade to his throat. The killing moment had arrived but she hesitated. The Puritanic twisted half-way around in her grasp, and she saw his face. The night was dark, but not so much that she couldn't see the mistake she had made. The Puritanic she held was a smooth-faced boy.

Trib's gut twisted into a knot. This wasn't right. Puritanics were full grown, bearded men—merciless tyrants who killed children. This boy, for all his height, was no more than a child himself. He didn't look merciless, he looked terrified, the whites of his eyes showing in the dark as he tried to see who or what had attacked him.

Trib was losing control of him as he thrashed about. The others would hear and come running soon. She knew she had to kill him now. She could feel his face under her hand, his beard no more than a few straggling wisps on his chin. He was probably younger than she was, not much older than the Native boy.

"Hush," Trib whispered into his ear as if he was a baby to be soothed. "Hush."

He was sobbing now, gasping against her hand. He felt so alive and strong in her arms. This was some woman's son. Suddenly the last thing Trib wanted to do was end this boy.

Suddenly he reared up and nearly threw her off. He managed a choked cry, and there was a shouted reply in the distance. She had no choice. The others were coming for him. Trib forced her right arm to pull the blade across his throat. She put all her strength into it, fearing the blade would be dull and he wouldn't die quickly enough. "'Dess, help me," she gasped. Unlike the times she had killed in the past, now she was horrifyingly aware of everything she did. She felt every bit of flesh she cut through as skin and muscle parted under her blade. She gagged as she felt the boy respond to what she was doing to him, heard the horrible sound he made when he tried to cry out. His body continued to move, at first trying to escape, and then convulsing involuntarily. She had killed him, but he wasn't dead yet. He was watching her, his face inches from hers as blood poured through the gaping hole where his throat should have been clean and whole.

Trib's hand was slick with blood, and she let go of the blade. Through the sound of sobbing, which she recognized as her own since the boy was no longer capable, she heard the Puritanics shouting, crashing through the underbrush towards her. She struggled to push the boy's weight off of her, her own muscles stiff and unresponsive as if she were the one dying. She staggered to her feet and yanked her sword out of the boy's neck. Then she limped in the direction she thought the Natives had gone, throwing up as she went. She almost hoped she wouldn't find them, afraid they might have seen what she had done.

Two shapes rose from the ground in front of her, one tall, one small. They stood calmly, without horror, and she knew they hadn't seen.

"Run!" she croaked as a cry went up behind her. The body had been discovered. The Natives turned and did as she bade them. It was all she could do to keep up with them as they moved swiftly and silently through the dark forest.

CHAPTER TWELVE

Peyewik

Peyewik and Kwineechka slowed their pace so Flame Hair could keep up. She was gasping for breath, and every now and then a tiny sob escaped her.

"What has happened?" Peyewik whispered. "She is hurt?"

"I do not know," Kwineechka replied. "I do not think we are being followed." He came to a halt and listened. All Peyewik could hear was Flame Hair's ragged breathing. She was too winded to speak, but she gestured that they should keep going. Kwineechka started to argue, but she ignored him and resumed her awkward half-run.

"Little brother, you are tired," the storyteller said. "You can keep going?"

Peyewik was more tired than he had ever been in his life. Beyond exhaustion, he felt like he was moving weightless through a dream. He started to jog again.

"She cannot go much longer," the storyteller said, pacing alongside.

Sure enough, after a short while Flame Hair tripped, tried to rise, and fell again. She stayed where she was, sprawled on the ground.

"She is hurt?" Peyewik asked again. Kwineechka bent down to look at her.

"She is breathing." He poked her with a stick. "No new injuries. I think she sleeps."

Peyewik knew there was something wrong with her, but the story-teller shrugged, unconcerned.

"You should sleep too," he told Peyewik, untying the small bundle strapped across his back. "This is a good place to stop."

They were surrounded by tall trees that blocked out the stars overhead. It was still very dark and Peyewik could not tell if they were closer to the beginning of the night or the end. It felt like three nights had passed since he had last seen the sun.

The storyteller handed him a sleeping skin. "I carried an extra in case of cold, lucky for you. We should not make a fire, in case the Pure Men are near."

Peyewik peered into the darkness nervously.

"Do not worry," the storyteller said. "If they come, we will hear them long before they get too close."

Peyewik took the sleeping skin and said, "Thank you." Then he knelt beside Flame Hair and untied the bundle on her back. He pulled out her sleeping skin and draped it over her.

The storyteller sat cross-legged on the ground, watching him. "You are kind," he said.

"She would get cold."

"This is true." The thought didn't seem to bother him, and he changed the subject. "We were far from your village when you appeared. How did you find us?"

"There was a man in the forest. He brought me to you."

"A man? Of the People?"

"He spoke the language of the People, but strangely. He knew your name."

"This man told you his name?"

"No. He would not let me see his face either. You know him?"

The storyteller was silent for a moment. Then he said, "If I do, he is a friend."

Peyewik wanted to know more, but the storyteller asked him another question.

"Why were you out in the forest alone at night?"

Peyewik pulled his knees up to his chest. "I ran away."

"Why?" The storyteller wasn't shocked or upset. He just sounded curious.

"Chingwe was killed," Peyewik explained. "It was my fault. I had to leave so that no more of the People would be hurt. Chingwe's spirit..." He glanced up at the storyteller but could not see his face in the darkness. "His spirit came to me."

The storyteller waited for him to say more.

"He came to me as a panther and led me to the Pale Ones. I think he wanted me to go to them so that they would be satisfied and leave the People alone."

"You did not go to them?" Kwineechka asked.

"The stranger caught me and brought me to you."

"Maybe your friend's spirit led you to the stranger, not the Pale Ones."

"It was my fault," Peyewik insisted.

"Tell me how it was your fault," the storyteller said patiently.

"An angry spirit clings to me. It drew the Pale Ones to the village, and the Pale Ones killed Chingwe."

Kwineechka was quiet for a few breaths, then he said, "I have heard people talk about you. You are the boy who dreams and is visited by many spirits."

"Yes," Peyewik whispered. He was dismayed to learn that he was talked about even in the village of the Away People.

"Do not be sorry for it," Kwineechka said. "You are a gift to the People. They are the ones who should be sorry for not recognizing this."

Peyewik was stunned. He had been sure the storyteller would be wary of him just like everyone else.

"You did not bring Snakebrother to the village," Kwineechka continued. "She did." He pointed at the dark lump on the ground that was Flame Hair. "She does not know it, but Snakebrother walks beside her. He hisses in her ear and she does his bidding."

Peyewik wondered if this could be true, if Flame Hair really was the one to blame for the coming of the Pale Ones.

"If Snakebrother walks with her, how can her people help us?" Peyewik asked.

Earlier, while they were hiding, the storyteller had whispered a brief explanation of what he and Flame Hair were doing out in the forest together, where they were going.

"Your chief thinks they can. He is a wise man, but I am not so sure. I will tell the fighting women our story, as your chief asks, and they will decide how they will be a part of it, for good or bad."

"You think it will be bad," Peyewik said.

"She is a man-killer," the storyteller replied. "She may not mean to do evil, but anger and violence are the way of her people and of Snakebrother. I do not see how they can help us."

Peyewik struggled to take this in. He was too tired to think anymore.

"Do not worry for now, little brother," the storyteller said. "All you need to do is sleep. I will keep watch."

Peyewik lay down obediently and let the storyteller tuck the sleeping skin around him. The nearness of dreams made him anxious, and he did not think he would be able to sleep.

As if he could hear thoughts, the storyteller said, "I will sing a prayer to Manito for your dreams to leave you in peace."

He began to hum, and Peyewik felt immediately comforted. Within moments he slid gratefully into a dreamless sleep.

CHAPTER THIRTEEN

Trib

Trib didn't know where she was when she woke up, but she could tell dawn wasn't far off. It was still dark, but the birds were starting to make noise and the treetops were becoming visible overhead. Nearby she could see the outlines of sleeping bodies. Her first thought was that it was Cuss and the other apprentices, but there were only two bodies, and one was small. She remembered through the fog in her head that she was traveling back to the bay with two Natives, and that Cuss was dead.

She sat up stiffly. Her head felt heavy and her whole body ached from lying on the exposed roots of a tree. She wondered why she'd chosen such an uncomfortable spot for her bed. She reached for her sword, but it wasn't beside her. She felt around her bedroll, and then crawled in widening circles, growing more frantic with each turn. She breathed a sigh of relief when her palm came down on the hilt, but it was odd that the weapon lay so far away from her bedroll, as though she had tossed it away before sleep. And there was something wrong with the blade. She brought it close to her face so she could see in the meager light.

There was blood on the blade. She'd forgotten to clean it.

Then she remembered. The Puritanic boy came back to her like a blow to the gut. She could feel him struggling in her arms, his hot blood gushing over her hands from the gaping wound in his throat.

Her fingers clenched reflexively around her sword, her left hand on the blade. She could feel it biting into her palm and welcomed the pain.

"What've I done?" she moaned.

"You are ill?"

The storyteller was sitting up, his face blurry in the gray light.

"No," she gasped. She tried to let go of the sword, but couldn't. She needed to be strong in front of the Native, but she kept seeing the boy's eyes rolling in his head, hearing the gurgle of his dying breaths.

"Blood." The storyteller pointed.

Trib looked down. Fresh, red blood was running down the blade, mixing with the black, dried blood of the Puritanic boy.

"I killed a boy last night!" Trib hadn't wanted the storyteller to know what she had done, but the words came of their own volition, like a poison being expelled from her body.

He recoiled visibly, but he didn't flee from her. He held himself steady and said, "You have killed many."

"Aye, but this one was just a boy, some woman's child..." Trib's stomach churned, and it felt as though a heavy weight pressed against her chest.

"All boys are some woman's child," the storyteller said. "All boys grow into men. Like the men you killed in the village of the Original People. What is the difference?" he challenged her, trying to understand.

"I used the Rage in the village. It can only be used against enemies. The Goddess wouldn't have let it work on an innocent boy. I didn't use the Rage on the boy, though. I just killed him. Dess forgive me," she said, "I don't know if he was innocent or not."

"If he is the son of your enemy, isn't he also your enemy?" the storyteller asked.

"Puritanics steal boys from their New Murian mothers," Trib replied. "Force them to their ways and beliefs. If the boys refuse, the Puritanics kill them."

"Only boys? They do not steal girls?"

"Don't bother with girls. Just kill them outright, like they did my sisters."

When the storyteller made no reply, she looked up. He was watching her, his face unreadable. He shifted forward onto his knees, no longer poised to spring away.

"I am sorry your sisters were killed," he said.

"They killed ma, too." She said the words without emotion because she felt none. The Puritanics had murdered her family a long time ago, before she was taken in by the Scath to be raised as a warrior. She had only one set of memories of the event and the people, and she kept them carefully guarded, recalling them only when she needed to summon a Rage.

"You're bleeding," the storyteller said quietly. He stood slowly, moved within arm's reach of her, and knelt down again.

"Dess forgive me if I've killed an innocent boy," Trib said again, vaguely aware of the storyteller's nearness.

He reached out and touched her clenched fingers lightly.

"If I could give him his life back, I would," she said.

She had killed before, but had never felt like this. It had never felt like anything before. The Rage had kept her numb. But without the Rage, the killing felt like Hell.

The storyteller sat in front of her, his knees touching hers. His eyes were on her hands as he carefully tried to loosen them from the sword. He started to sing. He was very quiet, but his head was close to hers and the vibrations of his voice buzzed softly in her ear, in her head. Her grip relaxed. He lifted the sword out of her hands and set it aside.

"What's the song about?" she murmured.

"It is a story," he said, holding her bleeding hand in his. "About a spirit crossing the River of Death and being happy to see the friends and family who have crossed before him."

Tears sprang to Trib's eyes. She wiped them away with her good hand, hoping the storyteller hadn't seen.

"Why are you helping me?" she asked. "You don't like me."

"I am helping you because you need help," the storyteller answered.

Trib lifted her head and looked straight into his eyes. She would've preferred disgust or hatred to the pity she saw there.

"I will find you a bandage," he said.

"No." She pulled her hand away and tried to stand, but her injured leg was stiff and she stumbled. The storyteller caught her elbow, but she shrugged him off.

"I don't need your help," she said.

The storyteller stood and walked away without a word.

Trib dug one-handed through her small bundle of belongings for something to stop the bleeding. The cut on her palm stung now. She found a strip of cloth and tied it using her teeth. She could hear the storyteller singing again, quietly, from a distance, and tried to ignore the sound.

When she heard the storyteller returning, she steeled herself, remembering what the Scath always said about never giving ground to a man. The storyteller would never see her vulnerable again. She stood up.

"What happened to the Puritanics that were following us last night?" she asked as he approached. She hated to admit that she didn't remember, but she needed to know.

"They did not find our trail. We were not followed," the storyteller said.

Trib realized how lucky this was. She would've been in no condition to fight them off if they had followed. She turned to look at the still sleeping form on the ground.

"The boy can't travel home alone," she said. "You'll have to take him back."

"The boy's name is Peyewik," the storyteller replied. "He does not want to go back."

"Why not?"

"He thinks the attack on the village was his fault."

"That's a damn-fool notion," Trib said. "Wasn't his fault."

"I told him this," the storyteller nodded, bending over to roll up his sleeping skin. "I told him it was your fault."

"You're blaming me again?" She took an aggressive step towards him.

The storyteller straightened up and stared at her, the half-rolled sleeping skin in his hands. There was a flash of anger in his golden eyes, but before he could say anything the boy, Peyewik, sat up.

He looked at both of them anxiously, trying to get his bearings. The anger left the storyteller's face as he spoke to the boy in the Native language. The boy looked reassured. He got up, walked a few paces away, then raised his arms and began singing, just as the storyteller had done a few moments earlier.

"What is he doing?" Trib asked impatiently.

"Giving thanks to sun."

"For what?"

"Rising."

"Oh." Trib had never thought about what made the sun rise every morning. She tried not to think about the Puritanic boy who would never see the sun rise again.

"Peyewik comes with us," she said to the storyteller. "He's your responsibility. If he slows us down at all, I leave both of you behind."

CHAPTER FOURTEEN

Peyewik

Peyewik hurried to keep up with the storyteller's long strides. The early sun was warm against his face and made him glad. The previous day and night had felt like an endless nightmare. And although he was now far from home and facing certain danger in the company of two near-strangers, he rejoiced in the new day.

His stomach gurgled with hunger and he tried to ignore it. The storyteller had been kind to him the night before, but he couldn't help being intimidated by Kwineechka, Storyteller of the People. Peyewik had never heard Kwineechka tell a story in person, but he had heard about stories of great power from others who had traveled to hear him. The Storyteller commanded almost as much respect as a chief, and Peyewik couldn't imagine bothering him about something as trifling as breakfast.

"I am sorry, little brother," Kwineechka said suddenly. "I was in such a hurry to get on our way..." He glanced back at Flame Hair stomping angrily behind and grimaced. "I forgot about breakfast. You must be hungry."

Peyewik had watched Kwineechka and Flame Hair arguing before setting out. He didn't know what it had been about, but the air between them had been charged like just before a lightning storm. The charge had dissipated once they started walking, but Flame Hair had been grumbling to herself all morning, and Peyewik saw the storyteller's jaw tighten every time she spoke.

The storyteller took a pouch from his waist and held it out. "Try some of this," he said. "It is cornmeal and maple sugar. Hunters carry it when they are away from the village for many days. A small handful will fill you up. I prefer porridge, but I did not bring a cooking pot."

He smiled and Peyewik scooped a handful out of the pouch. The storyteller turned and offered the pouch to Flame Hair, but she just shook her head with a grunt.

"Too proud to eat?" the storyteller muttered.

Peyewik didn't know if he was expected to answer.

"How can anyone think she is anything but an ally of Snakebrother, God of Chaos?" the storyteller continued. "She takes all sense and order out of the world. One moment she cries as if she is truly sorry for killing someone. The next moment she is like this..." He gestured over his shoulder at her. "Rude, thoughtless, and disgusting."

Peyewik looked back at Flame Hair. Her garishly colored hair was a snarled mess and her robe was stained. She moved awkwardly and made so much noise it seemed as though she was deliberately stepping on every twig in her path. The ones she didn't step on she tripped over.

Peyewik had to agree with the storyteller that she did not make sense. It was impossible to match the lithe, happy spirit animal he'd seen with this clumsy, belligerent girl.

"I will not try to understand her anymore," Kwineechka said. "Snakebrother has made her crazy. Think of the wife she would make."

Peyewik couldn't help laughing at this. "She would have to take a bath first," he said.

The storyteller shook his head. "I do not think it would help. I am sorry for the man who becomes husband to Walks-Like-Moose-Smells-Like-Rancid-Bear-Grease-Woman."

Peyewik laughed again and it felt good. He hadn't laughed in a long time, not since he and Chingwe had stopped being friends. Then he remembered that Chingwe was dead and his laughter faded.

70

"I understand the burden you carry, little brother," the storyteller said. Peyewik looked up, surprised.

"When I was your age," the storyteller explained, "I received my blessing, and it was that I would be the next Storyteller of the People. My parents were glad, for this was a great honor. But I was no longer allowed to play with my friends. I spent all my time with the old storyteller, learning how to let the ancestors speak through me. That is where the stories come from, from the spirits of those who lived them. They no longer have voices and bodies of their own so they must use mine. The Storyteller of the People receives much respect, but my friends no longer know what to say to me. And when it is time to tell a story, my body and voice are not my own."

This sounded familiar to Peyewik, except for one thing.

"The People do not respect me," he said bitterly. "They are afraid of me."

"They do not understand yet. In the stories there are always messages and warnings before something happens to the People. Nothing has happened to the People in a long time and, they have forgotten this. But change is coming. Your grandfather thinks so too. Your dreams and visions are a warning to the People. Something is coming, and it is not good. Flame Hair is proof of it."

"Why do the spirits choose me?" Peyewik asked. "I am just a boy. I do not understand any of this, and I am afraid!"

The storyteller's golden eyes were full of sympathy. "Your dreams and visions are a gift from Manito, just like my stories. They are also a burden. I know this. I did not want to come on this journey with Flame Hair, but now I am glad I did. It is good that you and I are together."

"You are not afraid of my dreams or of what may come?" Peyewik asked.

The storyteller stopped walking and turned to face Peyewik. "I will tell you a story," he said.

A thrill shot through Peyewik. A story from the Storyteller of the People! He turned to see how far behind Flame Hair was, but Kwineechka was already speaking, drawing Peyewik's attention like a moth to flame. His voice grew deep and powerful and became the sound of many voices speaking as one.

⚏

"Manito's children lived in peace on Mother Earth's belly."

Peyewik felt the ancestors' voices resonate in his bones.

"Manito loved his children very much, and they wanted for nothing. They knew neither cold nor hunger, and they were content..."

Peyewik felt as though he was traveling a great distance without moving from the place where he stood. The forest around him faded and was replaced by a vision of another forest. Manito's children walked among the tall trees of this forest, exploring Mother Earth, full of wonder. Peyewik shared their happiness as they rejoiced in the glorious sun overhead, and in the quenching rain that fell on the sweet, rich soil. He joined Manito's children in their songs of thanks and love. He felt many seasons pass and saw many generations live with the same joy and wonder.

Then Peyewik heard a strange hissing sound. Manito's children heard it too, and they listened, curious, as the hissing grew louder. It was Snake, jealous of his brother Manito's love for his children. He had come to spread lies and discord. Manito's children did not know better and they listened to his lies.

Peyewik felt the world grow cold and his teeth began to chatter. Snakebrother's lies had brought Winter into the world. Hunger gnawed at Peyewik's belly, and he watched Manito's children become weak and sick. The hissing grew louder still, and Peyewik could hear what Snakebrother was saying.

"Manito has forsaken you...he does not love you anymore...."

Manito's children argued that Manito would never do this.

Then Snakebrother said, "There is still a warm place in the world, but my brother does not want you to know about it."

Some of the People continued to fight Snakebrother's lies, for they had learned to build houses, and they were warm and protected from the cold. But there were others who wanted to go and find the warm place that Snakebrother told them about. They were angry with Manito for betraying them, and they became angry with those who still believed in him.

Peyewik felt the first act of violence as if the blow had fallen on his own body. He cried out in pain as the snow became red with the blood of Manito's children, spilled by their own brothers and sisters. He cried out in sadness too, for Snakebrother had achieved his end, and Manito's children were divided.

But then the snow began to melt, and Peyewik felt the world growing warm once more. Manito's children put down their weapons and lay down to rest. In their dreams they could hear the spirits of the trees and the rivers speaking to them. When they woke from their dreams, Manito's children knew that Manito had not forsaken them, that he had brought Spring into the world for them. They also knew that he was always with them, no matter how hungry, cold, or scared they might become. All they had to do was listen and they would hear him and know.

Then Manito's children, the People, rejoiced. They sang songs of thanks and love again, and Snakebrother went away to a far part of the world, and many generations lived untroubled by him.

The voices of Kwineechka and the ancestors fell silent. Time caught up with itself and resumed its normal pace. Peyewik blinked and looked around. Flame Hair was still limping towards them as though nothing had happened. The storyteller's eyes were vague and far away. Slowly they came back into focus and he fixed them on Peyewik.

"The spirits speak to the People through you," he said, "just as the ancestors speak through me. It is always Manito reminding us that he is with us. I am not afraid of you, and I am not afraid of what may come."

Flame Hair caught up then and looked at them questioningly, wondering why they had stopped. She barked at Kwineechka, who started walking quickly to get away from her, and everything was back to normal.

Peyewik jogged to keep up with the storyteller and thought about what he had seen and heard in the story. It made him feel better about the spirits who spoke to him, Manito's messengers. He was still scared, though. If his dreams really were messages from Manito, then the People were not listening, and the way was open for whatever strife and suffering Snakebrother would bring.

CHAPTER FIFTEEN

Trib

Each step had become excruciating, but Trib wouldn't let herself lean on a crutch or ask the Natives for help. It wasn't until the shadows in the forest began to grow long that she called out to the storyteller.

"Reckon it's time to stop for the night," she said, trying to keep the strain from her voice. "The boy'll be getting tired."

The storyteller and the boy stopped and waited for her to catch up. She gritted her teeth and tried to hide her limp as she drew close.

"Peyewik is not tired," the storyteller told her. A smile lingered on his face, as if he and the boy had just been laughing about something. "We will walk until dark. Unless *you* are tired."

Trib glared at him, wishing she'd never agreed to bring him along. All day she'd been walking behind him, watching his long, black hair swing over his smooth, coppery back. He hadn't spoken to her since taking the blade out of her hand, except to offer her some inedible food. He walked ahead as if he were in charge, without bothering to consult her about their route. She wondered where a storyteller got such nerve. There were storytellers in the settlement, but they told their stories for entertainment, when the real work of the day was done. If this arrogant Native couldn't do anything more than tell a tale, he was less important and more useless than the lowliest, chamber pot-emptying houseboy.

"Damned disrespectful," Trib muttered. No man in the settlement would behave this way in the company of a warrior. Manservants, farmhands, and houseboys all knew their place.

Trib knew it was her own fault, though. She had let him see her in a moment of vulnerability. She hadn't meant to, but killing the Puritanic boy without the Rage had affected her in unexpected ways. She realized she needed to get control of herself, act like a warrior and put the killing behind her. And then make the storyteller show her some respect.

"If you are tired, we will stop now," the storyteller said.

A half-smile still played across his lips, and Trib was sure he was laughing at her.

"No. I ain't tired," she barked. "We'll keep going." She took a step and it was all she could do not to yell out in pain.

The boy, who had been watching Trib, spoke up.

"Peyewik wants to stop," the storyteller translated.

"Aye, he's tired, like I said."

The storyteller made no reply except to look pointedly at her injured leg. She turned her back on him and made for the nearest fallen log.

"Thank Dess…" she hissed as she sat down and stretched her leg out in front of her.

The storyteller and the boy set up camp, chattering away in their strange, flowing language. Trib wondered what the Scath would think to see her following this insolent, pretty-eyed man around like a docile cow. The old warrior would show him who was in charge in no time. She would wipe that smirk right off his face. The thought pleased Trib immensely.

She noticed that the boy had begun gathering sticks.

"No fire," she said. "Puritanics might see it."

"To cook," the storyteller explained. "We must eat."

"To cook what? Are you going to hunt us some fresh meat and make a stew? Where's your cooking pot?"

The storyteller looked offended. "Cooking is women's work," he said.

Trib went rigid. "What did you say?"

"Cooking is women's work," he repeated.

Trib saw flickers of red at the edges of her vision. "Not where I come from," she growled. She felt a Rage coming on and embraced it gratefully. It was time to teach the storyteller some respect.

She threw herself at him, her hands closing around his throat. She could feel his pulse under her thumbs. And suddenly she thought of the Puritanic boy's eyes, terrified in the darkness.

Her Rage disappeared as quickly as it had come.

She pushed away from the storyteller, feeling strangely ashamed.

He was on his knees, clutching his throat and coughing, but Trib was barely aware of him. All she could think of was the Puritanic boy dying in her arms.

"I'm sorry!" she cried. "Forgive me."

Then she covered her face with her hands and roared in frustration. She had been taught that the Rage was her Goddess-given right as a warrior to use against her enemies, who were the Puritanics and any man who wronged her. The boy she had killed was an enemy, and the storyteller had wronged her with his disrespect. But if this was true, why did she wish with all her heart that she hadn't killed that boy, and why had using the Rage on the storyteller suddenly felt so wrong?

There was a touch at her elbow and she jumped. It was the boy, holding out a piece of dried meat. She was impressed by his courage, being willing to get near her after what she'd just done to the storyteller. She looked around for him, but he was nowhere to be seen.

"Thanks," she said, taking the meat and biting off a hunk. She held it in her mouth to let it soften before trying to chew it. She expected the boy to scamper away, but he stayed beside her, gnawing away at his own dinner.

"Kid, I never been so lost and confused in my life," Trib was surprised to hear herself saying. The boy turned to look at her, and, although she knew he couldn't understand her, he seemed to be listening carefully all the same.

"All I want is to get back to my people, back to a life I know and understand, and back to following the Scath's orders. I've been following orders all my life, and never once have I had to figure out what's right or wrong."

She chewed and swallowed.

"Once," she told him, "I was passing through the gates of the settlement and looked up to see a severed head on a pike. I reckoned it belonged to a Puritanic raider who'd been burning outlying houses and crops, but I was told it was the head of a manservant. I asked what he'd done, and they told me he'd broken a dish and disrespected the householder he worked for."

Trib felt sick to her stomach and couldn't eat any more.

"I remember that didn't seem right to me, but I was a warrior and it wasn't my problem. So I just forgot about it. Until now."

She looked up then to see the storyteller standing nearby, watching and listening. She could see the marks her fingers had left on his neck. She remembered the look of pity in his eyes earlier that day. It was gone, replaced by a look she couldn't quite place. There was anger and disgust, which she understood, but there was something else. She didn't have time to figure it out because he turned away and didn't look at her again for the rest of the night.

CHAPTER SIXTEEN

Peyewik

Crow perched in a tree. On the ground below stood a group of women, including one to whom Crow felt a strong affinity. This woman wore long black robes, her face was as pale as the moon, and the other women followed her as a leader.

There were also men on the ground below Crow, but most of them were dead. Crow had witnessed the slaughter. They hadn't stood a chance against the fury of the women. Only three men remained alive, and these knelt before Crow's woman. Crow cawed impatiently. She had sampled the remains and was hungry for more.

Bear sniffed the wind. She smelled humans. They were too far away for her weak eyes to see, but her nose told her everything. Men lay dead, bleeding into the forest floor. Angry women held metal weapons in their sweating hands. Crow was there with her human counterpart. Bear did not trust Crow. She was a carrion feeder, insatiable and unpredictable.

Bear recognized the scent of her own counterpart among the humans, an older woman with a storm of rage contained and controlled within her. Bear was not generally interested in humans but she respected this one, the devastation she could unleash at will. Bear saluted her with a roar before turning away.

Crow ruffled her feathers at the sound of Bear's roar. She could tell Bear was far away and not looking for a fight or dinner. Crow flew down

*and pulled at her woman's hair, impatient for the last three deaths. But
her woman did not kill the men. Instead she sang to them, a song that
Crow had heard her sing before, always to men. It sapped their wills
and bound them to her body and soul. When the song ended, the men
remained kneeling with their heads bowed until Crow's woman told
them to stand and walk.*

Peyewik woke shivering. It was still night and a chill wind was blowing
through the branches overhead. It felt as though autumn had come early,
but this wasn't the only reason Peyewik shivered. He had dreamed again.
He thought of the storyteller's words: The spirits speak through you.
It is Manito's voice... and tried not to be afraid, but the cold crept into
his chest and clutched at his heart. He could not imagine why Manito
would want him to see the disturbing things he had seen through the
eyes of Crow and Bear. He longed for his grandfather. Muhkrentharne
would know what the dream meant. But Muhkrentharne and the rest of
the People were far away, and Peyewik kept shivering.

There was movement in the dark, and Peyewik realized Flame
Hair sat beside him. He felt her cloak, warm from her body, fall over
him. It didn't smell very good, but it eased his shivering.

⚙

When Peyewik woke again, it was daylight, and Kwineechka and
Flame Hair were already awake, sitting a good distance apart with
their backs to each other. The silence between them was heavy.
Flame Hair kept glancing over her shoulder at the storyteller. Peyewik couldn't read the expression on her face. The storyteller sat rigid
with an air of grievance.

Peyewik got up and handed the cloak back to Flame Hair. He
thanked her for it and looked to the storyteller to translate, but
Kwineechka didn't move. Peyewik went and stood in front of him.
The storyteller crossed his arms and stared straight ahead.

"The marks on your neck are gone," Peyewik pointed out.

"That does not mean they were not there yesterday, that she did not attack me like a wild animal," Kwineechka huffed.

Peyewik couldn't help smiling. "You are angry because you got knocked down by a girl."

Kwineechka frowned sourly. Then he looked at Peyewik for the first time. "Little brother, you look tired. You did not sleep well?"

"I dreamed."

"Tell me," Kwineechka said gently.

"I saw the Fighting Women," Peyewik replied.

Kwineechka's frown deepened. "What did they do?"

"They killed many Pure Men. There were two...Crow Woman and Bear Woman. The Crow Woman sang a strange song that made the Pure Men obey her."

"This Crow Woman is a sorcerer? This is magic like Flame Hair's Rage?"

"I don't know," Peyewik shook his head. "We should ask Flame Hair about her."

Kwineechka's back went rigid again. "I will not speak to her. She tried to kill me."

"She did not try very hard," Peyewik said, looking over the storyteller's shoulder at Flame Hair's hunched form. "Her Rage was not strong. I think she does not know what else to do when she feels bad."

"This means she is allowed to behave like an animal?" the storyteller demanded. But he turned grudgingly and spoke to her.

Flame Hair jumped at the sound of his voice but listened attentively. When he was done, she looked confused and shook her head.

"She does not know a Crow or a Bear Woman," the storyteller said.

"One of her chiefs wears black robes and carries a crow on her shoulder," Peyewik said. "Ask her." Then he waited for the wary look.

It came and Flame Hair answered slowly, staring at him.

"Flame Hair knows this woman. She is..." Kwineechka struggled to understand what Flame Hair was saying. "She does not fight. She is a priestess. Her sister is the warrior, the one who taught Flame Hair how to fight."

"This is Crow Woman, and her sister is Bear Woman," Peyewik confirmed.

Flame Hair pointed at Peyewik and said something in a questioning tone, but Kwineechka ignored her.

"What do you think the spirits are trying to tell you about the Fighting Woman and their leaders," he asked.

This question made Peyewik anxious. "Between the Rage and Crow Woman's spell-song, the Fighting Women are stronger than the Pure Men. Maybe the spirits want us to know we have made the right choice, that the Fighting Women can protect us against the Pure Men?"

He hoped this was what the dream meant, but he couldn't forget that the vision had been frightening, and he had awoken from it with the cold clutching at his heart again.

Kwineechka looked skeptical. "A whole village of women like Flame Hair is terrifying to think of."

✳

Later, after they had started the day's journey, Kwineechka offered Peyewik the pouch of cornmeal. Peyewik took some and then watched the storyteller struggle internally before turning and offering it to Flame Hair as well. She surprised them both by smiling and grabbing a large handful. She slapped the whole thing into her mouth and then gagged as the dry grain caught in her throat.

"Greedy," Kwineechka rolled his eyes and thumped her on the back harder than he needed to.

Flame Hair shoved him away and choked out a few angry-sounding words.

Kwineechka froze, staring at her.

Peyewik held his breath.

Then the storyteller burst out laughing. "She said now we are even! We have both tried to choke the other and failed so now we must call a truce."

Flame Hair smiled weakly between coughing fits.

"You agree?" Peyewik asked nervously.

"It does not sound like any apology I have heard before," the storyteller said. "But she made me laugh, so I will accept for now."

For the rest of the morning Flame Hair kept pace with Peyewik and Kwineechka. Her leg didn't seem to be bothering her as much and while she still walked loudly, she wasn't quite as loud as the moose Kwineechka proclaimed her to be.

Around midday they stopped to refill their waterskins from a stream. Peyewik knelt down to drink and was slapped in the face by an arc of cold water. He spluttered while the storyteller laughed from a rock in the middle the stream.

"I got you, little brother!" he crowed.

Peyewik sprang to his feet and started kicking water at him.

"Now you are in trouble," Kwineechka said stepping onto the bank. "Now you take a bath."

He moved to pick Peyewik up, but Peyewik stepped one foot behind him, locked his knee in place, and pushed him off balance, right into the stream.

"Now *you* take a bath," Peyewik said, grinning widely as Flame Hair cheered in approval.

Kwineechka climbed out of the creek, dripping from head to foot. "How did you do that?" he asked, ignoring Flame Hair's taunts.

"Flame Hair showed me."

The storyteller looked surprised.

"I can teach you if you want," Peyewik offered.

Flame Hair was still laughing. Kwineechka raised an eyebrow at her and then shook out his long hair, spraying her with water.

"Teach me," he said quickly, before Flame Hair could retaliate.

It soon became clear that the storyteller had indeed spent more of his youth learning stories than playing with other boys. The move did not come easily, and he kept cheating, picking Peyewik up, or tickling him until he fell down. Finally Flame Hair put a hand on Peyewik's shoulder, indicating that it was time for her to take his place. He stepped aside, laughing at how quickly the storyteller's face went from playful to anxious.

After many bruises and rolls in the dirt, Flame Hair managed to show the storyteller how to knock her down. He threw his arms up in triumph and made up a song for himself on the spot.

Mighty Kwineechka!
Felled the Flame-haired monster.
Such a strong storyteller, such a brave storyteller.

He translated it for Flame Hair, which earned him a punch on the arm.

"Ow ow ow..." Kwineechka rubbed his arm and kept singing.

Wounded storyteller
Treacherous Smells-Like-Rancid-Bear-Grease-Woman...

Peyewik laughed, his dreams from the night before all but forgotten.

They continued their southeastern journey in good spirits for the first time, laughing and joking as they went. As the afternoon light turned gold and the shadows began to stretch, Peyewik noticed that the terrain was changing, the ground was flattening out. The soil underfoot was sandy, and there were more short pine trees among the taller sycamores and oaks. He also noticed that Flame Hair grew quieter and moved more slowly.

"Her leg is bothering her again?" he asked.

Kwineechka shook his head. "We are close to the bay."

Peyewik nodded, realizing this meant they were also close to the camp of the Fighting Women. His good mood evaporated as well, and their meager supper was eaten in silence.

Before he slept, Peyewik murmured a prayer of thanks to Manito for his odd traveling companions. He thought of his dream the night before, and of what might come tomorrow when they arrived among the Fighting Women, and he felt his heart grow cold again. He heard Flame Hair sigh restlessly and wondered why she wasn't happier about being back among her people when she had been so anxious to return earlier. It made him think of how much he missed his grandfather. Just before sleep overtook him he sang a prayer of well-being for Muhkrentharne.

Owl swooped low over the village of the People. He looked down with his night vision and gave a hoot of warning. There were pale-faced men creeping through the forest towards the sleeping village. There were many of them, and they all carried weapons in their hands.

CHAPTER SEVENTEEN

Trib

The boy cried out in his sleep, waking Trib just after dawn. She reached out to wake him in return, wondering what his nightmares looked like.

Just then the storyteller began to sing his morning prayer. Trib couldn't see him, but his voice came from a cluster of pines near the river's edge. The boy seemed to hear it as well, and was soothed by it. He rolled over with a sigh and slept peacefully. Trib let him be and climbed to her feet, groaning at the pull of sore muscles. As she packed up her bed roll, she listened to the storyteller's song with half an ear. When it ended, she was surprised to feel her heart skip a beat and looked up to see him emerging from the pines.

His long hair was wet. Beads of water, crystalline in the morning sun, sparkled on his neck and chest. His skin was flushed a coppery red, and Trib sent an uncharacteristic prayer of thanks to the Goddess that her attack two nights earlier had not left a mark.

"You bathe every day?" she said, trying not to stare at the tiny bumps raised by the cold across his chest and arms. "You ain't afraid of getting sick?"

The storyteller gave her a familiar look, incredulity bordering on disgust.

"You never bathe," he observed. "You are not afraid no man will want a wife who smells like rotten bear grease?"

Trib snorted. "I got no plans to take a husband. Even if I did it wouldn't matter how he wanted me to smell. I don't like water." She scratched vigorously at her scalp for emphasis.

The storyteller studied her quizzically. "The Fighting Women do not marry?"

"None of the New Murians do," Trib said. "We got rid of that along with the rest of the Puritanic's oppressive ways."

"There are no children in your settlement?" he asked.

"There's plenty of kids," Trib replied.

"How do you get them if you have no husbands?"

He seemed completely at ease asking the question, but Trib wasn't used to discussing such matters with pretty-eyed, half-naked men. She noticed glints of blue where the sun struck his black hair. She wanted to touch it, to let the shining strands slide through her fingers. She cleared her throat, hoping her blush wasn't giving her away.

"Children are, uh, gotten...from whoever a New Murian fancies. If we want him, we just take him."

The look of incredulity and disgust deepened. "Your men choose to live this way?" he asked. "How do they know which children are theirs?"

She shrugged. "The choices of manservants and farmhands ain't important," she said. "We don't put much stock in fathers anyway."

"Fathers love their children as much as mothers do," the storyteller said.

"Not where I come from," Trib replied, remembering the fierce-looking man she'd seen in the village, his simple delight in the company of children. Native fathers didn't treat children the way Puritanics did. "I told you what Puritanics do to kids," she said.

"But these men who still live in your settlement, they are not Pure Men."

"They used to be," Trib explained. "Until Aoifa made them give up their old ways and swear to serve the Goddess and New Murias."

"Who is Aoifa?"

"The Scath's sister, the woman in black robes that Peyewik dreamed about yesterday. She's the head priestess in the settlement."

"Peyewik said she sang a song that made the men obey her," Kwineechka said.

"Aye, her siren song. The Goddess taught it to her to make sure the former Puritanics truly serve us, so their strength and skills can be put to good use in the settlement."

"This woman sings this spell song to these men, and then you use them for whatever you want? You just *take* them?"

"Well, no..." Trib said, flustered. "I never..."

The truth was that she didn't have any experience in taking a partner in New Murias. She only knew about it from listening to Cuss and the other apprentices brag about it.

"But I always heard that they liked it," she said defensively. "Or at least they didn't mind..."

"You cannot *take* a person or any being with a spirit," the storyteller said, and Trib could hear both revulsion and fear in his voice. "Why would you want to?"

Trib didn't know what he meant. Cuss had never mentioned anyone's spirit when she talked of being with men.

"Your ways are not right," the storyteller said, turning away from her. "Such people cannot help us," he said over his shoulder. "We should never have come."

He began to gather his belongings. Trib felt a sinking in her stomach and wondered if there was anything about her that *wasn't* repulsive to him.

"We're almost there," she said. "We'll reach the camp by afternoon."

The storyteller shook his head. "We will go back. I will explain to the chief of the Original People that he was wrong..."

Just then the boy sat up with a cry, his eyes wild with fear.

The storyteller dropped to his side and began speaking in a low, soothing voice. Slowly the boy's eyes cleared of his nightmare visions. He spoke and tears ran down his face.

"He has seen the Pale Ones attacking his village," the storyteller translated.

"Seen? You mean dreamed?"

"Yes. He has seen it in a dream."

"He had a nightmare?" Trib struggled to understand.

"No," the storyteller said impatiently. "He has seen it. This thing has happened or it will happen."

Trib remembered the boy's uncanny description of Aoifa the morning before. He had called her a crow woman, echoing the warriors' irreverent title for the black-robed priestesses. This ability of his to see things happening far away reminded her of the priestesses, of the powers they were rumored to have, and sent a shiver up her spine.

"If it's true that this thing has happened," Trib said, "then you got no choice but to ask my people for help. We're the only ones who can save you from the Puritanics."

The storyteller shook his head. He looked as though his mind was made up until Peyewik spoke again, his voice frantic.

"He is saying you must help us," the storyteller said resignedly. "We must go to your people..."

Trib suddenly felt the weight of her promise and realized she couldn't guarantee anything. But she told herself the Scath would do the right thing. She had to.

"We will help you," she said, trying to sound confident.

⚙

They traveled through pine barrens that day, moving as fast as they could. Trib's leg hurt, but she told herself she could rest when they got to the New Murian camp. Around mid-day, the boy uttered an exclamation and stopped.

"What's the matter?" Trib asked, afraid that he had *seen* something else.

The storyteller smiled briefly. "Peyewik has never smelled the ocean before."

Sure enough, Trib could taste the tang of saltwater in the air. She hadn't noticed until her attention was drawn to it.

"You have?" she asked the storyteller.

"My village is not far. A day's journey to the north and east."

By early afternoon gray clouds had covered the sun and a light rain was falling. The boy paused again, this time raising his hands to the sky as if to catch the raindrops before they hit the earth.

"Surely he's seen rain before," Trib grinned, but the storyteller only frowned in reply.

A few minutes later the sky grew darker, thunder rolled, and the rain became a downpour. The boy grabbed at the storyteller's hand and spoke in an agitated voice.

"What is it?" Trib shouted over the rumble of thunder.

The storyteller didn't answer. He had stopped in his tracks and was staring straight ahead. A flash of lightning revealed a landscape of tree stumps stretching before them.

"He said the spirits are weeping," the storyteller said finally. "No one thanked the trees for their sacrifice. They were just... taken."

He turned to face Trib slowly and the look in his eyes made her cringe. There was no hope in them, only a growing fear. A sudden thought burst into her head. *Run! Take the boy and run as far away from here as you can!*

She opened her mouth to say it out loud, but there was another flash of lightning, and she saw that they were surrounded by brown-cloaked figures with drawn swords.

"By the Goddess! I'm one of you!" she shouted, afraid that in the poor light and her animal skin clothing the New Murians wouldn't recognize her.

The weapons didn't falter. She spun around, trying to find the leader of the group.

"Tribulation," someone said, "we thought you were dead." The speaker's face was hidden in the shadow of her hood. "Who are these strangers?"

Trib recognized the voice. It belonged to a master warrior named Jezebel, who had been left behind on the bay when the mapmaking expedition set out.

"They're Natives whose village isn't far from here," Trib explained. "Puritanics are attacking them and they need our help. We need to see whoever's in charge of the camp."

"That would be the Scath herself."

"The Scath's here?" Trib's gut wrenched.

"Aye. Aoifa and her priestesses as well. Got here not too long after we found the remains of your expedition and brought them back for burial. Aoifa performed the rite herself."

There was a beat of silence and Trib knew what was coming.

"How is it that you alone survived?" Master Jezebel asked.

Trib realized she had been waiting for this question since she'd first regained consciousness in the marsh three weeks ago. There was no good answer.

"I reckon Aoifa and the Scath will want to be the first to know the answer to that," she replied.

After a moment Master Jezebel lowered her sword. She gave an order, and the company closed in around Trib and the Natives. "I'll take you and your *allies* to Aoifa and the Scath directly," she said in a hard voice.

They didn't have far to go before the beginnings of a massive timber palisade loomed over them, and Trib understood what had happened to the trees. Someone had been working fast. There hadn't been anything but tents when Trib left with the mapmakers. There were two high mounds of earth just outside the wall. Burial mounds. They hadn't been there before either. Trib felt grief rising as she thought of Cuss and the other warriors. She had to be strong when she went before the Scath, so she pushed the grief back down.

The hooded warriors led them through a newly constructed gate. It was twice as high as the huts in the Native village and required five men to open it. The gatekeepers were farmhands from New Murias. They stood bare-headed and cloak-less in the rain, their faces blank until someone shouted at them and they moved to close the gate behind the warriors and the travelers. Trib wondered why she had never noticed before that there was something strange and vacant about them. She glanced at the storyteller and the boy, hoping they hadn't noticed the men, but the boy was looking right at them. She saw his eyes fill with panic as they pushed the gate shut. Trib couldn't blame him. After so many weeks out in the open she felt penned in, trapped by the high walls even though they were incomplete. She couldn't imagine what it must feel like to the two Natives.

"It's all right," she tried to reassure Peyewik. "These are my people. They're going to help you..."

The boy made a strangled sound and pitched forward, his eyelids fluttering. She caught him before he landed in the mud. She looked around for the storyteller to help her. He was standing nearby, but when she called his name, he didn't move. His golden eyes were vacant and staring, just like the farmhands'.

"What in Dess's name...?" she cried.

"They are overwhelmed," said a cool voice.

Trib's head snapped up, and she found herself looking into the moon-pale face and ice-blue eyes of Aoifa, the head priestess of New Murias.

CHAPTER EIGHTEEN

Peyewik

ark wings enfolded Peyewik. He could see nothing, but he could feel a softness like feathers all around him and hear a soothing lullaby that filled his mind. All is well, *the lullaby claimed.* Do not worry, just sleep...*But Peyewik did not want to sleep. He knew that all was not well, and he struggled against the soft darkness. It became suffocating, and he began to understand the singer's true intent. The lullaby faltered and ended with an angry caw.*

Peyewik sat up, instantly awake. He looked around for Crow Woman, but she wasn't there. He was lying on a straw pallet in the center of a cramped, airless room. The only light came from a small lamp beside the pallet. He could see the shape of a body slumped in the corner.

"Kwineechka?" he said softly.

The storyteller groaned and leaned forward into the light. Peyewik barely recognized his clay-like features and dull eyes. He looked like the men who had opened the massive gate to the Fighting Women's camp.

He crawled to the storyteller's side. "What has happened to you?"

The storyteller couldn't answer.

Peyewik put his hands on either side of Kwineechka's face and instantly the lullaby filled his mind again. He dropped his hands, stricken.

"The Crow Woman has trapped your spirit with her song. I do not know how to help you," he said.

"Little...brother..." Kwineechka gasped. Peyewik saw the flicker of recognition in his eyes and knew the storyteller was trying to fight the song. Desperate to help, he replaced his hands on Kwineechka's face. The lullaby flooded in again and he resisted it with all his might. *No!* he shouted in his mind. *Do not listen!* He could feel Kwineechka's spirit struggling, feeble against the overwhelming softness and darkness. *The song is a lie. Think of something true.* Peyewik began to sing out loud, a song of home. He sang about the rush and splash of the river, the gentle roar of the wind in the pine trees, and the chittering of insects in tall grass. He sang about the People—laughing children, hunters giving thanks over a fallen deer, women talking and singing as they wove mats. The lullaby grew fainter and fainter as the sounds and images of home filled Kwineechka's mind.

Peyewik dropped his hands and looked anxiously into Kwineechka's face. The storyteller blinked and his eyes focused on Peyewik. He was free.

"What happened to me?" he asked. "I could not think or move..."

"It was Crow Woman's song, the one I saw her use in my dream. She sang it to us, and it made us like the men at the gate, it gave her power over our spirits."

"Why did she sing it to us? We are not her enemies. She does not need power over us."

Peyewik didn't know what to say.

The storyteller's face went suddenly dark with anger. "Where is Flame Hair?"

Peyewik had wondered this himself. "I do not know," he whispered sadly.

"What is this place?" The storyteller picked up the lamp and began exploring the room. It was made of wooden planks, walls, floor, and ceiling. It was more like a box than a house. Every surface was extremely hard. Peyewik felt bruised every time he moved, and suffocating with every breath.

"There are no spirits here," he realized. "They cannot get in."

"It is a dead place," Kwineechka agreed. The lamp light fell across the hinges of a door set into one wall. He grasped the latch in the center of the door and pulled. When nothing happened he set his shoulder against the door and pushed.

"It does not open," he said through clenched teeth. "We are prisoners."

Peyewik felt the airless, spiritless space closing in on him. He felt drained and hopeless.

"Flame Hair lied to us!" the storyteller shouted suddenly. "I told the People that the Fighting Women could not help us. They are greedy. They use their magical strength to take what is not theirs to take—even the spirits of trees and people. You cannot tell me this is not Snakebrother's doing. If the Pure Men don't destroy the People, the Fighting Women will!"

CHAPTER NINETEEN

Trib

Aoifa spoke again. "Your companions will be well cared for."

Trib blinked and looked around. The storyteller and the boy were gone. She didn't remember seeing them go, or who had taken them. "But we need…"

"Come with me," the priestess cut her off. She turned, her black cloak flapping like dark wings in the rain.

Trib followed her with a strange feeling of detachment. There was a blanket wrapped around her shoulders, but she didn't know how it had gotten there. She didn't recognize the camp they were moving through. Split log barracks for the warriors were under construction. A few thatch-roofed cabins for priestesses were already completed. The skeleton of a barn showed through the fog. It was no longer a makeshift camp but the beginnings of a fort. The New Murians were here to stay.

There weren't many people moving about in the wet darkness, but each brown-cloaked figure she passed seemed like a ghost to Trib. She couldn't help searching for familiar faces, only to be reminded again and again that her friends were all dead.

Aoifa led her to a large cabin. The door opened and a young priestess stood aside to let them enter. As Aoifa crossed the threshold a large black crow swept out of the night and landed on her shoulder. "There you are," the head priestess cooed to the bird.

Trib followed her into the cabin and immediately wanted to be outside again. The walls were too solid, the air thick and stale. The smell of smoke and old cooking and unwashed bodies turned her stomach.

"Tea," Aoifa said.

The young priestess turned to the fireplace and hung a kettle over the flames. Aoifa lifted the bird from her shoulder and set it on a jutting hearth stone. The bird squawked and shook the rain off its feathers.

"Sit and warm yourself," Aoifa pointed Trib to a delicately carved chair by the fire.

Trib hesitated. Her muddy animal skins would ruin the fancy cushion.

"Sit," the priestess commanded.

Trib obeyed awkwardly, her palms sweating. This wasn't what she had expected. She had assumed she would see the Scath first. Aside from her Rage initiation she had only seen Aoifa from a distance performing rites on Feast Days. Up close, the priestess was ageless and flawless. Her hair was as sleek and black as the crow's wet feathers, and her face was like carved white stone. Her eyes were twin blue fires that never seemed to flicker or blink, and Trib could not meet their gaze.

Just then the younger priestess turned from the fire with two pewter mugs in her hands. Trib saw her face clearly for the first time and gave a start. She had been on the map-making expedition. Trib hadn't been the only survivor. But the young priestess gave her no sign of recognition in return, making Trib wonder if she was mistaken.

"That will be all for the night, Morrigan," Aoifa said.

"Goddess bless you," the younger priestess murmured. She bowed once and left the cabin.

"You look like you've seen a ghost," Aoifa observed.

"I...I thought that priestess was killed in the ambush. But I must be wrong..."

"Haunted by the spirits of your fallen comrades, perhaps?"

Trib nodded, still avoiding the high priestess's gaze.

"You're not wrong. My apprentice Morrigan was on the expedition. Like you, she survived, though she bears the scars. Unlike you, however, it took her only a few days to find her way home." She paused expectantly.

Trib didn't know where to begin. "Where's the Scath?" she asked in a small voice. She wanted the old warrior present when she tried to explain herself.

"My sister is out hunting Puritanics," Aoifa said. "She would want you to speak freely with me."

"Then I'll ask you for forgiveness," Trib said miserably. "For dishonoring you and my Fellow warriors."

"On the contrary. You have done well."

Trib thought she heard wrong. "I should've died with them..."

"Yes, according to my sister's code of honor, you should have. But I do not speak of the ambush," Aoifa said. "You have done well by bringing the Natives to me."

"The Natives?" Trib had momentarily forgotten the storyteller and the boy.

"I had intended to seek them out myself, frighten them with stories of the Puritanics' cruelty and offer my protection. Instead, you have saved me the trouble."

"Peyewik and Kwineechka—the Natives—came with me to ask you and the Scath for help. Their people took me in after the ambush, healed my wounds. Now their village is under attack by Puritanics. They're peaceful folk with no way of defending themselves. I promised them we could help."

Trib rubbed her sweating palms on her thighs, knowing it had been above her place to make such a promise.

"Independent thought and action are generally undesirable in a warrior, but you have done me a great service."

"I have?" Trib's thoughts felt very slow and cumbersome.

"Tell me, did the Puritanics attack their village before or after the Natives took you in?"

"After."

"Wonderful," Aoifa said.

Trib was beyond confused now. "Begging your pardon, but they killed an innocent boy and are set to attack again any time now. How is that wonderful?"

Aoifa gave her a cold smile. "I shall explain. The Puritanics came south to form an alliance with the Natives, just as they have done in the north. My hope was to get here before they did and form my own alliance first. By taking you in, the Natives did all the work for me. The Puritanics will have assumed the Natives are in league with us and therefore enemies. Originally the Natives might have had a choice as to whom they sided with, but you eliminated that possibility and altered circumstances in our favor."

"I didn't mean to!" Trib protested, horrified by the idea that the Puritanic attacks really had been her fault. If it was true, then the storyteller had been right to blame her for bringing Snakebrother to the village.

"Of course you didn't. Warriors rarely make good strategists off the battlefield. Not much for subtlety and nuance. I realize you lucked into it, but I will reward you all the same."

"Does the Scath think I've done good?"

"She'll come around eventually. What I'm trying to do here is beyond her warrior's ken."

The back of Trib's neck was tingling. Something was wrong, but she didn't know what yet.

"Before the ambush..." she paused, uncertain of herself.

"Speak up, girl," Aoifa said.

"They said the priestesses were making a map. Why?"

"The Rage has given us the advantage until now, but the Puritanics have been growing stronger in the north through alliances with the Natives and other settlements. They also have powerful supporters in the Old World who are sending them weapons and supplies that we New Murians cannot get our hands on. The scales may be tipped back in their favor unless I can establish a port of trade here and intercept all merchant and supply ships sailing between the Old World and the settlements in the north."

"What about the Natives here in the south?" Trib asked, her sense of danger growing.

"What about them? I have already said I intend to form an alliance with them. We will protect them from the Puritanics."

"They'll be able to live as they always have?" She thought of the tree stumps and the speed with which the fort was being built, before any thought was given to how it might affect the Natives. Kwineechka had said his village wasn't far.

"As long as they don't interfere with my new fortress and trade routes, they can do whatever they wish."

Trib felt some relief, but the priestess wasn't done.

"If, however, they refuse my offer of an alliance, I let the Puritanics have their way with them, and then I have my way with the Puritanics." She gave Trib another cheerless smile.

Finally Trib understood. Aoifa wasn't at all concerned for the Native's well-being. She only cared about making sure they didn't interfere with her plans.

"That ain't right," Trib said quietly. She wished the Scath were present. The warrior would know what was right and honorable.

The priestess went very still, her blue eyes fixed on Trib's face. Suddenly the hearth seemed less warm, less bright.

"Right? You speak of *right*?"

Her voice was so cold Trib shivered.

"Was it *right* that my sisters and I were forced from our home in the Old World for worshipping in the old ways, and cast out onto the street where there was nothing for us save whoring? Was it right that the Puritanics promised us freedom and plenty if we sailed on their cursed "brideship" to this New World, only to make us live like slaves once we got here? Was it *right* that the Puritanics hanged my youngest sister simply for singing some of the old songs to the other women of the brideship, so that the Goddess might give us strength in our troubles? Tell me, Tribulation, does any of this sound *right* to you?"

Trib shook her head mutely.

"No," Aoifa continued. "Those men would take everything from us if we let them. *And you dare to speak to me of right.*"

The crow above the fire gave an angry caw, and Trib had a brief, visceral awareness of the molten hatred boiling beneath the priestess's glacial surface. It was hotter than any Rage she'd ever experienced. Then Aoifa regained control, and Trib felt as though she were being torn apart from the inside out. The priestess's words had invoked a powerful connection to her people and to the Goddess. She could feel it all through her body, yet she could not release herself to it entirely. She had thought the tormenting confusion of the past few days would go away when she was among her people again, but it had only grown stronger.

"I killed a boy," she said slowly, her heart pounding. "He was with the Puritanics, but I don't know if he was my enemy. I don't know if he deserved to die."

"If he was with the Puritanics, he was your enemy," Aoifa said flatly. "You should feel no remorse."

"I killed lots of men using the Rage and didn't feel anything. I killed this boy without the Rage and his death will haunt me forever. Why?"

"Your only mistake was your excessive pride in not using the Goddess's gift of the Rage. Why did you do this?"

"I thought I didn't need it."

"Arrogance," Aoifa said. "Pray to the Goddess to forgive you for it."

"But..."

"My patience wears thin, Tribulation. Say what you need to say and be done with it."

"What's wrong with the men of New Murias?" Trib blurted out. "Why are they so...empty?"

"You know this. They were once Puritanics and capable of atrocity. They have sworn obedience to me and the Goddess, and they are doing penance." Aoifa's voice was calm, as if she were stating the most obvious fact. But her answer made Trib feel suddenly ill.

"Native men ain't like the Puritanics," she said, her voice wavering. "Will you make them swear obedience and do penance?"

The priestess narrowed her eyes at Trib. "So," she said softly. "It comes full circle."

Trib had no idea what Aoifa was talking about, but fear suddenly thrilled through her body.

"You are trying to tell me some men are not so bad," Aoifa continued. "Your mother once said the same about the Puritanics, that there were good among them, just as there were bad among the New Murians. For this reason she refused to use the Rage, just as you have. She let other women fight for her freedom, and when she had it, she spat on it. She defied my laws, and let a Puritanic into her home without making him swear allegiance to me and the Goddess. She treated him as an equal and insisted that she loved him."

"No," Trib croaked. "It ain't true. My ma couldn't do that."

"Do you even remember your mother?"

Trib shook her head.

"Then how do you know what she could and couldn't do?" Aoifa asked. "That Puritanic was your father. Eventually your mother grew tired of slaving for him and saw the error of her ways. She told him to leave, as was her right under my law. Do you know what your father did then?"

Trib couldn't reply.

"He went as she asked. But he came back. With many of his brethren..."

"No!" Trib cried. She put her hands over her ears. Aoifa bent forward and pulled them away.

"You will hear this!" she said. "That man, who tricked your mother into thinking he was good, killed his own children. You were the only survivor. You seem to have a special talent for that."

She released Trib and sat back with a cruel smile. "The Puritanics believe that all children are born sinful, but they also believe all children born to Puritanics are also Puritanics..."

"I ain't..." Trib whispered.

"You were never told this, to spare you the shame of your mother's treachery. I see now it may have been a wasted effort."

Trib couldn't speak. Her blood surged. A Rage was coming.

"Control yourself!" Aoifa cried, putting a cold hand on Trib's forehead. "Save your Rage until the enemy is at hand."

Trib felt the power slowly drain, leaving her empty and exhausted.

"Do you understand now what is right?" Aoifa said in a soothing voice. "Everything has been taken from you, from all of us. The Goddess brought us to this New World for a reason. Its resources will feed us and make us strong so that no Puritanic or any other man will ever harm us again. *The right is ours.*"

The crow on the fireplace cawed again. Trib slumped forward in her chair. "Aye," she whispered. "The right is ours."

CHAPTER TWENTY

Peyewik

Peyewik had lost all sense of time in the windowless room. He was dozing fitfully when a sudden spasm of cold pain in his chest brought him fully awake.

"She is coming!" was the only warning he could manage before the plank door swung open and Crow Woman entered, followed closely by Flame Hair. Flame Hair was no longer wearing the clothing of the People. She was dressed as she had been when Peyewik first saw her, in stiff leather leggings and a vest over a linen shirt. Her hair had been combed and braided in the style of the Fighting Women. She didn't look up when Kwineechka hissed at her.

Crow Woman went straight for the storyteller, already singing her spirit-trapping song.

"Do not listen," Peyewik wheezed. The cold in his chest was stronger than it had ever been, and he couldn't breathe. It felt as if his lungs were freezing solid.

The storyteller didn't stand a chance against Crow Woman. He sank to his knees after only a few notes. Crow Woman knelt behind him. She wrapped her arms around him and sang into his ear. She stroked his hair and face until his eyes went blank and his chin dropped to his chest.

Peyewik fought the spirit-trapping song. He tried to remember the sounds of home to drown it out, but Crow Woman was too close.

104

Her voice overpowered him and then lulled him, surrounding him in soft, warm feathers...he felt himself grow light and careless. He didn't need to worry, the song told him. Crow Woman had great power. She would take care of everything. All he had to do was trust her, turn himself over to her body and spirit...

When the singing stopped, Peyewik wanted to fill the ensuing silence with everything he had, to offer himself up to her completely...

CHAPTER TWENTY-ONE

Trib

Aoifa stopped singing.

"Your pretty young man broke my spell once," she said. "I don't know how he did it, but he won't be able to do it again."

"You said you wanted to ask him some questions," Trib said. "You didn't tell me you would use the siren on him."

"It's the only way. His will belongs to me and to the Goddess now. What shall I ask of him, Tribulation?"

Aoifa slid her hands slowly up the storyteller's bare arms.

Kwineechka's head was bowed, and he did not respond to the high priestess's caress. Trib looked away. The boy, Peyewik, was hunched nearby, also caught in the siren-song.

"You don't need to touch him," Trib said hoarsely.

"But I want to touch him," the priestess replied. "He is beautiful. You want to touch him too, don't you? This man you think is not like other men, with his golden eyes and stories and laughter."

Trib looked up sharply. These were things she had barely admitted to herself. She had taken pains to keep them hidden.

Aoifa laughed. "The siren works on everyone. I sang you a few notes earlier, in my cabin, while you were making yourself presentable. I asked you a few questions."

Trib suddenly felt sick. She had thought the siren was like the Rage, a gift from the Goddess, only to be used against enemies.

"Why'd you do that?" she asked. "I'm loyal to you and the Goddess. You know that."

"Yes, I know that because I asked you while you were under the influence of my siren and could not lie. I also asked you what you desire most. Do you know what you told me?"

Aoifa pushed the storyteller's hair away from his neck and stroked it lightly.

"Stop," Trib whispered. "I want you to stop." She couldn't understand why the high priestess was doing these things.

"That is not what you want," Aoifa laughed again. Her white hands were moving over the storyteller's chest now. "You want this man. You told me so yourself. You have never had a man before, and this is the one you want. Here he is. Take him."

"No." Trib wanted to shout but it came out as a whisper. She wanted to throw herself at the priestess, pull her away from Kwineechka and pound her with her fists. But she found that she couldn't move.

The head priestess narrowed her eyes. "I am offering you a gift. Why do you refuse it?"

"You can't do that," Trib said. "He ain't yours to give."

"You won't get another chance," Aoifa taunted her. "He will never choose you freely."

Tears of anger and shame ran down Trib's face. She couldn't speak.

"Very well," Aoifa said. "If you won't take him, I will."

Trib gave a cry of anguish as the high priestess began to sing again. She heard the words, heard Aoifa demand that Kwineechka offer up that which was most essential and sacred to him. With a wrench of her heart, she heard the storyteller's voice in reply. Aoifa fell silent as he began to sing his own song.

Trib had heard the storyteller sing many times, but never like this. His voice was amplified and impossibly varied in tone and pitch. It was as if many voices sang with him, a melody and multiple harmonies that created a sound so full and rich that she felt it with all her senses. She could see and feel his song, as well as hear it. It was a whole world unto itself and listening to it made her part of it.

Trib couldn't understand the words of his song but she knew what Kwineechka was singing, and why it had been his response to Aoifa's demand.

"Aoifa!" she growled, straining against the spell that held her as well as the storyteller. "He's telling you the story of his people. It's what he came here to do. He would've given it to you freely…"

The head priestess ignored her, enthralled by her own power, and the storyteller sang on because he had no choice. Trib felt heartsick for him as she remembered that the story was Kwineechka and his people's way of connecting to others in peace and friendship. And she hated herself for not being able to stop what Aoifa was doing to him.

Suddenly a sound like a thunderclap broke across the storyteller's song and shook the cabin to its foundation. Aoifa was thrown away from the storyteller and he sank to the floor, silent, eyes closed. Trib found that she could move and took two steps towards Kwineechka before seeing Peyewik's eyes on her, clear and free of Aoifa's siren song. She stopped. The air in the prison cabin felt somehow fresher, as though a summer storm had just passed by.

Aoifa's face was drawn and pale. "The boy has powers of his own," she gasped. Then she laughed. "Now I know how my spell was broken before. But it doesn't matter. I already have all I need."

"What do you mean?" Trib asked.

"The story," Aoifa said, and laughed wickedly. "I made him give me that which is most sacred to him. He gave me this story and, now that I have it, he is mine. It is only a matter of time before his people are mine too."

"What will you do with them?" Trib asked, terror rising.

Aoifa gave her a cold smile. "Nothing for now. I must rest. Help me back to my cabin."

Trib knew she couldn't help the Natives. She went to the high priestess and offered her arm in support. At the door she glanced back. The boy was kneeling next to the storyteller, who was beginning to stir. Neither of them looked at her, and she knew it was too late. They would never forgive her. They were right not to. She had betrayed them.

CHAPTER TWENTY-TWO

Peyewik

"Peyewik, what has happened?" The storyteller's voice was groggy. "I heard thunder."

The air in the tiny room tingled and buzzed, and for once Peyewik's chest felt warm.

"Crow Woman," Peyewik said hoarsely, his throat raw from the shout that had broken the spell-song. "She made you tell the Story of the People."

"You stopped her again?" Kwineechka asked.

"Yes," Peyewik replied. "At first she was too strong, and I was caught in her spell-song. I could see her touching you, and I heard her make you tell the Story of the People, but I couldn't help you. The Story gave her power somehow, I could feel it growing. I became frightened for you and for the People. She had to be stopped. So I called for the thunder spirit to come and break her spell...and it did," he added self-consciously.

Peyewik didn't like it when the spirits came to him of their own volition, but it was a whole new experience to have one come at his request and do his bidding. It was frightening, but no more frightening than feeling Crow Woman take control of the Story of the People.

"She is gone?" Kwineechka asked.

"Yes, but she will come back soon," Peyewik said. "She wants more from us."

110

Kwineechka flinched at this, and Peyewik saw the haunted look in his eyes. The stories of the People, all of them, were a part of Kwineechka's being and Crow Woman had reached in and taken that part of him without asking.

"Flame Hair was with Crow Woman," Kwineechka said in a low, ragged voice. "She meant to do this all along, to steal the story from me even though I came here to share it freely. Now do you believe me that she belongs to Snakebrother?"

"I do not know," Peyewik said quietly. The buzzing warmth generated by the thunder spirit was fading, leaving him sad and tired. He couldn't believe that Flame Hair had known what Crow Woman would do, but he couldn't deny that she had stood by and watched while Crow Woman violated the storyteller's body and spirit.

"You look tired, little brother. Rest while I find a way out of here." Kwineechka climbed unsteadily to his feet, still shaking off Crow Woman's spell. "We must escape before Crow Woman and Flame Hair come back."

Peyewik had the terrible feeling that there was no way out. He was terrified of what Crow Woman might do when she came back, and he knew he didn't have the strength to fight her off a third time. Summoning the thunder spirit had drained him. Eyelids heavy and body weary, he lay down on the straw pallet and surrendered to whatever nightmares would come.

CHAPTER TWENTY-THREE

Trib

Trib threw up in the slops jar.

She was alone in the new, roughly built cabin where Aoifa had sent her to get some sleep.

She guessed it was sometime around midnight. She had her sword, but the door to the cabin was locked from the outside. The cabin was empty except for the slops jar, a pallet, and a lantern.

Trib was exhausted, but she couldn't sleep. Her mind and stomach were churning over everything that had happened since passing through the gates of the fort at dusk. She continued to retch until her stomach was empty of the food Aoifa had fed her. She couldn't bear to think about what Aoifa had told her about her mother. Even more difficult was the thought that Kwineechka would have sung for Aoifa freely, as a gesture of friendship, but Aoifa had taken the song by force. It was wrong, but Trib didn't know what to do about it. She kept telling herself that it never would've happened if the Scath had been there and wondered when she would be allowed to see the old warrior.

Eventually she drifted into a troubled sleep, only to be awakened by someone shaking her shoulder. She reached for her sword before she was fully conscious.

"Tribulation, I am a friend."

It was the young priestess from Aoifa's cabin, Morrigan, the only other survivor of the ambush in the marsh.

"What are you doing here?" Trib sat up, her hand still on the hilt of her sword. "Did Aoifa send you?"

Morrigan held up her hands to show that she carried no weapons or tricks. "Aoifa doesn't know I'm here. I must speak with you."

"Then speak," Trib said warily.

The priestess removed her hood and knelt beside Trib's pallet. She was a small woman with delicate features and large brown eyes. Trib wondered briefly if her smallness was the reason she had become a priestess instead of a warrior. She wore her blonde hair in the style of all apprentice priestesses, neatly braided and wrapped in coils around her ears.

"I heard what you said to Aoifa about the Natives," Morrigan began.

"You were spying?"

"I knew it was wrong," Morrigan replied, "but I was so surprised to see another survivor of the ambush. I wanted to know what had happened to you. Now I think the Goddess willed it. I came here to tell you I agree with you. Aoifa's intentions towards the Natives are wrong. Your friends are in danger."

"They ain't my friends," Trib said, her empty stomach twisting painfully. They had been friends for a day, but no longer, not after what she had allowed Aoifa to do to Kwineechka. "And what you're saying is treason. You'd be hung if I told Aoifa."

"I don't think you'll tell her," Morrigan said.

"Why not?"

"Because you care about the Natives..."

"I never said that," Trib interrupted, feeling heat rush to her face.

Morrigan studied Trib for a moment and then smiled gently. "Just because you didn't say it doesn't mean you don't."

Trib started to protest, but Morrigan continued. "Even if you don't care for them, you gave your word as a warrior to protect them, and you know something is wrong with Aoifa's strategy."

"You're just saying all this because you heard what Aoifa said about my mother," Trib said, her voice hard. "You think I'm a traitor like her."

The priestess shook her head. "I don't think your mother was a traitor. I think the only thing she was guilty of was loving her family."

There was no judgment in her voice, just a hint of sadness that caught Trib off guard. She didn't understand how anyone could not condemn the shameful things Aoifa had said about her mother.

Still uncertain whether she should trust the priestess, she said brusquely, "How did you survive the ambush? I thought the Puritanics killed everyone."

"They left me for dead," Morrigan said.

She lifted her chin so Trib could see the ugly scar that ran from her right ear across her throat. Trib shuddered at the sight of it, remembering what she had done to the Puritanic boy.

"I thought I was dead too," Morrigan continued. "But the Goddess had other plans. She gave me the strength to stand up and start walking. I followed the river south and was found by the search party that came looking for us."

"Oh," Trib said. The story seemed legitimate, but Trib still wasn't sure. For all she knew Aoifa had sent the priestess to test her loyalty.

As though the priestess could read Trib's mind, she said, "I know you don't trust me. But I have known for a long time that there is something wrong with Aoifa and the way she runs the settlement. I know this because I pray to the Goddess all the time, and She often replies. The Goddess I speak to is nothing like the Goddess from whom Aoifa claims to gain her power."

Trib couldn't deny that some of what the priestess was saying rang true. What the head priestess had done to Kwineechka had been wrong.

"Aoifa told me that the Goddess has granted the resources of the New World to the New Murians because the Puritanics took everything from us."

"Aoifa is exploiting the name of the Goddess to her own ends," Morrigan replied. "What about all that your Native friends stand to lose at Aoifa's hands? Should they be sacrificed for our well-being?"

Three weeks earlier Trib would have answered yes immediately. Now she wasn't sure.

"Your friends are in grave danger if they stay here," Morrigan said softly. "I know what Aoifa will do to them because I've seen her do it to countless men before. She will use her siren magic to drain them of their wills. She will take all that is sacred to them and use them as slaves."

"I can't allow that," Trib said. She stood up and began buckling her sword onto her back. "The Scath wouldn't allow any of this if she were here. But I reckon there's no time to wait for her."

"No," Morrigan said. "The Scath can't help us."

"Us?" Trib said. "You ain't coming with me?"

"You'll need me," Morrigan replied.

"No offense, priestess, but like hell I will. Never had much use for praying and such."

The priestess went to the door of the cabin and pushed it open. Trib saw two warriors lying on the ground, unconscious.

"Aoifa set a guard on you," Morrigan said. "The siren can do things other than enslave. A deep and instant sleep for one. It attracts less attention than the Rage. There will be more guards at the cabin where Aoifa is holding them. Then I can show you how to get your friends out of the fort."

"Then I'd be much obliged for your help," Trib said, impressed. Her only plan had been to swing her sword at anyone who tried to stop her.

She stepped out into the darkness with the priestess close behind. Dawn wasn't far off and the fort was quiet. She was worried about the watch but they encountered no one until they arrived at the cabin where Peyewik and Kwineechka were being held. She hid in the shadows while Morrigan crept up behind the guards. The priestess sang so softly Trib couldn't hear her, but the guards were slumped on the ground within moments. Trib went to the door of the prison, noting angrily that it was barred from the outside, as if Kwineechka and Peyewik were animals or criminals to be penned in. She started to lift the bar and paused, her heart pounding.

"What is it?" Morrigan whispered.

"They got no reason to trust me," Trib replied. "They'll think I'm here to hurt them more."

"We must try," Morrigan replied. "It's their only chance."

The eastern sky was growing lighter by the moment. They were losing the cover of darkness. Trib lifted the bar, pulled the door open, and stepped inside.

CHAPTER TWENTY-FOUR

Peyewik

Peyewik woke to find the door of the windowless room open, and Flame Hair standing in it. Her face was pale in the lantern light, with dark smudges under her eyes. She stepped inside followed by a figure in black robes, but it wasn't Crow Woman. It was a yellow-haired girl about the same age as Flame Hair. She looked at Peyewik, and he instantly felt the presence of her spirit animal, a deer. Peyewik had never sensed a Pale One's spirit animal so quickly and easily. Even more surprising was the way the deer spirit seemed to reach out, not in a clutching, hungry way like Crow Woman, but in a gentle, welcoming way. Deer Girl smiled at Peyewik, and then she was gone back outside at a word from Flame Hair.

Flame Hair was closing the door behind her when Kwineechka sprang. She did nothing to defend herself, allowing him to knock her to the floor and pull her head back by her hair. He grabbed the knife from her belt and held it to her throat. His hand shook, and a red line appeared against her pale skin. Flame Hair still didn't speak or move, but she met Peyewik's eye with a look of pleading.

"Kwineechka," he said softly, "Flame Hair is here to help."

The storyteller looked up at him, his face twisted with a fury that made him unrecognizable. "She betrayed us," he hissed. "She should die for what she let Crow Woman do to me."

Without thinking Peyewik called out silently, summoning the story-teller's spirit animal the way he had summoned the thunder spirit. The spirit came to him almost at once, filling the room with the sound of a finned tail swishing through water. It was Carp, and in his presence Kwineechka remembered himself. The fury left him and he threw the knife away. Peyewik thanked Carp, and the sounds of water faded away.

The storyteller pushed away from Flame Hair. He leaned against the nearest wall and drew his knees up. "I have never wanted to kill anyone before," he said quietly. "Snakebrother is gaining power over me."

"But you did not kill her," Peyewik replied. "You did not listen to Snakebrother."

The storyteller dropped his face into his hands without replying.

Flame Hair spoke then, her voice tentative.

Kwineechka did not raise his head to translate.

"What is Flame Hair saying?" Peyewik had to ask.

"She says she will show us the way out," Kwineechka mumbled into his hands. "It is a trick. She came here with one who is like Crow Woman."

"Deer Girl is not like Crow Woman," Peyewik said.

Kwineechka finally looked up.

"I saw her spirit animal," Peyewik explained. "I think we can trust her, even if we can't trust Flame Hair."

Kwineechka stared at him for a moment, then nodded and stood up. He said something to Flame Hair without looking at her. Peyewik saw the relief in Flame Hair's face as she got up and went to the door. She opened it a crack and peered out, then gestured for Peyewik and Kwineechka to pass through.

Deer Girl met them outside and pointed to a place where the giant wall being built around the camp was not yet finished.

"On her signal we will run for that gap," Kwineechka translated her whispered instructions. "The river is on the far side and a ferry that will take us across."

Deer Girl and Flame Hair did one last check to make sure none of the Fighting Woman were nearby, then Deer Girl waved for them to go. Kwineechka took Peyewik's hand and they ran together. Peyewik turned for one last look at Deer Girl. Her hand was lifted in farewell, and he got the sudden feeling that he would see her again someday. Then he was running flat out, giddy at the feeling of fresh air on his face. The ground beneath his feet was muddy from the storm the evening before but the sky overhead was clear.

Flame Hair ran behind them, her longknife drawn, turning every few steps to look back. They reached the river bank without incident. The camp of the Fighting Women was silent as the stars near the eastern horizon began to disappear. Flame Hair ushered them onto a raft that was tied to a rope spanning the river. She put her longknife on her back and untied the moorings, then began poling away from the shore.

At the last possible moment a figure lumbered out of the shadows and leapt for the raft, landing heavily and nearly capsizing it.

It was a large, middle-aged woman with wild yellow hair and scars on her face. She held a longknife in her hand. Peyewik knew her from his dream. It was Bear Woman.

CHAPTER TWENTY-FIVE

Trib

Trib reached wearily for her sword. For weeks she had longed for nothing more than the Scath's presence and guidance. Finally the old warrior had appeared only to find Trib defying all her teachings of loyalty and honor.

"Leave your weapons till the far shore and man the boat, girl," the Scath growled.

Trib left her sword on her back and tried to focus on keeping the ferry moving across the current.

"I knew you were lying!" the storyteller spat at her. "I knew you wouldn't set us free."

Before Trib could answer, the Scath spoke up, surprised. "Aoifa didn't tell me the primitives could speak civilized."

"She didn't wait to find out," Trib replied.

"Trib ain't lied to you, boy," the Scath told the storyteller. "I reckon she aimed to set you free, just like she said. It's me and my sister she's betrayin' now, not you."

The storyteller said nothing, his golden eyes darting back and forth between Trib and the Scath.

The Scath gave him an appraising once over. "He's a pretty one. Almost can't blame you for trying to keep him outta my sister's claws." She chuckled as Trib flushed.

They finished crossing the river in tense silence. There was no movement on the shore behind. When the ferry bumped the landing, Trib waited for the Scath to make the first move.

"Off the boat," the old warrior ordered.

When they were all on shore, the Scath severed the line and set the ferry drifting downriver.

"Why'd you do that?" Trib asked warily.

"Need privacy for what comes next. Follow me to level ground." The Scath led the way up the river bank.

"Stay behind me," Trib whispered to Kwineechka. "Run at the first chance you get."

The Scath led them to a place that was flat and clear of underbrush. Then she turned to face Trib, feet planted, arms crossed, her sword still sheathed on her back.

"My sister wasn't sure of you, so she set me to watching," she said. "Betraying us for the sake of men-folk seems to run in your blood."

Trib said nothing but watched the Scath carefully, her body tense and ready. The Scath was old and heavy, but she was the commander of the New Murian Warriors, and still the fiercest fighter among them.

"Your ma would still be alive if she hadn't treated that Puritanic husband of hers like an equal," the Scath said. "Refused to summon the Rage, much less use a siren song to keep him in line."

"I know the price she paid for it," Trib said bitterly. "Whatever price you want from me, I'm willing to pay it, but this man and this boy didn't deserve the treatment they got at Aoifa's hands. They're good men, from good people. They deserved friendship and respect. Not to be locked up and abused."

Trib glanced at the storyteller. He was watching her, but his face was unreadable.

The Scath nodded slowly. "You might be right," she said, surprising Trib. "I don't hold with some of my sister's ways. She ain't always honorable. It's to be expected from one who's suffered as she has.

Life's been hard on me too, but I've had fighting and the Rage to keep me balanced. So I ain't here on account of the Natives. Judging from my sister's plan, I reckon their troubles are far from over, but I aim to let them go in peace today."

"If you ain't trying to bring us back, then why are you here?" Trib asked cautiously.

"To give you the chance your ma never got," the Scath replied.

"What are you talking about?"

"My sister told me to deal with you the same way I dealt with your ma, but I ain't going to do that. This time it's to be a fair fight."

Trib was confused. "My ma was killed by my father and a gang of Puritanics. Aoifa told me. How do you figure to make that a fair fight?"

"My sister didn't tell you the truth. I'll tell you now. It'll help you summon a strong Rage, keep you from holding back against me. Aoifa wants you dead, and these Natives recaptured alive. If you can best me, she'll have neither. You have my word, you'll all go free. If you lose, only the Natives go free, because you'll be dead. Either way I'll be free of this guilt I been carrying all these years, reminded every time I look at you."

"What in Dess's name are you talking about?" Trib demanded. The Scath was starting to scare her.

"I killed your ma," the Scath said simply. "It wasn't your father. It wasn't the Puritanics, like we told you. I summoned a Rage and killed your ma and your sisters."

It was such a ridiculous statement that Trib laughed. "You couldn't have," she snorted.

"I did. Your ma was warned about her behavior concernin' the Puritanic. She carried on, makin' my sister out to be a fool. So Aoifa made an example of her. Sent me to kill her and make it look as though your father did it."

Trib was becoming increasingly annoyed by this joke of the Scath's. "You couldn't have," she repeated. "The Goddess gave us the

Rage to defeat our enemies. We can't use it against good people, or each other."

"Anyone can use the Rage to kill anyone," the Scath said. "Aoifa and I taught you to believe otherwise, but I know its true nature. I used it when I killed your family and you'll use it now against me."

"*You*...killed my ma?" Trib couldn't take in the meaning of the words.

"And your sisters. Would've killed you too, but you hid. Didn't find you till I came back with some warriors. Told them it was Puritanics, and I couldn't kill you in front of them. It didn't matter. I already knew I'd made a mistake. Your ma was no warrior. She and her babes were defenseless. It was my duty to protect them. That was the oath I swore when I became a warrior. I knew what I did was wrong. Aoifa wanted me to get rid of you, but I wouldn't do it. So she used some of her tricks to clear your memories and told me you were my responsibility. I raised you to be a good warrior so one day you could restore my honor in a fair fight. I'd rather you were a little older and more skillful, but the time has come."

The Scath drew her sword and moved into an attack position. "Summon your Rage, girl."

It was a direct order from the Scath, from the voice that had been telling her right from wrong, and what to do her whole life. For the first time ever, Trib refused.

"I can't fight you," she said in a dull voice. Her hands and feet were numb, her thoughts sluggish.

"You have no choice," the Scath replied. "I taught you to obey me in all things, and you must obey me in this as well." Her blade swooped back and forth as she moved slowly forward.

"Mary," the Scath said.

Trib stared, uncomprehendingly.

"Your eldest sister," the Scath explained. "Crucible and Sorrow. Twins," she said, continuing to move forward.

Trib felt as though she had been hit in the stomach. "Stop!" she gasped.

"I killed the youngest last." At this the Scath's voice caught in her throat, but she kept coming. "No more than a slip of a girl. She cried for her ma, I remember. Calvary, she was called."

Trib's Rage came fast and furious.

"Kwineechka, run!" she shouted over her shoulder as she pulled her sword off her back. The blood-red veil was closing over her vision. She had never felt the Rage so strongly before, and she didn't think she would be able to control it. "Go!" she screamed, and the word became her battle cry as she launched herself at the woman who had been the closest thing she had known to a mother.

CHAPTER TWENTY-SIX

Peyewik

"We must run!" Peyewik heard Kwineechka say as Flame Hair's shriek died away. The storyteller was trying to pull him away from the river, into the forest, but it was as though his feet had grown roots. He stood transfixed as the two warriors came together in a clash of weapons that sent sparks into the pre-dawn light.

The yellow haired woman who was much older and had almost three times the bulk of Flame Hair, was thrown wide by their first contact. But Flame Hair landed on her feet and sprang back, her longknife moving so fast Peyewik saw only a blur. The two warriors seemed to become pure energy, like fire, their fury feeding on the air around them. The older warrior's form flickered, and Peyewik could see her bear-spirit, its claws slashing at Flame Hair again and again. So far Flame Hair had been fast enough to avoid them. Her form was flickering too, but her spirit animal was still struggling to make itself known. He could see that it was a creature of speed and agility, but its full identity and power were still hidden, obscured by the shadow of the bear. Flame Hair had not come into her full strength yet.

Flame Hair darted beneath Bear Woman's guard, and Peyewik saw the first blood as she whirled away again. Bear Woman let out a roar and seemed to grow taller and wider. Her eyeballs bulged in her crimson face, and she bore down on Flame Hair like an angry mother bear, ready to fight to the death. Flame Hair lunged and spun, her movement a thing of beauty, almost a dance, but Peyewik could tell she was beginning to tire. Her tricks of balance and shifting-weight would not be enough against this overpowering opponent. She slowed, and the claws began to graze her flesh. Soon they would tear into her deeply. Years of anger and fighting consumed Bear Woman. Flame Hair was trying to resist, to match the fury with her own, but Bear Woman's anger was too vast and unyielding. Flame Hair faltered and fell to her knees. Peyewik could see her magical fury dwindling, suddenly turning black and charred as a ribbon of grief snaked its way around her heart. She tried to lift her longknife, but the fury was gone, and her muscles had worked beyond their capacity.

Bear Woman roared again and raised her weapon for a killing strike. Peyewik saw her flickering back and forth between bear and woman. Then she roared once more, a sound full of grief and shame, and the sword fell from her hand. The fury had left her as well. She became just a woman once more, looking suddenly tired and old. She growled in a low voice and gestured for the trees. She was sparing Flame Hair, telling her to go.

Flame Hair didn't move.

"Leave her!" Kwineechka cried as Peyewik ran to her.

He tugged on her arm, but couldn't move her until Kwineechka came to help. Bear Woman watched as they dragged her towards the trees.

There was a distant shout, and Peyewik turned to see brown-cloaked figures running through the mist on the far side of the river. Flame Hair and Bear Woman's battle cries had been heard and it wouldn't be long before the other Fighting Women found a way across.

"She said she would kill Flame Hair," Kwineechka said. "I don't understand why she is letting her go now."

Peyewik looked back at Bear Woman, still and gray in the dull light. "She couldn't kill her cub," he said.

"We can't outrun the Fighting Women," Kwineechka said, struggling under Flame Hair's dragging weight.

Peyewik had no breath to reply as they pressed on into the trees where it was still dark. He held Flame Hair's hand and felt her stumbling blindly beside him, slowing them down.

"We must leave her," Kwineechka gasped.

Peyewik stopped suddenly, nearly sending Kwineechka sprawling. He stood in front of Flame Hair and looked into her flat, empty eyes. He couldn't sense her spirit animal anywhere. "Her spirit has traveled far from her body," he said, knowing it was true as he said it. "And it won't know how to return unless I help her."

"Why should you help her?" the storyteller demanded. "After what she has done to us."

"She didn't lie to us," Peyewik said. "It was Crow Woman who lied. To us and to her."

"Bear Woman lied to her too," Kwineechka said quietly, surprising Peyewik.

"What do you mean?"

"Bear Woman killed her family," Kwineechka explained. "Not the Pure Men. I heard her say so. All her life Flame Hair has believed it was the Pure Men."

Peyewik nodded. He had known that Bear Woman had said something terrible to make Flame Hair angry enough to fight, he just hadn't known what.

"That's why her spirit has gone. Bear Woman was like a mother to her. The betrayal is too much."

"You can't help her," the storyteller shook his head. "She is lost in all these lies, all this violence. She belongs to Snake-brother."

"She rescued us from Crow Woman," Peyewik said. "I must try to help her."

"There's no time to argue." Kwineechka glanced over his shoulder towards the river. "We have to keep moving."

He didn't look happy about it, but he pulled Flame Hair's arm across his shoulders and headed deeper into the forest, stopping again after only a short distance.

"What is it?" Peyewik asked.

"Someone is there," Kwineechka said, peering into the shadows under the trees.

Peyewik heard crackling and rustling and then fifteen or more Pure Men appeared, weapons drawn. He and the storyteller began backing away as the Pure Men advanced. Peyewik's heart lurched as a shriek sounded from behind. It was followed by a chorus of battle cries, and he turned to see the Fighting Women charging towards the Pure Men. He, Kwineechka, and Flame Hair were caught between them with nowhere to run.

"Peyewik!" Kwineechka cried, letting go of Flame Hair and lunging towards him. Peyewik whirled around to see a Pure Man running straight for him. He saw cornhusk hair and sky blue eyes, and froze. Then, just as the Pure Man was upon him, he forced himself to drop into Flame Hair's wrestling stance. All the practice with the story-teller had trained his muscles, and before he knew what was happening, the Pure Man was on the ground.

There was no time to congratulate himself. Another Pure Man was running for Flame Hair, who now stood alone, oblivious to the danger all around. The Pure Man's weapon was raised to strike when Kwineechka slammed into him from the side, catching him around the waist and pulling him down.

Another round of battle cries distracted Peyewik. More Fighting Women were charging from the direction of the river. He turned back to Kwineechka and found him on the ground, breathing hard and holding his side. The Pure Man he'd knocked down lay dead beside him, a bloodstain growing on his chest.

A second Pure Man, tall and thin, stood over the storyteller holding a bloody knife.

"No!" Peyewik cried.

But the tall Pure Man didn't attack Kwineechka. He put the knife away and knelt down to speak to him. The storyteller grimaced in reply, and Peyewik saw the blood welling between his fingers.

"Kwineechka, you're hurt!" Peyewik said.

The Pure Man looked up. "I am a friend," he said, and Peyewik recognized his voice. He was the stranger from the forest, the man who had stopped Peyewik from turning himself over to the Pure Men. He was a Pure Man himself, and he was carefully lifting Kwineechka to his feet.

"Follow me," he said.

Kwineecha leaned heavily on the Pure Man and let himself be led away. Peyewik had no choice but to follow, pulling Flame Hair by the wrist.

"We have to get away before the fighting stops," the Pure Man said.

"Why are you helping us?" Peyewik asked.

"No time to explain," the Pure Man replied. "By Manito, trust me."

So Peyewik followed the Pure Man, fearful that at any moment one of the Pale Ones would come after them. But they were too caught up in their skirmish and gradually the sounds of fighting faded behind.

Though the Pure Man was slowed by Kwineechka's weight, Peyewik saw again the ease with which he moved through the forest. He looked and dressed like a Pure Man, but he could speak and move like one of the People.

The sun had risen far above the horizon and was shining down through the treetops when the Pure Man finally came to a stop beside a large outcropping of rock. He pulled aside some trailing vines and ducked into a small cave where he gently lowered Kwineechka to the ground.

"This is my home," he said simply. "You will be safe here while I go to the village of the Away People for help. I will return as quickly as I can. Kwineechka has lost a lot of blood and needs a healer."

Peyewik let go of Flame Hair's hand, and she dropped into a corner, hunched over and silent.

"You know Kwineechka? And the Away People?" he asked, studying the Pure Man. His eyes were blue, like Sky Eyes' had been, but there were many care lines around them, and they did not frighten Peyewik. Flame-colored hair grew on the lower part of his face, but the hair on his head was darker, except for patches of gray around his face, and it sprang out of his scalp like the curling tendrils of a pea vine.

"I know the Away People," the Pure Man replied. "I am an old friend of Kwineechka's father. I was the one who taught him the language of the Pale Ones, but there is no time to tell the whole story. Just know that I have been watching out for you."

"Why did you hide your face from me that night in the forest?"

"I didn't want to frighten you or anger the New Murian. I thought it was best if no one saw me."

"Kwineechka knew you were there?"

"He suspected it, but did not know for certain. I will tell you the rest later. Now I must go for the healer."

"If you bring me pine bark or sassafras, and some nettles, I can help slow the bleeding," Peyewik said.

The Pure Man looked surprised.

"My grandfather is the healer of the Original People," Peyewik explained. "I have seen him treat wounds like this. It needs to be closed with sinew and a bone needle, but I can slow the bleeding until you come back with the healer."

"The nettles and pink bark are nearby," the Pure Men said. "I will fetch them for you before I go."

When the Pale Man was gone, Peyewik tried to wipe the blood away from Kwineechka's wound with a torn cloth. Every time the storyteller took a breath more came gushing out. He sang a little prayer to Manito, asking for help remembering everything he had seen Muhkrentharne do.

The Pure Man returned with the nettles and pine bark. "There is also some valerian root to help him rest," he said.

As Peyewik took the plants from him, he was surprised and pleased to sense that the Pure Man had said the right prayers of thanks to the plant spirits. There was a firepit near the entrance of the cave, and the Pure Man lit a fire there, propping up a clay pot of water to heat. He brought in a pile of dry wood, and then said, "I must go now."

At the entrance to the cave he paused to look down at Flame Hair's huddled form, and Peyewik was startled by the expression on his face. It was a strange mix of fear, hope, and sadness. When he was gone, Peyewik wanted to ask Kwineechka about him, but the storyteller was feverish and in pain.

Peyewik gave him the valerian to chew and then blanched the nettles in the simmering water to remove the sting. He pounded them with a rock to draw out the juices and pressed them against the wound, the edges of which were starting to look red and angry. Fever would set in soon. He let the pine bark steep in the warm water until it softened and then placed it over the wound like a bandage. It would dry and hold the edges of the wound together, slowing the bleeding until it could be stitched closed.

When Kwineechka had slipped into a fitfull sleep, Peyewik turned to Flame Hair. He was exhausted, but she still needed his help. Except for startling once when Kwineechka cried out in pain, she hadn't moved from her huddled position in the corner.

Peyewik crouched down beside her. He reached out and covered her heart with his hand, then closed his eyes. Her spirit couldn't be too far away if her heart was still beating and her body lived, but he could not sense it. It wanted to be gone. He understood this because his spirit had felt the same way after watching Sky Eyes die, and again after Chingwe was killed.

He had been so sure that he could help her earlier, but now he was tired and his head was spinning. He didn't know where to begin.

"Peyewik."

He looked up and saw a panther slink into the cave. "Chingwe, my friend," he smiled, thinking he must have fallen asleep and started dreaming. "Have you come to help me find Flame Hair's spirit?"

The big cat stared at him with its yellow eyes.

"Follow me," Peyewik heard the familiar voice. "I will show you the way."

CHAPTER TWENTY-SEVEN

Peyewik

The panther passed through an opening at the back of the cave that Peyewik hadn't noticed before. Peyewik followed and found himself in cold, damp, absolute darkness. When he looked back for the firelight in the cave, there was nothing but black.

"Chingwe," he said, panic rising. "I cannot see."

"Walk forward. I am right in front of you."

Peyewik could hear the cat purring. It was the only sound in the dense darkness, and he moved towards it. He tried to stay calm as he followed the sound, but the darkness only grew heavier. It seemed to press on his chest, making his heart strain to beat, his lungs struggle to draw air. More than once he slid towards panic, only to hear the voice in the darkness say, "I am with you," and the panic subsided.

They seemed to be making a gradual descent. The air grew colder, and he began to shiver. Eventually he lost all sense of time and felt as though he had been walking down through the darkness for years. He thought he was imagining things when the air began to get warmer. He stopped shivering and the darkness seemed somehow less dark. He blinked a few times and saw an earthy reddish brown instead of pitch blackness.

"We are almost there," came the voice, and Peyewik could just make out the shape of the panther moving ahead of him.

The descent ended abruptly. Peyewik took a few more steps and his sight was completely restored. The panther had stopped and was looking back the way they had come. Peyewik turned and gasped at the sight of a mountain so high he couldn't see the top. He could see the path they had followed down the mountainside, winding and narrow, sheer rock face to one side; a long, cold drop to the other.

"Come," the voice said. Peyewik followed and found himself on the sandy shore of a lake so large he could not see the other side. Then he saw that there was a current, moving fast in one direction, and knew that it was not a lake but a river. It was twilight, but he could see the stars overhead clearly. None were familiar. He drew in a breath so clear and pure it felt as though his lungs had become the air itself.

"You do not need to breathe here," the voice said. "You felt the darkness lift as we descended, did you not? That was your spirit casting off the weight of your body. We have arrived in a land of spirit. The River of Death flows at your feet."

Peyewik didn't feel concerned by this news. Strange as this place was, he felt at home here.

"There is nothing to fear," the voice confirmed. "Your body will be safe until you return. Though the longer your spirit is away from your body, the harder it is to come back. The girl you call Flame Hair, the one called Tribulation by the New Murians, she has been away from her body for a long time."

Tribulation. Flame Hair. Peyewik remembered why he had followed the panther to this place. "She is here?" he asked.

"Call her name. She will come if she can."

"Flame Hair?" he said timidly. There was no reply but the quiet rush of the river. "Tribulation?" The word was awkward in his mouth and throat. He tried again. On the third try the name rang out loud and clear. "Tribulation!"

At the sound of her name, Tribulation felt a tug in the place where her heart used to be. She tried to resist, but the voice was too loud to ignore. With only a vague memory of speech she said, "What do you want from me?"

Peyewik turned towards the whispery voice but could see nothing. "Your body lives," he said. "It is not time for you to leave it."

A shadow flickered at the corner of his eye and he turned towards it.

"That body ain't anything but pain," the shadow that was Tribulation said.

"You are afraid of the pain?" Peyewik asked her.

"A warrior ain't afraid," Tribulation said, feeling herself grow more solid under Peyewik's steady gaze. "Not even of death."

Peyewik heard her voice growing stronger and watched her shape emerge from the shadows. "If you do not fear death," he said, "then you do not fear living. Come back to life with me."

"Why?" Tribulation asked. "I'll never become a master warrior. I'll never defend New Murias against its enemies and win the Scath's approval. Aoifa, the Scath, the Rage—all of that was a lie. There's nothing for me anymore... " Her shape began to fray at the edges.

"I am not a lie," Peyewik said. "Kwineechka is not a lie. He risked his life for you. We are your friends. Come back to us."

"The storyteller should've let me die. You saw what I let Aoifa do to him..."

"No!" Peyewik shouted. Her spirit was fading away again, and he didn't know how to make her stay. He thought of Chingwe's mother, her wail of grief over her son's body. He thought of his own mother, long dead to a fever. And he thought of Muhkrentharne and the Original People. He didn't even know if any were still alive after the attack he had seen in his dream. What Flame Hair had said was true: there was too much pain in life. Maybe she would be better off if her spirit stayed lost.

"Chingwe!" he cried. "Why did you bring me here?"

The panther stood nearby, still as a carving.

"I thought you came to help me," Peyewik said. "Do you refuse because it was my fault you died?"

The panther stared at him, its yellow eyes unblinking. "Chingwe's death was not your fault. You must endure the pain of his loss, but that does not mean it was your fault."

"Then why won't you help me bring Flame Hair's spirit back? Why have you led me here?"

"All you can do is ask her to come back. It is up to her to accept your invitation or not. She is not the only reason you are here. You have a task of your own in this place. You must release the angry spirit you carry with you. It was not your fault the Pale Ones came. You do not need to carry that burden."

Peyewik put a hand on his chest, felt the familiar cold ache. "It is the spirit of Sky Eyes. He clings to me. I do not know how to make him let go."

"Angry spirits can only take hold where there is already anger. Or fear. Sky Eyes feared death and clung to life. What do you fear?"

There was still enough of Tribulation in one place to hear these words, and though they were spoken for someone else, they pulled at her, pulled her back into herself.

"I fear the things spirits tell me, and I fear that the People will blame me for saying things they do not want to hear," Peyewik replied. Then, to his surprise, he heard Tribulation's voice.

"The world ain't as I was told," she said. "And I no longer know my place in it. This makes me afraid."

"Peyewik, the spirits bring you messages that are not always easy to hear," Panther said. "But they are messages from me."

"From you?" Peyewik asked. "You are not Chingwe? Who are you?"

Panther did not answer. Instead, he spoke to Tribulation, whom Peyewik could now see clearly again.

"The world is not as you were told, but it is my world, and it is up to you to find your place in it."

"Your world?" Tribulation asked. "You're the...Goddess?"

"I am the spirit of a boy called Chingwe, and I am the Goddess worshipped by the New Murians. You can also find me in the holy books of the Puritanics."

Sudden understanding struck Peyewik and filled him with great joy. "Manito!" he cried. "Spirit in All Things!"

"I also answer to that name," Panther replied.

Tribulation was confused. "You can't be both the Goddess and the God of the Puritanics," she said. "They ain't anything alike."

"I am all those things, depending on how my children choose to see me," Panther said. "I have many faces. I can be a nurturing mother or a punishing father. I can also be the Devil or Snakebrother. These are the faces that fear gives me, and they cause much pain and suffering."

"I didn't understand your Snakebrother at first," Tribulation said to Peyewik. "Now I do. The Scath told me Aoifa hurt people because people hurt her. That's why she hurt me, and why she'll hurt the People. It's all she knows."

"That is Snakebrother's work," Peyewik agreed.

Then Tribulation and Peyewik spoke at the same time:

"Manito, you will protect the People from those who would harm them?" Peyewik asked.

"Goddess, did you give Aoifa and the New Murians the right to gain power by any means necessary over those who would harm them?" Tribulation asked.

Suddenly Panther disappeared, obscured by a blinding light.

"It is for you to decide," came the voice out of the light. "Choose fear, or choose love. I will appear accordingly. This is the Blessing I bring to both of you."

Slowly the radiance faded, and Panther stood before them again. The cat stared at them for a moment, then turned and padded away.

Peyewik felt deep happiness and peace. He had just received his Blessing from Manito himself, and he would never choose fear again.

"Come back to life with me," he said to Tribulation.

She hesitated, uncertain. "I don't know the way."

Peyewik held a hand out to her. "I do."

CHAPTER TWENTY-EIGHT

Trib

The first thing Trib saw when she opened her eyes was Peyewik kneeling beside her.

She sat up and said, "I dreamed of you. I was lost and you came looking for me."

Peyewik smiled and said, "Tri-bu-layshun."

"My name!" she said in surprise. "Just call me Trib. It's easier."

The boy smiled again, and Trib studied him. There was something different about him, though she couldn't say what. For some reason, as she looked at him, she felt hopeful. Her memory of recent events was fuzzy, except for everything that had happened with Aoifa and the Scath. She remembered their betrayal with crystal clarity. Her whole life had been a lie, and her world was in chaos, but as the boy smiled down at her, she felt as though she sat in the calm at the center of the storm.

"You called me your friend," she said, remembering something more from her dream.

Peyewik said something in his language.

"Wish I knew what you're saying," Trib replied.

"He said he *is* your friend," came an unfamiliar voice behind her.

Trib sprang up and whirled around. There, in a corner of the cave, sat a Puritanic. She pulled Peyewik close and reached for her sword. It wasn't on her back and she tried to feel around for it one-handed, keeping her eyes on the Puritanic. She couldn't remember where she'd left the weapon, but there was a lot she couldn't remember, including how she'd come to be asleep in a cave occupied by a Puritanic. Trib gave up on the sword and straightened to her full height, trying to look menacing. She pointed at the Puritanic and said, "You'd be dead right now if I had my weapon."

"I do not doubt it," the Puritanic replied. He held his hands up to show that he too was weaponless.

Peyewik tapped at Trib's arm.

"He says you're holding him too tightly."

Trib didn't release her protective grip. "Why should I believe you?"

"Peyewik is also telling you that I am a friend," the Puritanic said patiently.

She was surprised that the Puritanic knew the boy's name, but it wasn't enough to convince her.

"You don't look like a friend," she pointed out.

The man's appearance was actually more bizarre than condemning. He didn't look like other Puritanics Trib had seen. He had curly red hair shot with gray, and an orange beard. Trib guessed by his weathered face that he was about the Scath's age, maybe a little younger. It was his clothing that baffled her most, though. He wore a regular linen shirt, like any man in the settlement might wear, but his trousers and shoes were of animal-skin, like those worn by the Natives.

He noted her confusion with a slight smile. "My name is Jonathan Green," he said. "The People call me Jongren."

Peyewik spoke again, struggling in Trib's grip.

"Believe it or not, he is telling you not to worry, that I am to be trusted," the Puritanic translated.

"I don't believe it," Trib replied, but she loosened her hold.

"Don't get too close to him!" she warned. "He's dangerous."

"I promise you I am not," Jongren said.

"What've you done with Kwineechka?" she demanded.

Jongren tilted his head towards the back of the cave, and Trib saw the storyteller lying there on a bed of leaves. She couldn't tell if he was dead or alive. She made a move towards him and then stopped.

"What happened to him?"

"You don't remember?" the Puritanic asked.

Her heart skipped a beat. The last thing she remembered of Kwineechka was shouting at him to run just before she summoned her Rage. She shook her head, barely able to breathe. Peyewik went to the storyteller and checked the bandage around his middle, causing him to shift in his sleep. Trib's knees went weak with relief at the sign of life.

"Peyewik told me your spirit left your body for a time," Jongren said quietly. "Perhaps that is why you don't remember."

"My spirit? I don't know anything about that," she said impatiently. "Just tell me what happened to Kwineechka."

"He took some Puritanic steel in the stomach yesterday," Jongren explained. "I was on my way to Aoifa's fort with a contingent of Puritanics. My hope was to set them on the New Murians and create a diversion so that I could get Kwineechka and Peyewik away. But you had already escaped when we arrived, and the New Murians were close on your heels. Thankfully the New Murians and the Puritanics became too caught up in fighting each other to notice us slipping away."

"You brought Puritanics to the fort?!" Trib's anger was automatic, and she was reaching for her missing weapon again before she remembered that she was now a traitor among the New Murians, as vilified as the Puritanics themselves.

"My intent was the same as your own," Jongren said. "I thank Manito you succeeded."

"Who are you?" Trib asked suddenly. "And what is this Dess-forsaken place?" She gestured around the cave.

"I live here," Jongren explained. "We are about one league southwest of the New Murian fort. I brought you here because Kwineechka could not have made it all the way back to his village without more help."

"What about the New Murians and the Puritanics? Are they looking for us?"

"I do not know for certain, but I hope they will be distracted long enough for us to get Kwineechka safely home."

"Why do you live in a cave, like an animal?" Trib asked suspiciously. "And why did you help us? You're a Puritanic, ain't you?"

"I was once, yes."

"You ain't anymore?"

"It is a long story," he said, giving her an odd look. "Some of it is only now coming clear."

"If you want me to start believing you ain't an enemy to be gutted on the spot—or as soon as I find my sword—you best tell me."

He gazed at her for a moment. "We might begin with you telling me your name," he said at last. He looked strained, as though bracing for something.

"Why should I?"

"I told you mine."

She frowned but couldn't find the harm in it. "Tribulation Sarahdaughter."

He breathed out slowly, as though he'd been holding his breath. "By Manito, how can it be...?" he said.

Trib wondered what the hell he was talking about. "You're insane," she decided.

"Not at the moment," he replied ruefully. "Though that's exactly what I was twelve years ago when Kwineechka's father found me wandering near here, naked and starving. You see, my wife and children had just been murdered, and it drove me quite mad."

Trib was puzzled. As far as she knew, no Puritanic could care that much about a wife and children.

"Who murdered them?" she asked.

"I had my suspicions, but I did not know for certain until recently."

He glanced at the boy, who sat quietly beside the storyteller, watching their exchange. "Peyewik told me what the Scath told you yesterday, about what she did to your family."

"What's that got to do with you?" Trib growled, suddenly even more on guard.

Jongren was staring at her, searching her face for something. He looked away. "Nothing. You have endured much hardship lately, and heard many difficult truths. I do not wish to burden you further with the details of my story just now."

Trib narrowed her eyes at the former Puritanic. There was something strange about him and it made her nervous.

"I don't trust you," she said bluntly.

Jongren sighed. "I do not blame you for that. There are two things you must know about me now. First, I parted ways with the Puritanics nearly twenty years ago. Second, Kwineechka's father, Nitis, saved my life and restored my sanity. I am forever in his debt, and that is why I am here, to help his son. And any friend of his son's," he added.

"I ain't Kwineechka's friend," Trib dropped her gaze to the ground.

"His actions say otherwise."

"What do you mean?" Trib glanced up again nervously.

"He saved your life," Jongren said. "I saw it with my own eyes. The Puritanic was intent on doing you harm. When you didn't move, Kwineechka came to your rescue and caught the man's knife in his side in the process. He must have been grateful to you for helping him escape."

Trib made an involuntary, strangled sound.

"What troubles you?" Jongren asked.

"Kwineechka had no reason to be grateful to me," she mumbled. "Or to save my life."

"Why not?"

"I promised to protect him and his village. I gave him my word of honor as a warrior. But Aoifa's got other plans for the Natives and I let her do something terrible to him." Shame flooded through Trib as she spoke, and she didn't know why she was making herself vulnerable by talking to this strange man.

"Peyewik told me much of what has happened to you," Jongren said softly, and Trib was startled by the sympathy in his face. "It is not your fault. You tried to do what you thought was right, but you have been deceived by those you trusted. The world is not as you were told."

"Aye, and I no longer know my place in it," she said. "That doesn't mean I ain't responsible for my actions."

Jongren smiled kindly. "Do not be too hard on yourself."

"What in Dess's Name do you know about it?" Trib spat in sudden anger, tired of his unwanted sympathy.

"I know what it is to lose everything. Kwineechka's father showed me unexpected kindness, and I found a new understanding of the world among the People. You shall find a new place as well."

"Maybe," Trib said doubtfully, "but it sure as hell won't be with the Natives."

She looked across the cave at Peyewik and Kwineechka. "I've done nothing but bring them trouble. The sooner I leave them, the better off they'll be."

She realized it was true as she said it and knew what she had to do. Jongren looked as though he wanted to say more, but she cut him off.

"You got no reason to concern yourself with me. Best forget you ever saw me."

She turned to Peyewik at the back of the cave. He smiled at her, and she remembered what he had said about being her friend. Her resolve wavered for a moment. This boy was the only friend she had in the world.

"I reckon you hid my sword from me so I wouldn't hurt this Puritanic," she said to him. "You have to give it back now so I can be on my way."

Peyewik looked at her, uncomprehending.

"Tell him," she said to Jongren.

Just then Peyewik's gaze shifted from Trib's face to the opening of the cave behind her. He gave a shout, and Trib turned to see someone entering the cave.

CHAPTER TWENTY-NINE

Peyewik

Muhkrentharne entered the cave, followed by a pair of hunters.

"Grandfather!" Peyewik shouted. "You are alive!" He ran to the old man and threw his arms around him.

"I am very glad to see you, little one," Muhkrentharne said.

"I am sorry I ran away," Peyewik said into the old man's shoulder.

Muhkrentharne held him tightly. "No, it is I who am sorry. Chingwe's mother told me what she said to you. She was crazy with grief over her son's death. She was not right to blame you. She has been full of remorse for causing the Original People to lose a second child that day. Now you are found, and the People will be glad."

Peyewik sighed and relaxed into his grandfather's embrace, letting his cares fall away for a few heartbeats. Then he stepped back and looked up into Muhkrentharne's wrinkled face.

"What has happened to the Original People?" he asked. "I had a vision of the Pure Men attacking the village."

Muhkrentharne looked sad. "Yes, the Pure Men attacked. We did as Flame Hair told us. We had a path of escape and hiding places. Most of the People got away, but the village was burned to the ground. Some were killed. Old Woman Menukan was one. She was too old to run away fast enough. We were not able to bury her properly, but we sang the songs so her spirit would not linger. Hunters have gone back to see if the Pure Men are gone. They will bury our dead if they can."

Peyewik had known something bad had happened to the village, but hearing the details filled him with grief. He held his grandfather's hand and prayed silently to Manito and the ancestors to look after Old Woman Menukan and the others who had been killed. At last he looked up and asked, "How did you find me in this place?"

"We went to the village of the Away People after our village was burned. We arrived yesterday. We were there when Jongren came. He told us that the Fighting Women held you and Kwineechka as prisoners and that you escaped. He told us Kwineechka was wounded and needed a healer. I came instead of the healer of the Away People because I wanted to see you."

"I am glad you came." Peyewik hugged his grandfather once more. "I have so much to tell you."

"I want to hear everything that has happened to you," Muhkrentharne replied. "But first I must tend to the storyteller."

Peyewik led him to the makeshift bed at the back of the cave. The storyteller was awake, and the two hunters who had entered the cave with Muhkrentharne were kneeling beside him.

"Little brother," Kwineechka said when he saw Peyewik. "Meet Nishingi and Nakismus, the best hunters of the Away People."

The hunters were both tall with broad shoulders and similar, good-humored faces.

"I am the best," Nishingi said with a grin. "My brother is only second best."

"It is true," Nakismus shrugged. "But I am better looking and my jokes are funnier."

"You are dreaming," Nishingi punched his brother in the arm. "I am the best at everything."

"Best at boasting, you mean," Nakismus punched him back. "There are two more hunters waiting outside to help carry you home," he told Kwineechka. "So you will not have to tire your dainty little feet with walking."

"As it should be," Kwineechka said. "I am the Storyteller, you know." He gave a weak laugh that turned into a grimace of pain.

"You will not die, will you?" Nishingi asked. "Before you tell me the end of the story of Moon Princess and Wolf Brother?" His tone was light, but Peyewik could see the concern in his face.

"It is a love story," Kwineechka told Peyewik. "Nishingi likes them as much as the women do. No," he said to his friend. "I will not die before you hear the rest of it. Now get out of the way. I have business with the healer."

"We will be outside when you are ready for us," Nakismus said, and then left the cave, teasing his brother about love stories and a girl named Kinteka as they went. Jongren followed, and Peyewik could hear them discussing which route to take back to the village of the Away People.

"Your friends are funny," he said to Kwineechka as Muhkrentharne examined his wound.

"They teased me endlessly when we were boys," the storyteller replied. "They were the only ones who weren't intimidated when I became Storyteller of the People. Now they stay friends with me because all the pretty girls like a good story." He tried to grin, but his face was pale and drawn with pain.

"My grandson did well with your dressing," Muhkrentharne told him. "But you are still feverish. I will give you a strong sleeping draught so that you will be asleep when I close the wound and during the journey back to your village."

"My thanks to both of you," the storyteller said.

"And mine to you for taking care of my grandson," Muhkrentharne replied.

He prepared the sleeping draught from herbs he had brought with him. Kwineechka drank it and was soon asleep.

"We should not have sent the storyteller to the Fighting Women," Muhkrentharne said as he prepared his bone needle and sinew.

"If you had not, he would not have been there to meet me in the forest," Peyewik pointed out. "I would have been lost and alone."

"This is true, but it was clear that Snakebrother ruled the Fighting Women. We should have known they could not help us."

"If all the Fighting Women were like Trib...like Flame Hair...they would have helped us," Peyewik said, realizing he had forgotten about Trib in the excitement of seeing his grandfather. He looked around and found her crouched in a corner of the cave, her eyes intent on the storyteller. "She did not understand that the spirit of her chief, the Crow Woman, was so damaged."

He remembered what Panther had said about the different faces of fear and anger. "Snakebrother has a strong hold on Crow Woman," he said. "She tries to make herself stronger and more powerful by stealing the spirits of others." He glanced worriedly down at the storyteller, wondering if he should tell Muhkrentharne what Crow Woman had done to him. Kwineechka was sleeping peacefully, and Peyewik decided to leave the telling to him.

Muhkrentharne nodded slowly, taking everything in. "The Away People and their chief, Mikwin, are preparing a Prayer Ceremony. It will be the first time in many years that the Original People and the Away People have come together to ask Manito and the spirits for guidance. We will ask them what to do about Crow Woman and Snakebrother."

This felt right to Peyewik. "A Prayer Ceremony will be good," he said.

Muhkrentharne began stitching Kwineechka's wound closed. Trib made a small sound of discomfort, and Peyewik looked up to see her watching the operation, her face slightly green. After a moment she stood up and went outside.

"Jongren told us Flame Hair helped you escape from the Fighting Women," Muhkrentharne said when she was gone.

"Yes. The Fighting Women lied to her, and she no longer belongs among them. I have decided she is my friend because her heart is good, but there is still much anger in her. I do not know what choice she will make."

"What choice do you speak of?" Muhkrentharne asked. He finished his stitching and prepared a fresh bandage.

"Love or fear," Peyewik replied. "The same choice we must all make."

Muhkrentharne smiled. "I see you have made your choice. You are no longer the boy who was too afraid to sleep in the same house with the fire-haired demon. You are confident in the wisdom the spirits grant you, and you are no longer fearful."

"I have received my true Blessing," Peyewik said happily. "I journeyed to the spirit world and received it from Manito himself."

Muhkrentharne's eyes filled with tears. "It is as I knew it would be. I am very proud of you, my grandson."

Peyewik felt his heart warm with the praise, and then realized that there was no feeling of coldness or tightness in his chest. There hadn't been since his journey to the spirit world. The angry spirit of Sky Eyes was gone for good.

CHAPTER THIRTY

Trib

Trib walked beside Kwineechka's litter with her sword drawn. She had intended to go her own way when the Natives left the cave, but Jongren had asked her to accompany them for protection in case they met any New Murians or Puritanics. The journey would take a day, and she would set off on her own as soon as Peyewik and Kwineechka were safely in the village. She didn't know where she would go, but it didn't matter so long as she went far away from the Natives.

In the meantime, she kept a close eye on the former Puritanic. Mid-way through the morning he stepped away from the litter-bearing party and disappeared into the trees. She followed stealthily, certain he was up to no good, but all he did was make his way around the litter in a wide circle, pausing every now and then to watch and listen. Trib noticed that he moved through the forest as silently as Peyewik or Kwineechka. Near the end of his circumnavigation he stopped and looked back at the tree behind which Trib had thought herself concealed.

"There is no need to spy on me," he said. "I am only making sure we are not being watched or followed."

Trib stepped out from behind the tree, scowling. "So you say," she said.

He smiled unexpectedly. "I am glad to know you take protection of the Natives as seriously as I do."

"You see any of your Puritanic friends out there?" Trib goaded him.

"Puritanics are no friends of mine, and I will need to go farther afield to be certain no one is hunting us."

Trib eyed him, still convinced of treachery.

"I will not go if you do not trust me," he said. "One of the hunters can scout instead."

"Aye, send a hunter," Trib said, moving back towards the others. "You stay where I can see you."

Jongren fell in step beside her. "Please believe that my main concern is the safety and well-being of my friends," he said.

"If you're such good friends with Kwineechka's father, how come he ain't mentioned you before?"

"I do not suppose he had a reason to," Jongren said. "He has known me his whole life and was never given a reason to connect me with either the Puritanics or the New Murians."

"Except you look like a Puritanic, talk like one, and act like one."

Jongren gave her a direct look and smiled again. "Surely you have noticed that I do not act like a Puritanic? Though I look more like one than usual today," he gestured at his linen shirt. "Kwineechka has only ever seen me in Native attire, browned by the sun, and living in the wild."

Trib was unwilling to accept his explanations. "Why ain't you a Puritanic anymore?"

Jongren looked off into the trees, his smile fading. "My wife."

Trib was surprised into silence.

After a pause he continued, "Puritanic tenets hold that women are too weak to know God directly. They can only achieve blessedness by serving their more spiritually capable husbands. I believed this until I met my wife. She was the strongest, wisest, most blessed person I had ever known, male or female. Thus my belief faltered."

Trib had never heard anyone say anything like this, least of all a man about his wife. There was so much emotion in his face and voice that it made her uncomfortable. She cleared her throat and looked at the ground.

"Forgive me if I speak too freely," Jongren said. "I loved my wife very much."

"So you ain't seen hide nor tail of a Puritanic in twenty years?"

Jongren made a visible effort to pull his thoughts back to the present. "Actually, I was among them not a month past. Perhaps it will ease your mind to know they were preparing to hang me for a traitor at the time."

"What did you do?"

"I was captured after leading them on a fool's chase that deprived them of some young quarry."

They had rejoined the litter bearers, and he looked over at Peyewik, who was chatting happily with his grandfather.

"I was sorry to learn that the Puritanics found the village anyway, and the very same boy I was trying to help was killed."

Trib stared at the former Puritanic. She had the strangest feeling that she knew him, or had seen him somewhere before. In a sudden flash of memory she recognized him.

"You were in the forest near Peyewik's village!" she exclaimed. "When I was chasing the Puritanics that ambushed my expedition."

Jongren cocked his head and gave her a wry smile. "Strange to think we had a similar goal. I was tracking the same Puritanics, ever since they arrived in the south, hoping they wouldn't find the Native villages."

Trib didn't return the smile. "You were tracking them when they ambushed my expedition in the marsh? You let them attack without warning?"

"No. I did not know about the attack until later. I am sorry if you lost friends that day."

"I did," Trib said, surprised that a former Puritanic would express sorrow over the deaths of New Murians. She thought briefly of Cuss, wondering what her friend would think of everything that had happened since the ambush.

"I found Peyewik right after I saw you," she told Jongren. "A Puritanic was trying to drown him in the river."

"As overzealous as my former brethren can be, and contrary to the rumors Aoifa spreads, they are not child-killers," Jongren said. "It is more likely that you rescued Peyewik from a forced baptism and kidnapping."

"You think it ain't so bad to take him from his family and all he knows?" Trib said defiantly. "What about all those kids who disappear from the settlement, the ones the Puritanics kidnap? You think they're happy being forced to live in the forest like animals with people who abuse them?"

"Some are kidnapped, it is true, but never with intent to harm. The Puritanics believe they are saving the children. But salvation is not the only reason they take children. Many Puritanics had to leave their children behind when Aoifa expelled them from the settlement and forced them to live, as you say, like animals in the forest. I have known men to steal their own children from New Murias simply because they could not bear to be without them."

Trib didn't understand this. "Why? They use them for servants or something, the way Aoifa uses captured Puritanics?"

Jongren looked at her sadly. "Because fathers love their children as naturally as mothers do," he said, reminding Trib that Kwineechka had said the same thing. "Some New Murian mothers willingly send their sons out to be with their fathers."

This was more than Trib could stand. "Lies like that could bring a Rage down on you," she warned him.

"Yet you do not summon one. Perhaps you have recognized what Aoifa does to young men of a certain age?" He looked over at the storyteller on his litter. "Many mothers would spare their sons the siren song and a life of servitude."

Trib followed his gaze but had to look away when her stomach flipped over at the sight of Kwineechka's sleeping face. She understood wanting to spare a loved one from Aoifa's manipulations. She tried to hide her feelings by asking another question.

"Where were you when Peyewik's village was attacked?"

"Tied up in the forest where the Puritanics left me. They were coming back for me after the raid on the village. As I told you, they planned to hang me as a traitor. I escaped while they were gone."

"You told them where Peyewik's village was," Trib accused, still looking for a reason to condemn him.

"No," Jongren said. "The first I learned that New Murians had arrived in the south was overhearing my captors talk about the ambush in the marsh and trying to find the New Murian who helped the Native child escape. The Puritanics found Peyewik's village while searching for you."

Trib's heart sank at this confirmation that the attack had been her fault, though there had been no accusation in Jongren's voice.

"What did you do after escaping?" she demanded.

"I was making my way back to warn Kwineechka's village when I found Peyewik and brought him to you."

"Why didn't you make yourself known?"

"You would have killed me on the spot."

"Aye, I would have," Trib agreed. "Also would've killed you on sight this morning, if I'd had my sword."

"Which is precisely the reason Peyewik and I hid it from you."

Trib frowned and said nothing. As much as she hated to admit it, there was a chance Jongren had not deserved to die on the spot.

"Something is troubling you," Jongren observed.

The kindness of his tone must have thrown her off guard, because before she could stop herself, she was telling him.

"What if you really are just trying to help the Natives?" she said slowly, working her thoughts out as she spoke them. "You're the only one who is. And what if I'd killed you this morning like I wanted to?"

Jongren remained silent, waiting for her to finish.

"Aoifa and the Scath trained me to think and act a certain way," she continued. "I used to think it was the right way and the only way. I don't know anymore if it was the right way, but I also don't know if I can do any differently."

"You can," Jongren said without hesitation.

"Who are you to tell me what I can and can't do?" she snapped.

"You will recall what I said earlier about how I lost my Puritanic beliefs? I never would have believed it possible before I met my wife. If I could change so drastically, you can as well."

Trib shook her head, not wanting to parallel her former beliefs with that of a Puritanic.

"You care about Peyewik and Kwineechka," Jongren said.

Trib didn't answer.

"Perhaps there is a place for you with them, as there was for me," he suggested quietly. "You might stay and continue to protect those you care about."

"The People were right to send me away the first time," Trib said. "I've done nothing but bring them trouble."

Jongren sighed. "Trouble has been looking for the People since we first came over from the Old World," he said regretfully. "It would have found them whether you were here or not."

"Why are you telling me this?" she demanded. "What do you care what I do or what happens to me?"

Jongren looked startled, almost frightened by this question. He opened his mouth to say something, then closed it. After a long pause he said finally, "I have faith that you can heal and change for the better."

"Dess damn your faith," Trib muttered.

After that, they walked without speaking for a time, until Jongren said, "The day wears on. I will ask Nishingi to scout the movements of the Puritanics and New Murians."

He started to approach one of the tall, young hunters carrying Kwineechka's litter, but Trib stopped him.

"You go," she said. "The hunters are busy. I don't think you'll betray us, at least not this time."

Jongren paused before leaving. "Do not set off on your own before I return," he said, then turned and disappeared silently into the forest.

CHAPTER THIRTY-ONE

Peyewik

Kwineechka's litter made for very slow going, but Peyewik didn't mind. It was the first time he had been outside since his journey to the spirit world. It was a warm, clear day, and everything felt clean and new, as if the world had been reborn while he was in the cave. It was as though a weight had been lifted from his shoulders and a veil from his eyes. His fears and worries were still there—what would happen at the Prayer Ceremony, what the People would decide to do in the face of such uncertainty and threat—but they did not rule him or dictate the shape of his reality. He walked beside his grandfather and listened to the birds, smelled the loam underfoot, tasted the breeze, and felt the sun soak into his skin. He was at home in the world, vibrating with life and full of joy. He told Muhkrentharne everything that had happened to him since he fled the village after Chingwe's death, and the old man listened with wonder.

"I've known there would be great and terrible things in your life since before you were born," Muhkrentharne said after Peyewik told him of his journey underground with Panther. "And I know it has been hard for you to be singled out this way."

"Yes, but it is also a gift," Peyewik gave his grandfather a reassuring smile. "I have seen amazing things, and they are helping me understand others who are different and the changes they will bring to the People."

He looked over at Trib, who was talking with Jongren. She was clearly wary of the man, but there was something about the two of them together that made sense to him.

"Grandfather, how will Trib be received when she arrives in the village of the Away People?"

"They will not be glad to see her, but Jongren says she plans to leave as soon as we get there. The People will not have time to get upset."

Peyewik was surprised to hear that Trib was leaving. He remembered Old Woman Menukan saying once that Trib had become part of the story of the People. Peyewik did not think her part was finished yet. Besides, he knew she had nowhere else to go.

Not long after, Jongren left the group to go find out what the Fighting Women and Pure Men were doing. Flame Hair continued walking beside the litter, stealing glances at the storyteller when she thought no one was looking. When Kwineechka woke up around midday, she quickly stepped out of his line of sight.

As soon as the brothers Nishingi and Nikismus realized their passenger was awake, they started teasing him.

"Flame Hair follows you like a wife," Nishingi goaded him. "Did you marry without telling us?"

Kwineechka grimaced and did not return their jests. Peyewik sensed that he was troubled. Whether it was about Trib or something else, he could not tell.

They arrived in the village of the Away People late in the afternoon. Everything was in chaos as Kwineechka was welcomed home, and the Away People continued to make room for the displaced Original People. Peyewik tried to keep track of Trib, afraid that she would leave without saying goodbye, but he lost sight of her as the Original People swept him up. Just as Muhkrentharne had said, they were overjoyed to have him back. Chingwe's mother wept and embraced him.

"It was not your fault the Pure Men came," she said. "I should not have blamed you. Chingwe loved you like a brother, and you are like a son to me. The People need you now. We will listen to all you have to say."

Peyewik cried with her when they talked of Chingwe and of Old Woman Menukan and the others who had been killed in the second attack on the village. Then she walked with him through the village, showing him where everything was, and introducing him to new people. The village was both strange and familiar to Peyewik. It was larger than the village of the Original People and surrounded by a cedar forest. The Away People were kind and welcoming, but he saw the anxiety in their faces and wished he could reassure them with some of the peace he'd found in the spirit world.

Towards sunset, Muhkrentharne came to find Peyewik for supper. The women of the village were cooking huge pots of stew in honor of their guests and the Prayer Ceremony that would happen the next day, and the delicious smell was making Peyewik's stomach rumble. On his way to the cooking fire he saw a disheveled figure lurking behind some huts. It was Flame Hair, uncomfortable and trying to stay out of sight.

"Have supper with us," he said to her, pantomiming eating so she would understand.

"That is not a good idea," Muhkrentharne tried to stop him.

"She has to eat," Peyewik insisted. He held out his hand to her, but she shook her head.

He went to her, took her hand, and pulled her towards the cooking fires. He saw Kwineechka surrounded by friends and family and started to walk to him. The storyteller smiled at Peyewik, but his face fell at the sight of Trib. Peyewik came to a stop as the people around the cooking fires fell silent, staring at Trib.

Trib tried to leave, but Peyewik held onto her, remembering too well what it felt like to be unwelcome among the People. He stood up as tall as he could and said in a loud, clear voice, "I ask you to extend your hospitality to my friend Flame Hair, called Tribulation by her people."

The People remained silent.

Peyewik looked at Kwineechka, but the storyteller dropped his gaze to the ground. Peyewik was disappointed and felt sorry for Trib. He was about to lead her away when someone said, "I speak for Tribulation as well."

It was Jongren. "Friends, to whom I owe my health and sanity, I ask another favor of you. Allow my daughter to sit and eat among you."

CHAPTER THIRTY-TWO

Trib

Trib didn't know what Jongren had said, but it drew a reaction from the Natives. There were surprised murmurs, and they began to point at her as well as stare. She thought she even heard someone laugh.

"Dess damn this," Trib said, pulling her hand from Peyewik's grasp and starting to turn away. A tall man stepped forward, blocking her escape.

"Move," she growled, trying to sound intimidating.

The man looked slightly bemused, but held his hand out to her and said something in the Native language.

"What does he want?" she asked over her shoulder.

"He is Kwineechka's father, Nitis," Jongren explained. "He is inviting you to eat with his family."

"Why?" Trib asked warily. "The Natives are all looking at me like I have two heads. Now he's asking me to supper?"

She glanced at Kwineechka, expecting him to look away. Instead, he too was staring at her, his golden eyes wide with shock.

She whirled towards Jongren.

"What the hell did you say to them?" she demanded.

"I told them you were my daughter."

It took a moment for the words to sink in. When they did, flickers of red appeared in the corners of her vision. "That's a dirty lie," she said in a low voice.

"I am sorry to tell you this way," Jongren replied. "I knew the People would welcome you if they knew. I wanted you to know you could have a place here."

He took a tentative step towards her.

"I ain't your daughter," she hissed. "Come near me again, liar, and I'll kill you,"

She turned her back on him and stumbled away, barely able to see through the veil of red covering her eyes. She headed for the darkness at the edge of the village, knowing she needed to get away before her Rage took over. She wanted to hurt Jongren, but not any of the Natives.

"Trib-u-lay-shun."

She recognized Peyewik's voice.

"Get away," she warned him. "Rage coming...I'll hurt you..."

Instead, she felt the boy take her hand again, and all at once her Rage was gone. It hadn't been as strong as she thought. She sat down on the ground, feeling suddenly very tired and alone.

Peyewik sat down beside her.

"What in Dess's Name am I supposed to do next?" she said. "I got nowhere to go, no one to trust..."

Peyewik didn't answer, but just then Trib heard women's voices and a group of Natives appeared. They startled and drew back when they saw her, but Peyewik spoke to them reassuringly, and they came closer again, looking down at Trib shyly. A young woman with a round face had the courage to step towards Trib with her hand extended.

Surprised, Trib took it, and let the young woman help her to her feet.

"Thanks," she mumbled.

The other women were continuing on their way into the forest, and the round-faced girl gestured for Trib to follow.

Trib glanced at Peyewik, who nodded encouragingly.

Trib took a deep breath. "Reckon I got nowhere else to go..." she said, and followed the round-faced girl into the forest.

The Native women were sure-footed in the darkness, and before too long they came to a stream where, without a trace of modesty, they shucked off their minimal clothing and waded into the water.

"Oh no," Trib said, backing away. "I hate water."

Two girls came out of the stream and began gently tugging Trib out of her clothes. Too surprised to protest, she let them. She felt self-conscious about the scars that showed up so clearly against her pale skin, but the girls didn't notice. They giggled shyly and pulled her into the water, which became wide and deep a few steps away from the bank. Trib shivered and for a moment thought she was miserable. Then she realized the water felt good on her sweaty, grimy skin. She hadn't bathed since Aoifa's cabin, and that had only been a quick rinse in a wash basin. The women around her were laughing and splashing each other. Trib cupped her hands and scooped water over her head. She felt her muscles relaxing as the cool liquid sluiced down her body. One of the young women handed her a flat, gritty stone and showed her how to use it, scrubbing her skin until she was cleaner than she ever remembered being.

When they had decided she was clean enough, the women pulled her out of the water, allowed her to dress again, and led her back to a small, neat hut at the edge of the village. Inside, laid out on one of the sleeping platforms was a dress made of soft deerskin and decorated with intricate beadwork. There were matching leggings and boots as well. One of the women pointed to her, then at the dress, then back at her.

"You want me to wear that?" Trib asked, shocked. She had never worn a dress, much less such an elaborate costume.

"No chance in Hell." She started to back away. "I appreciate your kindness, and I reckon you're doing this on account of what Jongren told you about me being his kin. But it ain't true. So I should be going now."

The women laughed uncomprehendingly and swarmed around her. Their hands were gentle, and Trib gave up resisting as they pulled the dress over her head. Her skin still tingled from the scrubbing, and the dress was a soft caress against it. She had never felt such a thing.

The women stepped back and studied her. They twitched a shoulder seam here, tugged a legging there, and when they were satisfied, smiled and made appreciative noises at her. Trib was startled by this. No one had ever expressed anything positive over her appearance before.

Just then the sound of drums started outside and the women scattered. Trib found herself alone with the round-faced girl. She wondered if she should go too, but the girl smiled warmly and gestured for her to sit and wait.

"What's happening," she asked the girl. "Why are they drumming outside?"

The girl didn't understand. She just smiled and shrugged herself into a dress similar to Trib's. The beadwork was equally intricate and Trib wondered if it had been done by the same person. The round-faced girl pulled out a set of combs and held one out to her with a questioning sound. Trib peered at the delicate carvings on it and shook her head.

"Ain't got the first notion what to do with it."

The girl indicated that she could do it for her.

Trib hesitated. "If you really want to," she said. "It ain't necessary. I don't know what all this is for." Then she couldn't help laughing at the worried look on the girl's face as she held the comb and studied Trib's red hair.

"It won't bite you," Trib said, reaching back to untie the leather thong that held it back. "Though I reckon there were things living in there before I combed out the rat's nest."

The girl smiled nervously and touched Trib's head. When nothing happened and she was reassured that it was like any other hair, aside from the color, she set upon it and with a few deft strokes lifted and pinned it away from Trib's neck. Trib felt the complicated knot on the back of her head and watched as the girl replicated it with her own hair.

"That's really...lovely," Trib said, the last word awkward in her mouth. It wasn't a word she was used to saying.

"So is this," she said, pointing at the beadwork on the arm of her dress. "Did you do this?"

The girl gave her a sad smile and said something in the Native language. At first Trib didn't understand, but then she realized the girl was telling her the name of the person who made the dress, a person who was no longer here or she would be wearing it herself.

"I'm honored," Trib said solemnly.

The drumming outside had grown louder. The girl smiled one last time and led Trib out of her house and into the center of the village where a huge fire had been lit. The drummers sat near the fire, pounding out a rhythm for the dancers who circled the fire.

"What in Dess's Name is happening?" Trib asked, but the round-faced girl was gone, caught up in the circle of dancers.

She spotted Peyewik on the far side of the circle with his grandfather, and decided it would be better if she left without talking to anyone else. She was trying to find the round-faced girl's house and her own clothes when she heard the singing. The sound tugged at her and she followed it to another circle around a smaller fire. Instead of dancing, the people in this circle sat close together and sang.

Trib stood in the shadows outside the circle and listened. She couldn't understand the words, but the melody was sad and made her think of everyone she had known who had died. Not just her friends and family, but the men she had killed as well. More than just thinking of them she seemed to feel the places they had occupied in her body and heart, whether in anger, hate, or love, and she felt the spaces left behind when they died. The sensation was unbearable, and she stepped away from the singing circle, hoping to escape it.

There was a touch at her elbow and she jumped, spinning around to find Jongren beside her.

"I apologize for startling you," he said. "I was afraid you had gone."

"I ain't your..." Trib started to say, but Jongren interrupted.

"Your mother's name was Sarah and your sisters, my daughters, were named Mary, Sorrow, Crucible, and Calvary. You and the last three were named for the circumstances into which they were born."

An odd, disconnected image came into Trib's mind then.

"Calvary," she repeated the name.

"Yes," Jongren said. "The youngest before you. "

"She wore a blue striped pinafore." Trib didn't know where the memory came from, but she suddenly could see the little dress clear as day.

"Yes," Jongren confirmed, his voice catching. "You wore a matching one. Your mother cut them from the same piece of cloth."

"She was wearing it the day she died," Trib said, seeing a bright red stain seeping through blue striped fabric.

Jongren couldn't answer her at first. Then he cleared his throat and said, "The People are singing to the ancestors, those who have traveled to the spirit world before us. They are saying they miss them and will see them again."

After a pause he added, "You could sing with them. Your voice can do many things besides summon a Rage."

"I can't sing that song," Trib countered. "I ain't strong enough to face all the people I sent to the spirit world ahead of me."

To change the subject, she asked, "Why are the Natives singing and dancing when Aoifa or the Puritanics could attack any moment?"

"They are celebrating now because they are glad to be alive and together. There is a Prayer Ceremony tomorrow. They will ask

Manito and the spirits for guidance as to what to do about the Puritanics and the New Murians."

"It'll take more than prayer to deal with them," Trib said.

"I agree," Jongren said, surprising her. "Whether you believe I am your father or not, I would ask for your help in protecting the People."

"How?" she asked warily.

"You can speak to the New Murians on behalf of the People, and I will speak to the Puritanics."

Trib snorted. "That ain't going to work. I already tried asking Aoifa for help. She locked Peyewik and Kwineechka up like prisoners and…"

She couldn't bring herself to say what Aoifa had done to the storyteller. "Aoifa won't help," she finished quickly.

"And Scathach follows her orders, regardless of how many innocents are harmed?" Jongren asked bitterly.

Trib started to say "yes" but paused, remembering what the Scath had said as she tried to goad Trib into fighting her. It was difficult to think of it, to remember again how the Scath had betrayed her, but some of the things she had said…

"The Scath still values her honor as a warrior. She knows killing my family was wrong. It goes against her warrior's code to attack those who are weaker."

Jongren frowned. "If this is true, then deep in her blackened soul she may feel averse to attacking the People?"

"Aye," Trib replied, feeling sick to her stomach as she realized what this meant she would have to do.

"Would you consider approaching Scathach on behalf of the People?" Jongren asked. "Circumventing Aoifa all together?"

"Dess knows, the only time I thought to see the Scath again was to get revenge," she said through clenched teeth.

"If you could convince her to leave the People in peace, think of the lives you would save."

"Even if I could get her to leave the People alone, what about the Puritanics? You told me yourself they want to hang you for being a traitor. I don't reckon they're looking to do you any favors."

"You must trust that I know my former brethren better than you. I believe they can be persuaded to see God's plan in this."

"And you can see God's plan more clearly than the rest of us?" Trib sneered.

Jongren gave her a small smile. "I cannot. Neither God's, nor Manito's, nor the Goddess's. But no more can the Puritanics, until I convince them otherwise."

Trib shook her head. She didn't like the plan at all, but she thought of how Peyewik's grandfather had saved her life and how Peyewik had named her a friend. She thought of how she felt about Kwineechka and of the kindness she had been shown that very night by the Native women. She remembered her first impressions of the Natives as backwards and primitive and how she had thought her own people so superior. She blushed at how wrong she had been on both counts.

"I'll do it," she told Jongren. "It ain't a great plan, but my Rage ain't enough to hold off both the Puritanics and New Murians."

"It is precisely my hope that any use of the Rage, on anyone's part, may be avoided," Jongren said.

"Good. If I had my choice, I'd never use it again," Trib said, surprised by how much she hated the idea of ever summoning another Rage. It made her feel again like she no longer knew herself or her place in the world. And it reminded her of something Aoifa had told her.

"Aoifa said my ma refused the Rage," she said. "If she really was your wife, you can tell me why."

"Aoifa tried to teach Sarah the Rage when she needed warriors to expel us...I mean the Puritanics...from the settlement. Your mother refused."

"Why?" Trib asked, torn between a feeling of shame at her mother's refusal to fight and an intense curiosity as to why she had done so.

"Sarah described to me how Aoifa taught others to Rage. She used her siren powers to dig through a person's memories. She sought those who had been through something terrible because they were easiest to influence. She would call forth horrific experiences, buried deeply in the mind and body, and allow them to consume their owner, creating a terrible strength based on fear and anger. Then she manipulated them further so that this strength could be called upon at will."

The details of Trib's Rage Initiation a few months earlier came rushing back to her. She hadn't spoken about it to anyone, not even Cuss, but all of a sudden she found herself wanting to tell Jongren everything.

"It was just as you say," she told him. "Aoifa took me alone into a cave. I had no weapons, just a shirt and breeches. It was cold..." Trib shivered, feeling the chill of the dark cave again. "Aoifa told me to kneel down. She asked me if I was worthy of the gift the Goddess grants her warriors. I said I was. She asked me what I'd sacrificed in the Goddess's name. I didn't know what she meant, but she told me to remember..."

Trib's voice faltered. She felt Jongren's hand on her shoulder.

"What did she tell you to remember?" he asked quietly.

"The day the Puritanics murdered my family. She told me to remember as if I were there again. She said my greatest strength would come from my greatest suffering."

"Did you remember?" It sounded as though the question pained him.

Trib nodded. "I remembered the sounds of screaming and breaking in the other room. Then it was quiet, and I went to see what happened."

"You do not have to tell me. I saw it myself..." Jongren's voice was thick with grief.

"I should have died with the others," Trib said matter-of-factly. "I don't know why I wasn't in the room with them." She looked up.

"Where were you?"

"You were in your bed, sick," Jongren explained. "I wasn't there because I had gone to the apothecary for your medicine. I had to go all the way to one of the Christian settlements because the one in New Murias wouldn't serve me."

"Aoifa told me it was you who killed my ma and sisters," Trib said, and watched Jongren turn pale, his eyes go wild.

"That lying witch!" he exploded. "I saw her sister leave the house. I saw her! And to tell my only living child that it was me...Manito forgive me. I went mad at the sight of my wife and children murdered. I thought you were all dead and I ran from there raving. If I had known you lived..."

He closed his eyes and struggled to regain control.

"The Scath used the Rage on them," Trib told him, closing her eyes and seeing the room as if she were there again. "My ma and sisters were torn apart. There was blood everywhere...Aoifa asked me what it felt like when I saw them, but there ain't words for it. It was so bad I wanted to die so I wouldn't have to feel it anymore...Then Aoifa asked me who made me feel this way. I told her it was the Puritanics, and she asked me what I wanted to do to them. I said I wanted to tear them apart the way they tore my ma and sisters apart, so that the bad feeling would go away. She asked me where I felt the wanting to tear them apart. I told her it was in my belly, and she told me to let it move through me until I felt it in my arms and legs and hands and feet and everywhere in my body. I did this, I don't know how, but I did it. She told me to feel it in my throat, and I said it made me want to scream. She said 'Scream,' so I did, and the first Rage came to me. I saw red and just wanted to kill. I could still hear Aoifa's voice. She said, 'This is your Rage, Tribulation. This is your gift from the Goddess. Let it consume you...'"

"Do not," Jongren whispered. "Daughter of mine, do not let the Rage consume you."

Trib opened her eyes. She looked at Jongren, who still gripped her shoulder, and knew that it was true. He had been there the day her family died. Whether he really was her father or not, she felt a strange sense of relief, as if she no longer carried the burden of that day alone.

"I don't remember all that every time I summon a Rage," she told him. "All I have to do is think of one thing from that day, and the Rage comes. But that day is all I remember of my ma and sisters. The Scath told me Aoifa did something to the rest of my memories."

Jongren let go of her shoulder. He was no longer weeping, but he looked tired.

"Did my ma think the Rage was a gift from the Goddess?" she asked him.

"Sarah did not believe that the Goddess she prayed to would use such a tool of pain and destruction. You must see that this tool has been used against you as much as you have used it against others. Aoifa manipulated the horrors of a child to create more horrors."

Tribulation was silent for a long time, thinking of the terrible things the Rage had enabled her do without feeling any remorse.

"Maybe I'll remember other things about my ma and sisters, if you remind me..." she said.

"It would be my joy to do so," Jongren replied. "You will stay and help with my plan to create peace for the Natives?"

"Aye," Trib said.

"Thank the Goddess," Jongren sighed and closed his eyes briefly. "We will talk more about it later. For now though, singing and dancing is what is needed."

"I don't dance," Trib said.

"You used to. You loved to dance when you were small."

Trib snorted in disbelief, and Jongren smiled at her before going to join the singing circle.

Trib wandered back towards the dancing circle, but felt conspicuous standing outside it, watching while everyone else danced. She didn't dare join in. She didn't know if she'd be welcome, and more importantly, she couldn't remember ever dancing a step in her life, regardless of what Jongren had said.

"I don't reckon today's the day I'll take it up again," she muttered, just as the round-faced girl swung by and grabbed her arm, pulling her into the circle.

"What in Dess's Name?!" Trib cried. She stumbled through the first few steps and nearly fell, her face burning with embarrassment. She tried to leave the circle, but the round-faced girl had linked arms with her and wouldn't let go. She found her balance and trotted after the round-faced girl for another few steps. Then she started to hear the rhythm. She watched the round-faced girl's feet and before she knew it her own feet were moving in the same way. By the time the round-faced girl let go of her arm, Trib was dancing. She was so surprised that it didn't occur to her to stop. The drumming sped up, and the steps changed. To her amazement she followed the shift easily, throwing herself into leaping twirls that made her giddy. Her leg muscles were burning, and the old wound on her thigh complained, but she didn't care. She had never felt like this before. Fighting had always felt right to her body. It was the only time she wasn't clumsy. This felt right to her too, but it was different. Her body felt warm, smooth, and unified—with itself, with the rhythm of the drumming, and with the people around her. There was nothing but joy in her movement.

CHAPTER THIRTY-THREE

Peyewik

Peyewik sang songs of grief for Chingwe and Old Woman Menukan, and for the village of the Original People, the only home he had ever known. Then he went to the dancing circle and leapt for joy at being a part of Manito's beautiful world.

At one point he looked up and saw Trib in the circle. She was wearing a beautiful white, beaded dress, and her hair was pinned up in the style of the People. But most astounding was her dancing. The grace that he had only ever seen when she was fighting found a new and greater expression. She moved in complete harmony with the sound of the drums and the chanting and the people around her. Peyewik could hardly believe she was the same awkward, aggressive girl he knew. She looked happy as she danced. As Peyewik watched, he saw her spirit animal clearly, leaping and turning around the fire. It was a lynx, full of pure, joyful energy.

Peyewik couldn't believe he had once thought Trib a demon or a shape-shifter. Now, watching her dance and feeling her joy, he couldn't help feeling that having the fate of such a person intertwined with that of the People couldn't be such a bad thing. He laughed out loud and threw himself into the dancing.

Some time later Peyewik needed a rest and went to sit with Kwineechka, who was still too weak from his wound to do more than watch.

"Are you enjoying yourself even though you can't dance?" Peyewik asked.

"I am glad to be home," the storyteller replied. "But it reminds me that your home is gone. I'm sorry, Little Brother."

"It's sad and strange that my village is gone," Peyewik said. "But if I am with friends and family, then I always have a home."

They sat in silence for awhile, listening to the drums and watching the dancers, and Peyewik noticed that storyteller was distracted, his gaze returning again and again to the flame-haired figure in the white dress.

"I cannot believe she is Jongren's daughter," Kwineechka muttered at last. He tore his gaze away to look at Peyewik.

"I have known Jongren most of my life. He took me for walks in the woods when I was a boy and taught me to speak his language. I did not know he was strange among the People until I got older. He is a good man."

He looked back at Flame Hair, studying her intently. "They cannot be of the same people, much less related."

"They look alike," Peyewik pointed out.

"They are both pale-skinned..."

"Tall and thin with flame-colored hair," Peyewik added more specifically. "Maybe she is a good person too, just like her father."

Kwineechka shook his head in bewilderment.

"If you think she is bad, why did you help her when the Pure Man attacked?" Peyewik asked.

Kwineechka frowned, as if he wasn't sure of the answer himself.

"I have seen her spirit animal," Peyewik said, and smiled at the surprised look on Kwineechka's face.

"Pale Ones have spirit animals?"

"I do not see them as easily as I see the spirits of the People," Peyewik said. "I did not see Trib's until tonight when she began to dance. When she dances, she is free from the anger, the pain, and the violence. If she keeps dancing, Snakebrother will never have power over her the way he has power over Crow Woman."

The storyteller's face went pale at the mention of Crow Woman. "Then I pray to Manito she keeps dancing," he said.

Peyewik was about to reply when a handsome, middle-aged woman approached them.

"You are feeling well, my son?" she asked Kwineechka.

Kwineechka gave her a forced smile. "I am well. Muhkrentharne and Peyewik took good care of me."

The woman turned to Peyewik. "You are Peyewik, the Seer of the Original People."

Peyewik had never been given a title before and didn't quite know how to reply.

"I am Shikiwe, mother of the Storyteller of the People," the woman introduced herself. "Thank you for helping my son."

"You are welcome," Peyewik said, smiling because the woman had given herself a title as well. She was a good-looking woman and he could tell she was accustomed to a certain amount of attention and respect. She turned back to her son.

"You are sure your wound is not bothering you?"

"I feel so well that I think I will dance soon," Kwineechka teased her. His tone was light, but Peyewik noticed that the mischievous twinkle was missing from his golden eyes.

"You will not!" Shikiwe chided him. "You will watch and that is all, even though there are many who will be disappointed not to see you dance."

She gave a slight nod over her shoulder at a group of young women who kept looking over at the storyteller and giggling. Kwineechka hadn't looked in their direction once all evening.

"Mother," he said, embarrassed.

Shikiwe bent down and patted his cheek as though he were a small boy. "You are the Storyteller of the People, and you are old enough to take a wife. All the girls hope you will choose them. This is as it should be."

She sighed happily and straightened up.

"I must go and find your aunties. No dancing," she warned him once more. "Save your strength for telling a story at the Prayer Ceremony tomorrow."

She left then, failing to notice that her son's face had gone pale in the firelight.

"You do not want to tell a story tomorrow?" Peyewik asked.

"I have not tried since...Crow Woman," he said. "I do not know what will happen."

"You did not tell your mother about her." Peyewik observed.

Kwineechka's face darkened. "My mother is very proud that her son is the Storyteller of the People. It would shame her to know how I let Crow Woman take the Story of the People from me."

"You had no choice."

"No one can know of it!" Kwineechka said forcefully.

Peyewik sat in silence for a moment, then said, "It is for you alone to tell what Crow Woman did to you, but do not forget that I know what it is like to have a shadow cling to your spirit. Only you can release that shadow."

The storyteller shook his head. His eyes glittered with unshed tears and he couldn't speak. Peyewik said no more but stayed with him until the singing and dancing ended and the People went to their beds.

�֎

Sometime near dawn, Peyewik dreamed. When he woke, his face was wet with tears and there was a deep sense of peace in his heart.

✖

Early the next morning, Peyewik watched as every man, woman, and child of the Away People and the Original People came together in a great circle, many rings deep, around the ashes of the dancing fire. Traditionally, Prayer Ceremonies were held in the Ceremony House, but the combined villages were too many to fit inside. The chiefs of both villages, Okahoki and Mikwin, sat at the center of the circle, looking out at their people, solemn-faced in their ceremonial best. The elders of both villages sat in the first ring of the circle, closest to the chiefs.

Peyewik also sat in the first ring, with Kwineechka on one side, and Muhkrentharne on the other.

"The singing and dancing did the People some good," Muhkrentharne observed.

Peyewik turned to watch the arriving People and saw that they moved and smiled a little more easily than they had a day earlier. Nonetheless, even the small children knew something important was happening. They set aside their games and sat quietly, looking around wide-eyed.

When all of the People were settled, Mikwin, the chief of the Away People, stood to speak first. Peyewik had met Mikwin the day before and liked him. He was a friendly, generous man who had welcomed the displaced Original People into his village with open arms. He wore his hair in the same hunter's crest as Okahoki, but it was clear from the size of his belly that it had been a long time since he chased game in the forest.

"Hear us, Manito, Spirit in All Things," Mikwin sang the opening prayer, *"as we come together for the first time in many years to pray for guidance in this time of trouble..."*

When the prayer was over, Mikwin signaled for Kwineechka to stand and tell his story.

But the storyteller did not rise. Peyewik turned to him and saw that he was pale and shaking.

"What is wrong?" he asked.

"I cannot do this," Kwineechka replied. "Not after what Crow Woman did."

"You are the Storyteller of the People," Peyewik tried to reassure him. "No one can take that from you."

The People were silent, waiting for the story to begin. Kwineechka looked at Peyewik, his golden eyes full of fear.

"I cannot feel them," he said in a low voice. "The ancestors are no longer with me. I cannot tell a story without them."

Peyewik tried to help him by reaching out once more to the storyteller's spirit, but this time Carp did not come, and Peyewik could not sense him beyond the growing shadow on Kwineechka's spirit.

Peyewik turned to Mikwin. "His wounds have tired him. He cannot tell a story right now."

The chief nodded and gestured for Chief Okahoki of the Original People to continue with the ceremony. The People were disappointed, but no one could complain for Okahoki had already begun speaking.

"Brothers and sisters," he said, "the Original People have suffered great losses recently. Our village was burned to the ground by the Pure Men. Some of the Original People were killed."

Peyewik looked closely and saw scars on the chief's body and streaks of white in his hair that hadn't been there before. As Okahoki spoke, Peyewik realized that Kwineechka wasn't the only one who carried a new shadow on his spirit. A darkness now clung to the chief of the Original People as well, and the sight of it made Peyewik sad.

"We sang to their spirits, but the Pure Men would not let us bury them properly," Okahoki continued. "Our hearts are full of grief, and I fear that this grief will come to the Away People as well. Jongren, friend of the People, will tell us more of the danger we face."

Jongren stood. "I thank you for letting my daughter and me share in the sacred Prayer Ceremony. We were not born of the People, but you have saved both our lives at different times. We are indebted to you and have vowed to do all that we can to help you in this time of trouble."

"You will tell us what you know of the intentions of the Pale Ones?" Okahoki asked.

"The Fighting Women and the Pure Men fight each other for power. The People are caught between them. The Pure Men seek others to share in their beliefs," Jongren said. "They want to destroy the Fighting Women, but they do not want to hurt the People."

"They destroyed our village!" one of the Original People called out.

"They saw my daughter in your village," Jongren replied. "They thought the People were friends of the Fighting Women despite evidence to the contrary.

"What do the Fighting Women want?" Mikwin asked.

"The Fighting Women want things they can trade for profit. Land, timber, pelts...They want to be rich. Then they will have power over the Pure Men."

"They want power over the People?"

"They are not concerned with the People," Jongren said. "I believe they can still be convinced to leave the People in peace."

Peyewik didn't think this was true. He glanced at Kwineechka, who sat hunched in on himself, still shaking slightly. Crow Woman had demonstrated an insatiable appetite for power over all things, not just the Pure Men, and the storyteller was proof.

Jongren continued speaking. "My daughter and I ask that you allow us to go to the Fighting Women and the Pure Men in your name," he said. "We will tell them the People have no place in their conflict."

"They will listen to you?" Okahoki asked. Peyewik heard the doubt in his voice. "We already tried to ask the Fighting Women for help once."

"We must try," Jongren said. "I pray to Manito for success in this. No matter what you decide today, there are difficult choices and times ahead. This is all I have to say."

The outcry began before Jongren was off his feet. It went against all tradition and manners, but suddenly everyone had something to say and was saying it at once. Voices grew louder, arguments started, people jumped to their feet.

Peyewik looked at his grandfather anxiously, but Muhkrentharne returned his gaze with absolute trust and confidence.

"Tell them what you dreamed last night," his grandfather said, barely audible above the din.

Peyewik stood. No one noticed until Okahoki stepped to his side and lifted his arms.

"Silence!" the chief thundered. "Do you hear what I hear? I hear the People fighting amongst themselves. I hear whispering and hissing. I hear Snakebrother's belly scraping the ground as he crawls among us. Now we will listen to this boy instead of Snakebrother. That is all I have to say."

He gave Peyewik a nod and sat down.

The People gazed up at Peyewik, contrite and anxious.

Peyewik looked back at them and knew he belonged there, and it was his time to speak.

"I dreamed last night," he said. "Chingwe, who was like a brother to me, was one of those killed by the Pale Men and I grieved deeply for his loss. His spirit has returned to me many times and shown me many things. Last night he came to me in a dream and told me that these bodies of ours are merely clothing for our spirits. When we remove the clothing we see the truth, which is a light brighter than the sun. It is a truth that is always with us, but it is harder to see when we wear our bodies, for we fear the pain they can feel. Chingwe told me that though these bodies can be injured, spirits remain whole. A great injury has been done to the body of the People, and there is more injury to come. Our form has been altered and we will never again appear as we once appeared. This is very sad, but our spirit will remain whole as long as we do not allow fear to poison it. Chingwe spoke these things, and many spirits spoke with him until their voices became one and I knew I heard the voice of Manito. I hear it now in my heart, as we all do. I ask you to listen to this voice, and not be too afraid of the change to come. Approach it with as much love and faith in Manito's beauty as you can. That is all I have to say."

He sat down and waited.

"It is just as in the story," one of the elders said. "Manito has spoken to us through this boy's dream."

"What does it mean?" Kwineechka's father, Nitis, asked.

"The meaning of this boy's dream is clear," the elder replied. "If we keep our faith in Manito, all will be well in the end."

There were murmurs of agreement from the People.

"Do we ask Jongren and his daughter to speak to the Pale Ones on our behalf?" someone asked, raising his voice to be heard from the back of the great circle. "The dream tells us nothing of that."

"In the stories, fighting and violence divide the People and make us weak," another elder replied. "Manito does not want us to shed blood. He is offering us a peaceful solution to the situation with the Fighting Women and the Pure Men by bringing Jongren and his daughter to us..."

Peyewik saw Mikwin nodding in wholehearted agreement, but Okahoki gave no sign as to what he thought of Jongren's plan for peace.

Afraid of being reprimanded by Okahoki again, the People entered into a discussion that moved around the circle in an orderly and polite manner, the chiefs seeing to it that everyone who wished to speak was heard. Peyewik took the opportunity to turn his attention back to the storyteller. Kwineechka was no longer shaking, but he looked pale and drawn.

Just then, Mikwin addressed the circle.

"Because the story tells us that our strength is in our brothers, the elders and chiefs will not make this decision on their own. Each of you will have a say in it. Take time to pray and call upon Manito for your own guidance. Then we will vote."

After a period of silent prayer, the vote was passed around the concentric rings of the great circle. Mikwin kept track of each person's reply. It took a long time, and it was nearly nightfall by the time the final person had spoken. Mikwin took a moment to tally and then stood up.

"The People have decided, and the elders and the chiefs stand by their decision. Jongren and his daughter will go to the Pale Ones to ask for peace on behalf of the People."

CHAPTER THIRTY-FOUR

Trib

Trib crouched behind a large rock and watched ten Puritanics sneak up on a group of Native women. The round-faced girl, whose name Trib had learned was Kinteka, was among the women. They were pulling a fishing net out of the river, seemingly unaware of the approaching threat.

The Puritanics stopped a few paces from Trib's hiding place, and her muscles twitched with the urge to attack. They were the same monsters that had killed Cuss and destroyed Peyewik's village. But she forced herself to stillness, remembering Jongren's careful plan for securing peace.

"Approach these primitives with caution," said the man who appeared to be the leader of the Puritanics. Trib thought he looked older than Jongren, with a scraggly beard and hair that had turned from black to mostly gray. He was of middle height, and his build was solid, despite the effects of long-term hunger.

"There are no New Murians here to protect them," replied one of the Puritanics, a short, younger man with dark curly hair. "We should just kill them and be done with it."

Trib's lip curled into a silent snarl as flickers of red appeared at the corners of her vision. She was ready to forget Jongren's plan and launch herself at the Puritanics.

Their leader held up a hand and said, "You forget yourself, Josiah. Not all women are like the New Murians. Most are weak and vulnerable. It would be a sin to use our strength against them without provocation."

"But they are allied with the New Murians!" the man called Josiah argued. "They deserve to die for such an unholy allegiance."

"Who are you to condemn them with no proof?" the Reverend replied in a warning tone, surprising Trib with his lack of bloodthirst. "No Natives have attacked us yet. We will approach these women for the sole purpose of gaining information."

"If they resist?" Josiah asked, sulking.

"Do what you must," the leader said. Trib saw that he had a pistol shoved into his belt, but he was the only one. The others carried blades imported from the Old World, lighter and more refined looking than the Scath-made sword strapped to Trib's back.

"But only what you must," the Puritanic leader added. "Kindness to lesser beings is a virtue, and the Lord sees all."

He gave a signal, and the Puritanics left the shelter of the rocks and moved to surround the Native women. Kinteka and the others looked frightened, dropping the net and huddling together as the Puritanics backed them up to the river's edge.

Trib recognized her cue. She pulled her sword from behind her back and stepped out of her hiding place.

"Stop where you are!"

The Puritanics whirled around, weapons raised.

"A New Murian!" Josiah exclaimed. "I knew they were in league with the witches. Shoot her before she summons her Rage!"

The Puritanic leader pulled his pistol from his belt and pointed it at Trib.

"Coward," Trib said.

The Puritanic cocked the gun and took careful aim.

"I advise you against that course of action, Reverend," Jongren said, stepping out from behind a nearby tree. "Tribulation is not alone."

"Jonathan Green, the traitor." The Puritanic turned the gun on Jongren. "You escaped us recently, but I swear to God, you shall hang yet."

"Perhaps, but not immediately," Jongren replied.

There was the faintest sound of rustling, and Trib watched the Puritanics' faces as they realized they were surrounded.

"Now who's weak and vulnerable?" she sneered.

"Tribulation," Jongren said quietly. "Put your sword away."

She started to refuse but then caught sight of Okahoki, standing with the other hunters who had just made their presence known. He held his knife loosely at his side and watched the Puritanics impassively. If anyone had reason to hate the Puritanics, it was the chief of the Original People. Trib decided that if he could restrain himself, so could she. She replaced her sword on her back as Kinteka and the other women sidled past the Puritanics.

At Okahoki's signal, the hunters formed a semi-circle around the Puritanics, who now took a turn being herded back towards the water's edge.

Trib watched them with a mixture of curiosity and disgust. She had never been this close to Puritanics who weren't prisoners, servants, or opponents in battle. The first thing she noticed about them was that they didn't look well. They were thin and tired and dressed in rags with dirty beards and matted hair. The recent battles with the New Murians had left them even worse for wear, none free of ugly bruises or bloody bandages. She couldn't believe she had thought Jongren was one of them the first time she saw him. He was clean, strong, and healthy-looking, with more in common with the Natives than the Puritanics.

"Reverend Edward Wilson," Jongren addressed the Puritanic leader. "May I introduce you to Chief Okahoki of the Original People and a number of his hunters. You will be acquainted with them as the people whose village you attacked and destroyed three nights past."

The Reverend and his men eyed the Natives warily.

"Your souls shall be eternally damned for allying with the New Murian witches," the Reverend said.

Jongren smiled. "According to your laws my soul was damned long ago. This particular transgression won't make much of a difference, except perhaps to make the flames burn hotter. Nonetheless, you must hear our request. The Natives have no place in our quarrels. It is your duty as a man of God to repent of the damage you have done them already and leave them in peace."

The Reverend grew red in the face.

"How dare you tell me my duty to the Lord!" he cried, spittle flying out of his mouth. "It is my duty as a man of God to bring His Truth to all souls so that they may be saved. If you are allied with the witches then you are too far gone to be saved, and it is my duty to rid the earth of such irredeemable sinners."

"The Natives are not in league with the New Murians."

"How can you lie to me when one of the witches stands before me?" the Reverend spat.

"Tribulation is *formerly* of New Murias," Jongren replied. "My daughter is no longer in league with Aoifa either."

"Your daughter?" the Reverend said.

Expecting further condemnation and abuse, Trib was caught off guard as the Reverend stared at her with sudden curiosity.

"Daughter or not, she attacked us in the Native village," Josiah said impatiently.

"And you ambushed and murdered my friends in the marsh," Trib countered, itching to reach for her sword.

The Reverend's anger and contempt returned as quickly as it had gone.

"You murdered a boy," he accused Trib. "The son of a friend. His name was..."

"Stop!" Trib said, not wanting to hear it.

"Could it be your conscience trouble you?" the Reverend sneered. "I thought the witches were not bothered by such a thing."

He turned to Jongren. "How can you ask me to leave the Natives in peace with this murdering fiend in their midst?"

"Edward," Jongren said calmly. "New Murians and Puritanics alike have committed atrocities in this small war of ours. But the People are innocent. I have known you for a long time, Edward. We came to the New World together, and I know you to be a man of good conscience, as your God requires. These are peaceful people. They do not deserve your abuse."

The Reverend said nothing but crossed his arms and studied the Natives as if looking for proof of Jongren's words. Trib followed his gaze, her heart sinking at what she saw.

Far from looking innocent and wronged, two of the hunters, whose names Trib couldn't remember, were shaking with the effort of not laughing.

The brothers were both tall and muscular, intimidating-looking men, but Trib had learned the truth about them. They were pranksters who refused to acknowledge the seriousness of the situation, instead thinking of the whole thing as one big joke they were playing on the Puritanics. They had laughed the whole time Jongren tried to prepare them for this encounter.

Fortunately, the Reverend didn't notice the brothers' struggle. He stuck his pistol back in his belt and said, "Allow me a moment to consult with my brethren."

As the Puritanics huddled together, Jongren caught Trib's eye and nodded reassuringly. Trib frowned in reply, still doubting his claim that the Puritanics could be reasoned with. The idea went against all her training, and she stayed on her guard, expecting the Puritanics to attack at any moment, like the bloodthirsty savages she knew them to be.

Finally the Reverend turned back to Jongren.

"We will leave the primitives in peace," he said.

"Even though you consider them condemned souls?" Jongren asked. "Perhaps you are looking to convert them?"

"I would show them the light of God's Truth if I may," the Reverend said. "However, that is not my sole intent. We had thought them in league with the New Murians. This is the only reason we attacked them before. As you know, Aoifa harries us from dusk until dawn, both here and in the north. Over the past few days alone she has caught and killed or enslaved with her devil magic fifteen of my men, diminishing our numbers by half. It is all we can do to keep one step ahead of her and stay alive."

Trib heard the desperation in his voice and for the first time it occurred to her that he might regret the loss of his companions as much as she regretted the deaths of hers.

"Aoifa, ungodly harpy that she is, will not rest until we are exterminated," the Reverend continued. "We do not wish to inflict this same trouble on anyone who is still open to God's truth. It would be wrong to do so."

Trib remained suspicious, but the Reverend turned to Okahoki and addressed him directly.

"I deeply regret what we did to your village. We will leave you in peace if you can forgo the need for revenge and pledge to remain unallied with Aoifa."

Okahoki was silent for a time after Jongren translated. Trib was sure he would at last show some of his anger towards the Puritanics. Instead, when he spoke, his voice was clear and steady. Jongren listened intently and Trib noticed that the prankster brothers weren't laughing anymore.

"You are the men who destroyed Okahoki's home and killed his people," Jongren translated. "His grief is a pain so constant and terrible that he has wished he could die to escape it. He hears Snakebrother hissing in his ear all the time, tempting him with visions of vengeance that will ease his suffering. But he is stronger than the Pale Ones who have given in to Snakebrother and spend their lives trying to kill each other. He agrees to your terms of peace."

"We ask for no more," the Reverend said, surprising Trib. She had expected him to at least try to attach more terms.

He extended his hand and Okahoki took it, grasping his arm at the elbow.

"God be with you," the Reverend said.

He and the chief released each other, and Okahoki signaled for his hunters to allow the Reverend's men to pass.

The Reverend gave Jongren a curt nod and said, "We will meet again. This agreement was with the primitives, not you."

"You trust them?" Trib asked when the Puritanics were gone.

"Despite what you have been led to believe, my former brethren tend to keep their word. I pray to Manito that your meeting with Scathach goes half as well. When will you leave for the fort?"

Trib's stomach lurched at the thought of what she had to do next.

"I can go with you," Jongren offered. "You shouldn't have to face Scathach alone."

For a moment Trib was tempted. Even though Jongren was a near stranger and a former enemy, it would be easier to face the Scath if she wasn't alone.

She shook her head. "No point in both of us getting killed if I'm caught," she said, trying to sound casual.

Jongren looked stricken. "You must return safely!" he said.

He lifted a hand towards her but then dropped it and took a step back. "I...I have not had the chance to tell you more of your mother and sisters."

After an awkward silence Trib said, "I'll do my best," and then turned quickly away so that he wouldn't see her face.

Hours later Trib stood at the ferry landing across the river from the New Murian fort. It was almost midnight, and the first guard was about to change. After days and nights of keeping watch on the patterns and movements of the fort, Jongren had identified this as the best time to get in and out undetected. Trib had only moments to act, but she could not move. Fear was overwhelming her, rooting her to the spot.

She heard something in the darkness behind her and yanked her sword from her back, afraid she had been discovered. She gasped when, by the light of the half moon, she recognized Kwineechka coming towards her. He stopped a few paces away, leaning on a walking stick. His side was still bandaged where he'd been wounded trying to protect her.

"What are you doing here?" she hissed, lowering her sword. "You shouldn't have come all this way with your injury."

"Jongren told me you were coming here to speak to Bear Woman. I know what happened last time you saw her. You should not be alone when you do this," he replied. "So I am here."

"Why should you care what happens to me?" she said, taken aback.

"I care what happens to the People," he replied.

Trib started to turn away, to head for the ferry, but stopped. Heart pounding, she said, "Why did you save me before? When the Puritanic came after me. You should have let me die, after what I let Aoifa do to you."

Kwineechka was silent for a moment.

"I know how Bear Woman made you feel," he said, speaking haltingly, as if he was unsure of his own answer.

"She took away all the stories you knew," he said. "She made the world strange."

It was an odd way of saying things, but it was true. That was how Trib had felt when she learned that the Scath had killed her family and lied to her for as long as she could remember.

"How do you know that?" Trib asked.

"Crow Woman made me feel that way. She made me a stranger to my people, my world, and to myself."

Trib cringed, hating to hear how Aoifa had hurt him.

"Please don't let Bear Woman and Crow Woman do this to the People," Kwineechka continued. "I am here so you will not feel like a stranger, so you will not feel alone. So you will feel strong enough to make peace with Bear Woman and help the People."

Trib had thought she would never belong anywhere again, but as she looked at Kwineechka and took in his words, she suddenly felt as though it didn't matter. He was here now and if he needed her to help the People, that was what she would do. Or die trying.

She nodded once, then said, "Stay here. Aoifa can't be allowed to find you again."

"I will wait for you," he said.

"Hide if anyone comes. If I'm not back in an hour, I'm not coming back."

Then she turned and without hesitation strode towards the ferry and her confrontation with the Scath.

⌗

A short while later, Trib stood in the shadowed corner of a stuffy cabin, waiting for the Scath. The old warrior entered the cabin, went to the fireplace, and put a kettle on to boil. Then she sat down, pulled off her boots, and said, "Well? Ye gonna kill me or is there something else ye want?"

Trib chided herself for thinking she could sneak up on the Scath. She came out of the corner with her sword pointed at the Scath's neck.

"You said you were going to kill me after I helped the Natives escape," she said, relieved that her voice held steady. "Why didn't you?"

"Couldn't do it," the Scath replied matter-of-factly. "But I am willing to call for a guard and turn ye over to my sister."

"I'll cut your throat before you can make a sound."

"With one of my own blades? Ye wouldn't."

Trib pressed the tip of her sword into the Scath's neck and closed her eyes briefly as the image of the Puritanic boy's face flashed through her mind. Her eyes flicked open and she pressed the blade harder, drawing a thin red line of blood.

"Care to wager on that?" she said, thinking of her family and knowing she could kill the Scath if she had to, whatever it may cost her later.

"Besides," she continued, "turning me over to Aoifa is the same as killing me, ain't it? Or would you feel less guilty having her do the dirty work for you? Give her back some of the guilt she gave you when she had you kill my ma and sisters."

The Scath's eyes flashed with anger, but her body remained perfectly still, reminding Trib for an instant of Chief Okahoki and his hunter's stillness.

"Don't insult me, girl," the Scath said. "Ye know I take care of my own business. I'd turn ye over to her because I'm loyal to her above all else. She's my flesh and blood. We've been through too much together."

"Then the blade stays where it is. Inhale to shout, and I swear to Dess you're dead."

The Scath grinned. "That's the master-warrior I raised."

"I ain't a master-warrior," Trib said. "Never will be."

"No, I reckon ye won't," the Scath agreed. "Since I'm still breathing, I reckon there's something else ye want from me."

"Tell Aoifa to leave the Natives alone," Trib said.

"Ye like that pretty-eyed primitive of yers so much?" the Scath asked.

Trib thought of Kwineechka waiting for her out in the night. "I do," she replied. "I owe it to his people. And you owe it to me."

The Scath eyed her for a moment. "How do ye figure that?"

"You killed my family and you lied to me," Trib said flatly. "You took everything from me."

"Aye," the Scath said softly, with a hint of regret. "I did."

"Despite it all," Trib forced herself to continue, "I believe you're still a woman of honor. I've done things I ain't proud of, things that will haunt me for the rest of my life. I did these things because I didn't know better. I didn't know I had a choice because you never gave me one. Right now, I'm giving you a choice. You told me you knew you'd done wrong when you killed my family. Do the right thing this time, Master Scath."

"Aoifa won't listen to me," the Scath said, her eyes on the floor. "Especially since ye took off with those boys. Before that, she wanted at least the show of an alliance, but now I reckon she'd just as soon wipe 'em all out."

"You're the only person she'll listen to," Trib insisted. "Make her leave the People alone. They're good, peaceful people. You know what Aoifa will do to them if you don't stop her."

The Scath finally looked up and met Trib's eyes. "I'll do what ye ask," she said.

"Your word of honor as a warrior?"

"Ye have it. My word of honor as a warrior, my sister'll do no harm to the Natives."

"Thank you." Trib exhaled, relief racing through her body. "I'll go now. Since I can't have you raising the alarm..." She held up a gag and rope, but the Scath shook her head.

"I won't call out," she said. "Ye came to parley, and it's the honorable thing to let ye go in peace."

"Thank you," Trib said again, stowing her sword on her back and moving towards the door.

"Tribulation," the old warrior called quietly, "it don't mean much coming from one who's done what I've done, but ye would've made a fine master-warrior."

Trib slipped out the door without answering.

CHAPTER THIRTY-FIVE

Peyewik

*D*eer *tried to run from the attack, but Crow followed, swoop-*
ing and diving to peck cruelly at her eyes, beating her around
the head and body with her large wings. Blinded by blood
and feathers, Deer stumbled, and Crow attacked mercilessly...

Peyewik awoke full of dread.

The deer skin tent he shared with his grandfather was dark and stuffy. He could tell from the silence that Muhkrentharne was not there. He pushed away his sleeping skin and crawled outside. He didn't know exactly what the dream meant, but the possibilities terrified him. It was an ill omen and he needed to warn someone immediately.

It was as dark outside as it had been in the tent. The moon had already set and dawn was only a few hours away. Peyewik saw a dull glow in the center of the village and heard the murmur of low-pitched voices. One of the cooking fires still burned and around it sat his grandfather, Okahoki, Jongren, and a few of the elders, all smoking pipes. Kwineechka's friends, the hunters named Nishingi and Nikismus, were there as well. It was their voices he had heard.

"The Pure Men smelled like the village waste heap on a hot day," Nishingi was saying.

"One sniff could knock a man senseless," Nikismus chimed in. "And their faces were white as the underbelly of a fish. They looked like demons..."

"Smelled like them too," Nishingi added, causing his brother to giggle.

Peyewik saw Chief Okahoki smile around the pipe in his teeth, his eyes crinkling with a sense of humor that hadn't been seen since the attack on the village of the Original People. It made Peyewik want to turn around and go back to bed without telling anyone of his dream. He told himself that maybe this once it was just a dream like everyone else's dreams.

Just then Muhkrentharne caught sight of him standing at the edge of the firelight and greeted him through a puff of smoke.

"These young men could not sleep because they are still excited from their encounter with the Pure Men," he explained.

"And these old men could not sleep because they are old," said Okahoki, causing some of the elders to chuckle. "So they are letting the young men entertain them with their tales."

"They are not tales!" Nishinigi said. "The rest of the People sleep soundly because of the peace I secured from the Pale Ones!"

"You forget I was there," Okahoki pointed out.

Peyewik could still see the shadow on the chief's spirit, but it seemed lighter, which made him feel even worse about his dream.

"Yes, so you know it was mostly me, not my brother," Nikismus jumped in. "I intimidated them with my hunter's prowess, and they had no choice but to agree to peace..."

"Kinteka and the women were more intimidating than you," Nishingi interrupted, punching his brother in the arm. "*I* was the one who scared the Pure Men away..."

Peyewik hated to interfere with their feeling of victory and security, but he could not forget his dream.

"Has Trib returned from speaking to Bear Woman yet?" he asked.

"She has not," Jongren said, looking up from the fire. Peyewik could see the worry in his face.

"What is wrong?" Muhkrentharne said then, peering closely at Peyewik. A look of recognition crossed his face. "You have dreamed, haven't you?"

Peyewik nodded as all eyes turned towards him. He opened his mouth to describe the dream but stopped, drawn up short by the sight of something moving in the darkness on the far side of the fire. At first he thought it might be Trib returning, but the figure that stumbled forward into the light was not human.

It was a young doe. Peyewik gasped at the sight of her, but not because it was strange that she should venture so close to human. Her delicately pointed face was covered in blood and one of her back legs dragged sickeningly as she limped forward.

Peyewik heard the men around him reacting in alarm, but they already sounded far away. He felt the deer's spirit reaching out to him and knew she had not come by chance.

What has happened to you? he asked.

There is no time, she said. *You must come with me to the spirit world.*

CHAPTER THIRTY-SIX

Trib

I t was a long walk from the fortress back to the village, but the time went quickly for Trib as she walked along beside the storyteller. They hadn't spoken since she stepped off the ferry and said, "It's done. The Scath promised to make Aoifa leave the People alone."

His only reply had been, "Thank you," but she had heard the relief in his voice.

He was silent after that, but she had been intensely aware of the nearness of him as they walked together. He stayed close to her and she heard every twig he stepped on, every leaf that rustled under his feet. She was quick to notice when he started slowing down and for a brief moment hoped that he was trying to prolong their journey together. Then she realized that he was holding his side.

"It was stupid of you to come all this way with that injury," she said gruffly.

To her surprise the storyteller laughed. "Such stupidity never stops you, why should it stop me?"

His tone was lighter than she had heard it in days, and the sound of it warmed her insides.

"Well, I ain't carrying you back if you collapse," she blustered, though the sudden idea of touching him gave her goose bumps.

"This injury isn't so bad," he continued. "There are things that hurt more than wounds of the flesh."

His tone was still light, but Trib knew he was talking about Aoifa and the warmth she had been feeling disappeared instantly. In its place rose a sickly feeling of guilt and wrongness. She stopped walking.

"I...I'm sorry," she said, her voice catching, "for letting Aoifa...do what she did to you. I'm sorrier for that more than anything I've ever done before."

The storyteller didn't say anything. He kept walking without even looking at her.

Suddenly Trib wanted him to get angry at her, to yell at her or hit her, to make her pay for her wrongs. But he did nothing, leaving her to punish herself.

"I told Jongren I'd stay and help him secure peace," she said, hurrying to catch up with him. "I've done that, so I'll go away as soon as I can. Tomorrow maybe."

Kwineechka still didn't respond, and she let herself fall behind again, berating herself for all the foolish things she had been feeling about him. He could never care for her, just as Aoifa had said. He had found her strange and repugnant from the beginning, and after she had stood by and allowed Aoifa to do what she did, he had every right to hate her forever.

Then she tripped over a tree root. A stream of annoyed curses came out of her mouth as she hit the ground. Before she could pick herself up again Kwineechka was standing over her, holding out a hand. She grabbed it reluctantly and tried to let go as soon as she was on her feet. But he held on. Her heart gave an involuntary flutter that annoyed her even further.

"You do not need to leave," he said. "Not soon."

"Why should I stay?" she whispered, wishing she could see his face more clearly.

After a slight pause he said, "Your father will be sorry."

Trib pulled her hand out of his grasp. "Never had use for a father before," she said shortly. "Why should I start now?"

"So you will have a place," Kwineechka said quietly. "With him."

It was what Jongren had offered her the night before the Prayer Ceremony, a new place in the world despite everything she had lost.

"What about you? Where is your place now?"

"I do not know," he said.

"If I can find a new place, maybe you can too. With someone..."

He didn't say anything, but Trib realized with a thrill that he was staring at her through the darkness. She stared back at him, wondering desperately what he was thinking.

"I know you don't want it," she muttered, "but you'll always have a place with me."

"Trib," he started to say, reaching out to touch her shoulder and sending an electric shock through her entire body.

"Behind you!" he warned.

Trib turned and saw a dark shape looming towards them.

"Stay behind me!" she cried, pulling her sword off her back as the shape resolved into human form and staggered forward.

"Tribulation."

The figure spoke her name in a cracked, exhausted voice, and then collapsed at her feet.

"What in Dess's name?"

Trib crouched down and pulled away the folds of a cloak. The face beneath was barely recognizable as human. Kwineechka made a sound of distress behind her and moved away.

"I know her," he said.

Horror gripped Trib as she realized she knew the beaten, bloodied face as well.

"No..." she whispered.

The figure groaned and turned its head, revealing the scar, dark and ugly against the white flesh of its throat.

"Morrigan," Trib said. "What happened? Did Puritanics do this to you? Those murdering bastards..."

She looked over her shoulder at Kwineechka, who had his hands on knees and his head down as though he might be sick.

"I don't know if she can make it," she said, "but we have to try to get her back to the village."

The storyteller didn't move.

"She freed you from Aoifa's prison. We have to help her!"

Kwineechka straightened up, as if throwing off a bad dream, and came to help Trib lift Morrigan to her feet.

"I'm going to kill the men who did this..." Trib swore.

They had to stop many times to rest. Trib began to fear that the storyteller might collapse as well. Sometime around dawn, however, he said, "We are nearly home," and soon Trib could smell the smoke from the fires of the village.

"Thank Dess," she said, grateful that Morrigan was still alive. "We'll need Peyewik's grandfather."

"Muhkrentharne is there," Kwineechka said as they entered the village, nodding towards a group of people standing around one of the cooking fires. Trib saw Okahoki and Jongren as well.

"They must've been waiting for us all night," she said.

Morrigan groaned in pain.

"Don't worry," Trib tried to reassure her. "The old man is a great healer. He patched me back together..."

"Trib!" Jongren cried.

She could see the relief in his face as he hurried to meet her.

"What has happened?" he asked. "Who is with you?"

"Lay her down," Trib said to Kwineechka. As soon as she was safely on the ground, Kwineechka dropped beside her, exhausted and holding his side. Trib was worried about him, but Morrigan was in more danger.

"The priestess who helped us escape from the fort," she told Jongren quickly. "Puritanics beat her and left her to die in the forest. She needs the old man..." she said, looking around for the healer.

"What in hell is going on?" she hissed suddenly, seeing Peyewik's body for the first time. The old man crouched beside him and a few paces away lay the bloody body of a deer.

"Peyewik has fallen into a trance," Jongren explained. "The spirits are speaking to him."

CHAPTER THIRTY-SEVEN

Peyewik

Peyewik knew better than to question such a summons. He closed his eyes and felt his body falling. Before it hit the ground, he found himself travelling the long, dark tunnel downwards. The deer spirit did not offer comfort and reassurance as Panther had done last time he made this journey, but Peyewik no longer needed such things. He knew where he was going. He could hear the deer moving before him, its breath labored and painful until it no longer needed to breathe. The journey went much faster this time, and soon Peyewik found himself standing beside the River of Death. There he saw why it had been a deer spirit sent to summon him.

"Deer Girl!" he exclaimed. Before him stood a pale, yellow-haired figure dressed in black robes. It was the young woman who had helped him and Kwineechka escape from Crow Woman's prison.

She smiled. "Hello Peyewik. My name is Morrigan."

"Mor-gun," Peyewik tried the name, awkward at first. "Morr-i-gan, why are you here?" he asked, alarmed as the meaning of his dream about the crow and the deer began to come clear.

"I need to warn you," she replied.

"You sent a deer spirit to summon me," Peyewik said. "You speak to the spirits, as I do?" he asked.

Morrigan frowned slightly. "I don't know. All I know is that my body is close to death. I prayed to the Goddess for a way to speak to

203

you before I died. And here you are. The Goddess has even made it so that we can understand each other when we speak."

She smiled again with a warmth that felt like the sun on Peyewik's face, but his heart felt heavy. He hardly knew Morrigan Deer Girl, and yet from the first moment he had seen her in the fortress of the Fighting Women she had felt like an old friend, someone with whom he had much to talk about.

"What happened to you?" Peyewik asked, afraid to hear the answer.

"Aoifa found out that I helped you escape," she said. "I was beaten and left to die in the forest…"

Her voice faltered. She drew herself up and continued. "But there is no time to dwell on that. Aoifa told me of her intentions towards you and your friend, the storyteller. You are both in danger."

"Tribulation has gone to ask the Bear Woman for peace," Peyewik said. "If she agrees, surely Kwineechka will be safe."

Morrigan shook her head sadly. "The Scath may agree to peace, but Aoifa never will."

"Why?" Peyewik said. "What is wrong with her? What does she want?"

"Aoifa has not always been like this. At one time the Goddess was her source of strength, as she is mine. But Aoifa has forgotten the Goddess. She found a new source of power, and it is making her greedy. She can never get enough of it."

"What is the new source of power?" Peyewik asked.

"Using her siren song to drain people of their wills and make them do as she wishes," Morrigan said. "You've experienced it yourself."

Peyewik remembered how the song lulled him into wanting to give everything he had to Crow Woman. He would have given up his spirit if she asked for it, before he figured out how to break her spell, and understood how this gave her strength.

"Kwineechka escaped from her," Peyewik said. "She can't hurt him now."

"Aoifa experienced great power when she took your friend's will, unlike anything she has felt before. She is hungry for it now and won't stop until she has it."

Suddenly Peyewik understood.

"But that power wasn't Kwineechka's," he said. "She took the thing that was most precious to him. It was the Story of the People. Our story is our power. Is it our connection to our ancestors and everything that has happened to us. It's about our connection to Manito and the spirits. It's how we know who we are and where we belong. It is the source of our strength."

"Then it's worse than I thought," Morrigan said. "Aoifa doesn't understand this yet, but once she does, not only you and your friend will be in danger, but all of your people. She will do them great harm."

Peyewik thought back to the Prayer Ceremony and Kwineechka's inability to tell a story.

"She is already doing us harm. Our storyteller believes he can no longer tell stories. He is the People's connection to their power. Without him, the People will be lost before Crow Woman ever comes near them."

"You must warn them," Morrigan said.

"But what can we do?"

"Run," Morrigan replied.

"We cannot leave the land of our fathers," Peyewik said.

"If your people wish to survive without becoming her slaves, then you must go."

Peyewik could see that Morrigan's form was beginning to fade from sight.

"There's another thing," she said. "Aoifa is afraid of you. You were able to stop her siren. No one has been able to do that before. She sees you as a threat and will try to kill you."

Her voice was growing faint.

"By the Goddess, I wish I could have done more to help you..."

"And I wish you did not have to die for helping me," Peyewik replied.

"I hoped we would meet again and that we would be friends..."

"I hoped so too," Morrigan said, her voice no more than a whisper. "Good bye, Peyewik."

"Morrigan, do not go!" Peyewik called out suddenly.

But Morrigan Deer Girl was gone.

And Crow Woman was coming after the People.

Peyewik dropped to his knees on the silvery sand and wept in sadness and fear.

CHAPTER THIRTY-EIGHT

Trib

The old man made no move to help Morrigan, but stayed beside Peyewik.

"By Dess, she needs help now!" Trib said, starting towards him.

"Trib!" Jongren grabbed her arm.

She shook him off. "He best come now or I'll make him..."

"Tribulation, the priestess is dead."

Trib stopped. "No. She can't be. Peyewik's grandfather can help her, like he helped me..."

"I'm sorry," Jongren said. "Consider it a blessing that she is no longer suffering."

"It ain't a blessing! It's wrong, and everyone here is to blame for not helping her," Trib cried, glaring around at the Natives who were keeping their distance.

"They have never seen one of the crow women before," Kwineechka said. "They are frightened."

Trib noticed that even he had moved away from Morrigan's body.

"Dess damn their fear. And yours. Dess damn all of you!" The tell-tale flickers of red appeared at the corners of Trib's vision.

"Kinteka says we can bring Morrigan to her house."

Trib blinked and the red haze faded. She saw the round-faced girl kneeling beside Morrigan's body without a hint of fear or revulsion.

"She will sing for her and prepare her body for burial," Jongren continued translating.

"Thank you," Trib said hoarsely.

Jongren stooped to lift the priestess in his arms, and Kinteka started singing. Some of the Natives joined her in singing but continued to keep their distance. Trib followed Jongren to Kinteka's house, aware that Kwineechka stayed where he was.

When Kinteka began to clean the blood off Morrigan's face, Trib had to step outside. Jongren followed her. "I'm sorry about the priestess," he said. "But you haven't said yet what happened with the Scath. The People are anxious to know, and the girl's death is not a good portent."

"She promised peace. The Natives have nothing to be afraid of," she said bitterly.

"Do not blame them," Jongren said quietly.

"I don't blame them. I blame the Puritanics who beat her. They're the ones who murdered her!" Trib felt her Rage coming again.

"It wasn't the Puritanics..." Jongren started.

"Of course it was! It's what those murdering bastards do! Attack the innocent and unarmed..."

"Why was Morrigan alone in the forest?" Jongren interrupted.

"How should I know? What difference does it make?"

"You know as well as I do that no priestess would be out in the forest without an escort of warriors. And yet there was no one to take her for help. Did you see any other bodies?"

"No," Trib said, "but that doesn't mean anything."

"I know you don't want to hear this, but the Puritanics didn't attack your friend."

"You're defending them because you're still one of them!" Trib shouted.

Jongren stayed calm. "It can't be a coincidence that this is the priestess who helped you escape."

"Shut up," Trib hissed. "You're just like them. I'm ashamed that my mother took up with a liar and a coward like you." It was instantly clear from the look on Jongren's face that she had hurt him, but she couldn't stop herself.

"You're Puritanic to the core. Only a Puritanic coward could let his family die the way you did."

"Please," Jongren gasped as if she was causing him physical pain. "Don't say that..."

Trib felt a twinge of remorse, but still couldn't face the truth.

"Trib, Morrigan's death is not your fault," Jongren said. "Aoifa did this. She alone is responsible."

Trib knew he was right, but she couldn't help lashing out once more. "I ain't going to listen to you. I never needed a father before, and I ain't going to start now, especially not a coward like you. I'm ashamed we share the same blood."

Trib regretted the words before she was done speaking them, but it was too late. To make matters worse, she looked up and saw Kwineechka standing nearby, staring at her.

"Crow Woman killed the girl?" he said.

She saw the fear in his face and knew what he was thinking. If Aoifa would do this to her own apprentice for helping the Natives escape, she would never agree to the Scath's request to leave the Natives alone.

Morrigan was dead and their attempt to secure peace for the People had failed. Jongren had said it wasn't Trib's fault, but she knew better.

CHAPTER THIRTY-NINE

Peyewik

Peyewik tried to sing Morrigan's spirit across the River of Death, but he was crying so hard he could not find his voice.

As he cried, he felt rather than heard the approach of padded paws. He looked up into the yellow eyes of Panther.

"Manito," he whispered.

"Do not despair, Little One," Panther said. "It is not time for her to go. There is still much of the story to come, and she still has a part in it."

As Peyewik watched, Morrigan's form began to reappear, shadowy at first but growing more solid until he felt her take his hand.

"Thank you, Goddess," she whispered to the panther, and Peyewik wondered how Manito appeared to her.

"Manito," he said. "Crow Woman has taken the Story of the People from Kwineechka, and he is no longer connected to the ancestors. He can't tell a story without them. How can there be more of the story without a storyteller?"

"I have heard, seen, and told every story there is," Panther replied. "They do not always come from the past, and they do not require the voices of those who have come before to tell them. Anyone can tell any story at any time. This is one of the greatest gifts and powers granted to my children."

"Then we don't need the Storyteller and the ancestors?" Peyewik asked.

"You need them more than ever."

"I don't understand. Does Crow Woman have power over the People now? How do we stop her?"

"You will understand in time," Manito replied. "You too have a part in what is to come. Now you and Morrigan must return to the living."

"Will I see you again?" Peyewik asked.

"I am always with you," Manito replied.

CHAPTER FORTY

Kwineechka

Kwineechka stood outside Kinteka's house, his head echoing with the sound of Crow Woman's spell song. He thought he had escaped her spell once and for all, but it came back the moment he realized she would not leave the People in peace. He tried to fight the spell song but felt it slowly filling him, sapping his will.

"Kwineechka."

The spell-song faded, and he saw Trib standing close to him.

"Peyewik is here," she said.

Kwineechka turned and saw the boy approaching. He had returned from walking among the spirits, no doubt bearing a message or warning.

"Crow Woman is coming," Peyewik said in lieu of greeting.

As if the words were a summons, the spell song came flooding back, so loud and commanding that Kwineechka couldn't fight it. It felt as though he was in the airless room with Crow Woman, powerless against her as she ran her hands over him and made him tell the Story of the People, forced him to give her that which was most precious to him. From somewhere deep in his own mind, Kwineechka knew that all was lost, that Peyewik wasn't there to save him this time, that Crow Woman had him for good.

Then he felt a touch on his arm. It was warm and firm, not cold and caressing like Crow Woman's hands, and it acted as a beacon, drawing him back to the present moment. His eyes refocused and he found Trib watching him with a frown on her face.

"What's wrong with you?" she asked.

Her grip on his arm tightened, tethering him more firmly to the present. But before he could answer, there was a startled cry from inside the house. He pushed through the doorflap to find Kinteka staring down at the crow woman's body.

"She is breathing!"

Kwineechka stepped back in alarm when he saw the woman's chest rising and falling once more, but Peyewik swept past him with a whoop of joy and went to kneel beside her.

"My friend has returned with me from the land of the spirits," he said happily.

"You said she was dead," Trib said to her father.

"She was," Jongren said.

The woman who had been dead opened one eye. The other remained swollen shut.

"Peyewik," she said, her voice barely more than a whisper. "Have you warned them?"

Peyewik was smiling down at her, but when he looked up again his face was serious. "Crow Woman is coming," he repeated firmly. "The People must flee."

⚙

The sun had barely risen above the treeline as the People gathered once more in the center of the village. There morning air was cold, warning of the coming of winter, and everyone huddled close to the cooking fires for warmth as well as food.

Kwineechka looked around in a daze. It felt like just moments ago they had gathered for the Prayer Ceremony in exactly the same manner. He turned to Peyewik.

"You...you remember when I told you I was not afraid of what may come?" he said haltingly.

The boy nodded.

"That was before Crow Woman took the Story of the People from me. She did not want to know our story and become part of it. She only wanted power over me, so she took the thing I cared about most. I would have shared it with her in friendship, but she forced it from me. In doing this, she sent part of me into a darkness I cannot escape."

"I see the shadow that clings to your spirit," Peyewik said.

"I did not know one person could do something like that to another person," Kwineechka continued, hearing faint strains of the Crow Woman's spell-song. "None of the stories I have heard or told can explain such evil. Now I am afraid. I am afraid for the People. I am afraid of what Crow Woman can do to us."

"That is why the People must run from her," Peyewik replied.

"That is what the spirits told you?" Kwinecchka asked.

Peyewik was silent for a moment. "No. That is what Morrigan told me. The spirits did not tell me what the People should do."

Kwineechka wanted to ask him why he trusted the young crow woman so much, why he thought she was right, but just then Okahoki moved to stand before the People, and everyone fell silent, waiting for him to tell them why they had been summoned so early in the morning.

Trib appeared on Kwineechka's side, touching him on the shoulder to get his attention.

"You'll tell me what he's saying?" she asked in a low voice.

Kwineechka nodded, noticing that Crow Woman's song had faded to silence. Trib stayed close, leaning her head in towards his so he could translate quietly.

"The Seer of the People has brought a warning from the spirit world," Okahoki said. "Crow Woman is looking for the People and she will do us harm. Flame Hair's attempt to secure peace has failed, and it is said that the People must flee from Crow Woman and her Fighting Women."

The People responded with anxiety and dismay, but it was nothing compared to the distress caused by Okahoki's next announcement.

"The People must leave the land of the fathers," Okahoki said. "Mikwin will go with you and be your chief. But I will stay behind."

The People cried out in shock and denial, but Okahoki spoke over them. "There is a hole in my heart and a shadow on my spirit that no prayer can heal. This shadow makes me hungry for revenge and violence. I must stay here and fight whoever attacks my home next. But the People cannot stay with me or Snakebrother will put shadows on their spirits as well."

"He does not know how many others already carry shadows," Kwineechka heard Peyewik murmur.

"He can't fight Aoifa!" Trib said when she understood what the chief had said. "Even if he knew how to fight and had an army behind him, he wouldn't stand a chance against Aoifa, the Scath, and the Rage. I have to find Jongren, tell him to talk some sense into him."

As Trib walked away to find her father, Kwinnechka felt a sudden panic and a desire to call her back. Before he could figure out why, someone new started to speak, shocking everyone by interrupting the chief.

"I will stay with you, Chief Okahoki. I too feel Snakebrother's shadow on my spirit. If you are a danger to the People, then I am too. Violence has been in my heart for a long time now, ever since my sister was killed by the Pure Men. I will stay and fight with you."

It was Kinteka.

There was a few beats of silence and then Kwineechka heard a familiar voice say, "I will not let you stay here to die alone. I will stay with you."

Nishingi, whom Kwineechka had always known favored Kinteka but had never felt confident enough to tell her so, was now pledging to stay and fight with her. She looked at him for a moment and then nodded.

"I will stay with my brother," Nikismus spoke up, and all at once chaos broke out as the Original People rose to declare that they too would stay.

Okahoki shook his head. "I can no longer be your chief. I will give you my advice one last time. Go with the Away People to a new place where you can live and pray in peace and where the stories will make sense once more."

"You are our chief. We must go where you go," the Original People insisted.

"Stop this! Stop it now!" Kwineechka recognized his mother's voice cutting through the pandemonium.

"You cannot do this," Shikiwe said. "You are allowing Snake-brother to divide the People. The stories tell us that the People must not be divided or resort to violence."

"I do not want anyone to stay with me," Okahoki said. "But there are no stories that tell the People what to do in a situation like this. I have lived in peace with my brothers and sung my prayers to Manito every day, as the stories tell me to do. But this did not stop the Pale Men from destroying my village and killing my people. Stories and prayers can no longer help me. There is nothing left to do but follow my heart, and my heart is full of grief and anger. If others feel as I do, I cannot stop them from following their own hearts as well."

"Where is my son?" Shikiwe called. "The stories still make sense, as they always have. My son is the Storyteller of the People, and he will know what story needs to be told now. He will let the ancestors speak through him, and they will tell the People what to do."

Kwineechka felt sick as all eyes turned towards him.

"Come." Shikiwe gestured for him to stand in front of the People. "We need to hear the wisdom of the ancestors now, so that this fool-ishness will not continue."

Kwineechka stayed where he was, unable to move or speak.

"Kwineechka, what is wrong with you?" Shikiwe said. "You are the Storyteller of the People. You must do as you are asked."

"I cannot tell a story," he said, finding his voice at last. "I am no longer connected to the ancestors. I cannot hear them anymore. They no longer speak through me."

Kwineechka did not hear his mother's reply or the reaction of the People. Crow Woman's spell-song enveloped him and he heard and felt nothing else.

CHAPTER FORTY-ONE

Trib

Trib spotted Jongren through the increasingly agitated crowd of natives. He turned when she called out to him, but she could tell by his face that he was still hurt by what she had said earlier. She didn't know how to apologize so she spoke brusquely and without preamble.

"We can't let the People try to fight. Aoifa will massacre them."

"We've tried everything we can," Jongren replied. He sounded tired and wouldn't meet her gaze. "We failed. It's best if we don't interfere with what the People decide to do next."

"But they don't stand a chance!" Trib said. "And killing them isn't the worst Aoifa can do."

Jongren just shook his head.

"Are you acting like this because I was rude to you?" Trib asked.

"No. You were right about not needing a father. I have no right to interfere with your life, just as I have no right to interfere with the People's lives. Every time I meddle, someone gets hurt..."

"That ain't true," Trib said, trying to soften her voice. "You were right about Aoifa beating Morrigan almost to death. I...I'm sorry I wouldn't listen. I wanted to believe I'd stopped this from happening. I was a fool. You and I both know Aoifa can't be stopped once she's set her sights on something. Now she's set her sights on the People, and the only way they can survive is if they get away from here."

"If you wish," Jongren said, finally looking Trib in the eye, "I will speak with Okahoki, though I don't know what good it will do."

"Thank you."

"Something is wrong with Kwineechka," Jongren said, his gaze shifting over Trib's shoulder.

"What?" Trib turned and saw the storyteller on his knees, his face distorted with pain

"Dess damn it," she muttered, hurrying back to him. Her first thought was that his wound was bothering him, but as she drew close she saw him press his hands over his ears, as if the pain was in his head.

"What's wrong?" she asked, automatically reaching out to touch his shoulder. Immediately she felt his whole body relax under her hand. But just then someone grabbed her by the arm and pulled her away from him.

It was Kwineechka's mother and she was yelling at Trib.

"What in Dess's Name..?" Trib said.

Jongren, who had followed her, translated. "She is blaming you for the fact that Kwineechka can no longer tell stories."

Trib pulled away from the woman and turned back to Kwineechka, dropping to her knees in front of him. She took his face in her hands, once again feeling him relax under her touch.

"Tell me what is happening to you," she said.

He slumped forward, exhausted. "I cannot hear her when you are touching me."

"Hear who?"

"Crow Woman."

"Of course you can't hear her," Trib said, confused. "Aoifa's nowhere near here. She can't hurt you. Or speak to you."

"She is still singing to me. I can no longer hear the ancestors because of it."

"That's what your ma is blaming me for?" Trib asked.

"Please," he said, clutching at her wrists. "Do not tell anyone what Crow Woman did, that she took the Story of the People from me..." The shame in his face caused tendrils of red to appear once more in Trib's vision. The thought that Aoifa was continuing to cause the storyteller harm made her blood run hot.

A cry rang out, cutting through her Rage like a slap to the face. Kwineechka was holding his head again.

"She gets louder when your Rage comes," he said.

"This is crazy," Trib said. "What in the hell is happening?"

Kwineechka shook his head to say he didn't know.

Trib took a deep breath, clearing the Rage from her body. She was aware of Kwineechka's mother, still trying to interfere. Many of the People had begun gathering around with worried or curious looks on their faces.

"Enough," she growled. "We're getting you out of here." She put her shoulder under the storyteller's arm and pulled him to his feet.

"Out of my way," she said to his mother, and began to lead Kwineechka away from the press of people.

Peyewik appeared and gestured for her to follow him. He led them to a tent and indicated that she and the storyteller should go inside.

"He says he will bring his grandfather, and tell my mother I need to rest," Kwineechka said.

"Good. Then I reckon I best let you do that too." She started to back out of the tent, but Kwineechka caught her by the arm.

"Don't go."

"I ain't leaving the village yet. I'll stay for a little while longer anyway."

"Don't go now," he clarified, the desperation in his voice startling her.

"I...uh, reckon I could sit with you for a little while," she said.

She had been planning to go back outside and find out if Jongren had managed to speak to Okahoki. The faster the People could get away from Aoifa, the better, especially now that she knew the priestess's magic still had a hold on Kwineechka. But as she looked down at storyteller, she realized she didn't mind staying with him. Not at all.

She settled herself close to him, wrapping her arms awkwardly around her knees. "Aoifa ain't...bothering you right now, is she?" she asked tentatively.

The storyteller shook his head.

"Thank Dess I don't need to have a hand on you at all times," she said, laughing nervously. In truth she was a little disappointed not to have the excuse. She wondered again what was happening, why her presence seemed to counteract Aoifa's spell. She wondered if the storyteller minded having her near, but there was no chance to ask him because he had already fallen into an exhausted sleep.

CHAPTER FORTY-TWO

Kwineechka

"Wake up! The People are fighting."

Kwineechka came awake at the sound of Peyewik's voice. The boy was kneeling in the entrance to the tent. Another figure lay nearby, wrapped in a sleeping skin. The figure stirred and sat up.

"What's happening?" Trib mumbled sleepily.

Kwineechka was surprised to see her, unable to remember how they had come to be sleeping in a tent together.

"How long have I been asleep?" he asked Peyewik, hoping his disconcertion didn't show. He wondered how many of the People knew they had been in the tent together.

"Only a few hours," Peyewik told him. "It is just past midday."

"Why are the People fighting?"

"Come," Peyewik said. "Your mother will explain."

He backed out of the tent. Kwineechka started to follow him, but stopped to look at Trib, who was still bleary-eyed and disoriented.

"The People will not understand this," he said.

"What, that we slept together? We've slept together lots of times…"

"That was different. We were travelling," Kwineechka said, and gestured vaguely at the tent.

"Except it ain't," Trib said, waking up more. "It doesn't mean anything. You asked me to stay for awhile and I fell asleep. That's all."

Kwineechka noticed that she was blushing and couldn't look him in the eye.

He sighed and crawled out of the tent, followed awkwardly by Trib. He knew she was right, that it didn't mean anything. But the People loved to gossip. And he couldn't tell them the truth—that he had asked Trib to stay with him because she quieted the voice of Crow Woman in his head. He cringed at the thought of what his mother was going to say.

But Shikiwe's attention wasn't on her son's sleeping habits. Kwineechka found her standing in the center of the village, surrounded by provisions. Chief Mikwin stood beside her, but it was clear that she was the one in charge. The Away People were losing no time in their preparations to depart.

"Looks like trouble," Trib said, nodding at a group of Original People approaching the chief.

"We've come to ask for our share of the food stores you have gathered here," one of them said.

"No." Shikiwe surprised everyone by speaking for the chief. "That food belongs to the People. If you choose Snakebrother's path and stay to fight, you are no longer of the People."

"What are they saying?" Trib asked, but Kiwneechka didn't have time to translate.

"How can you say this of your own sister?" Kwineechka's aunt, Nichan, stepped forward. She caught his eye and smiled at him before turning to her sister. Kwineechka had always liked his Auntie Nichan. She was a kind woman who had married a man of the Original People and had lived among them for many years. Her home had been destroyed by the Pure Men.

"You will starve your own sister, your own nieces and nephews?" Nichan asked.

Nothing could have prepared Kwineechka for his mother's reply.

"Yes," she said quietly. "Better they starve to death than give in to Snakebrother as their mother has."

Nichan looked as though she had been slapped. Kwineechka saw pain in Shikiwe's eyes, but she didn't waver.

"Mother!" Kwineechka moved to stand beside her. "You don't mean that."

Shikiwe whirled on him. "This is your fault!" she said. "This would not be happening if you would tell the right story so that the Original People would know what they are doing is wrong. Instead you turn your back on them and run off with this...demon."

She glared at Trib, who responded by yawning hugely and then giving his mother a benign smile.

"What in Dess's Name is wrong with your ma?" she asked, looking at Shikiwe with mild curiosity. "Reckon she don't like me much."

Kwineechka's mother was known among the Away People as a woman to be reckoned with, but he realized that compared to Crow Woman and Bear Woman, Trib wasn't likely to be intimidated by her. He, on the other hand, was shamed by her words and said nothing to defend himself.

"You have no right to deny us," a man of the Original People said angrily.

"She does not, but I do," Chief Mikwin spoke up at last.

"You are not our chief," the man replied, stepping forward aggressively.

Kwineechka felt Trib nudge his shoulder, drawing his attention to a number of Away People gathering quietly behind Shikiwe and their chief.

The Original People and the Away People were squaring off.

Kwineechka heard the faint echo of Crow Woman's song, though it didn't grow any louder, presumably due to Trib's proximity.

"Stop this now!"

Chief Okahoki forced his way through the angry crowd and went to stand beside Chief Mikwin.

"My brother," he said to Mikwin. "I am sorry." He turned to the Original People. "If you wish to stay with me, then I am still your chief, and I say all the food supplies will be given to those who are leaving."

His voice was strong and decisive. The Original People looked dismayed, but no one argued with him.

"This is more of Snakebrother's work," he continued. "The People cannot fight among themselves like this. I ask you again to go with the Away People. If you stay with me, we have no chance of winning against Crow Woman and her Fighting Women. We will die."

"We are ready to die with our chief, in the land of our fathers," one of the Original People said, followed by sounds of agreement from the rest.

"What if we had Flame Hair's fighting magic?"

Kwineechka was instantly sickened by the idea, and surprised when it was Kinteka who stepped forward to continue addressing the chief.

"We would have a chance against the Fighting Women then, wouldn't we?" she asked.

"How can you ask this?" Shikiwe cried.

Kinteka ignored Shikiwe but turned to Kwineechka. "Ask her," she said. "Ask Flame Hair if she could teach us to fight as she does."

"Why is everyone looking at me?" Trib muttered.

Kwineecha hesitated, feeling nauseous.

"Tell me," Trib said, so he did.

Kwineechka realized his heart was pounding as he waited for her reply, as if it were suddenly the most important thing in the world. When Trib looked as sickened by the idea as he felt, he had a sudden urge to put his arms around her and kiss her.

"No," she said. "I couldn't even if I wanted to, which I don't. Only a priestess can do Rage initiations."

Kwineechka felt weak with relief. He saw his feelings echoed in Chief Okahoki's face, quickly replaced by sadness when one of the Original People said, "We will stay anyway. We will not abandon our chief or the land of our fathers."

Okahoki nodded resignedly. "Very well," he said. "But there will be no more talk of the Fighting Women's magic. Now, we must leave the Away People in peace to continue preparing for their journey."

CHAPTER FORTY-THREE

Trib

Trib spent the rest of the day close to Kwineechka, keeping a wary eye on the tension between the Away People and the Original People, and enduring disapproving looks from everyone. Many had seen her disappearing into the tent with Kwineechka earlier in the day.

"There's one thing the Away People and the Original People still agree on," she said when, at supper, an old woman refused to serve Trib from the communal pot. "You and me shouldn't be together."

"We are not together," Kwineechka said uncomfortably, handing her his bowl of stew. "They think I stay close to you because I want you, but they do not understand."

"Then explain it to them," Trib said shortly, stung by his words. Some part of her still hoped that more than necessity kept him near her, even though she knew it could never be.

"I cannot," Kwineechka said, the look of shame on his face triggering a rush of guilt in Trib.

"It ain't your fault!" she said. "It's Aoifa's. She's the one that should be ashamed, not you."

The storyteller didn't reply.

"Do you understand why she can't bother you when I'm around?" Trib asked.

The storyteller looked like he wanted to say something but then shook his head.

"You know I can't stay beside you all the time," she pointed out. "Eventually you're going to want to do things on your own. Like spend time with some of those women I see making eyes at you all the time."

She gave a rough laugh, but the storyteller didn't smile. He looked at her nervously. "Maybe once we leave with the Away People, she will lose her hold over me," he said. "The ancestors and the stories will come back to me, and I will not need you anymore. "

"By Dess, I hope so," Trib muttered.

"But you will stay with me until then?" he asked, his golden eyes anxious. "Until we are far away from her, and I am free?"

Trib looked away without answering. She watched the People eating their last meal together. She saw the begrudging looks that passed between those who were leaving and those who would stay to fight, and felt oddly torn.

"Yes," she said at last. "I'll stay with you. But we best sleep in the forest tonight. Reckon your ma will murder me in my sleep if she sees me going into your tent again."

⚙

Later, as they lay wrapped in their sleeping skins among the trees, Trib said. "It's just like old times, except you and I ain't trying to kill each other."

Kwineechka laughed, but the sound was cut short, as though he didn't have the heart for it. Trib suddenly missed the days of their journey, before they had arrived at the fort, when his mocking laughter had driven her crazy.

"We ain't trying to kill each other," she said softly as Kwineechka shifted uneasily nearby. "But everyone else is."

Eventually the storyteller fell into a restive sleep. Trib tried to follow suit, but she couldn't slow the thoughts racing through her mind. After a time, she got up and headed back towards the village, skirting the perimeter until she arrived at the little house set near the edge where Kinteka lived. She hesitated at the doorflap, not wanting to wake anyone, but she saw the glow of firelight and heard voices and was about to push her way in when someone spoke her name out of the darkness.

"Who's there?" she said in a loud whisper, reaching for her sword.

Jongren stepped towards her from the shadows.

"What are you doing here?" she asked suspiciously. He was the last person she wanted to see before doing what she was about to do.

"I'm glad to find you here," he said. "I need to speak to you about the storyteller."

"What about him?"

"Your..." Jongren cleared his throat, "relationship with him."

"You remember what I said about not interfering?" Trib growled.

"I do," he replied. "I just want you to understand that the People have different customs when it comes to a man and a woman..."

"It ain't like that," Trib interrupted impatiently.

"Then what is it?" he asked.

"It ain't your business," she said and turned to push her way into Kinteka's house.

Inside, she found Kinteka, Peyewik, and Morrigan all facing the door expectantly. Kinteka sat beside Morrigan on the sleeping platform, holding a bowl of broth. Peyewik sat on the floor nearby.

"You're awake," Trib said, suddenly nervous.

"We heard you and your father outside," Morrigan said, her voice barely more than a whisper through her cracked and swollen lips.

To Trib's annoyance, she heard Jongren entering the house behind her.

"I apologize if we disturbed you," he said. "I wanted to look in on you and came across Trib doing the same."

"How are you?" Trib asked, though she could see clearly that the priestess was a mess. She was alive but not well, and it was Trib's fault.

As if she had read her thoughts, Morrigan said, "It is not your fault, Tribulation. With Peywik and Kinteka's help I will mend."

Trib turned her attention to Peyewik, who smiled up at her. In all the excitement she had seen very little of him since her return from seeing the Scath.

"You've become fast friends," she observed.

Peyewik said something that made Morrigan smile, though with all the damage to her face it was more of a grimace. "He says we are kindred spirits," she explained.

"How is it that you understand the boy?" Jongren asked, a hint of wariness in his voice. Trib, who had gotten used to Peyewik's uncanny ability to communicate and understand without words, hadn't even noticed.

"I can feel what other people are feeling," Morrigan replied gently. "If they are close enough and open enough, I can understand what they are trying to say even if I don't know the language."

"It is some priestess trick?" Jongren asked.

"Aoifa tried to claim it was, just as she tried to claim the Rage was a gift from the Goddess that could only be used against our enemies. It was why she took me on as her apprentice in the first place. But the answer is no, it is not a trick. I was born with this ability."

Unsettled by this new information and the unexpected presence of Jongren, Trib found that she was having trouble focusing on the reason she had sought Morrigan out.

"You have something to ask me," Morrigan said, making the hair on the back of Trib's neck stand up. "Or would you prefer to speak to Kinteka first?"

"Aye," Trib replied nervously. She glanced at Jongren but looked away again quickly. "Since you're here," she said to him, looking at the floor. "Ask Kinteka for me why she asked for the Rage earlier."

At first Jongren was silent, and Trib was afraid of what he might be thinking. But then he spoke in the Native language, and Kinteka answered.

"The Puritanics killed her sister when they attacked the village of the Original People," he translated. "She was there visiting an aunt."

Trib remembered the beautiful beadwork on the dress Kinteka had lent her the night before the Prayer Ceremony and felt her heart sink.

"Kinteka thinks that if her sister had known how to use the Rage as you do, she would not have been killed."

Trib nodded slowly, her heart pounding.

"And your question for me," Morrigan prompted.

"Can you do Rage Initiations for the People?" Trib asked quickly, before the thought of what Jongren would say could dissuade her.

Morrigan replied with the same straight forwardness. "Yes. As Aoifa's apprentice I was taught how to instigate a Rage in someone and train them to access it at will."

"How long would it take?"

"It depends on how many wish to use it," Morrigan replied. "A few hours for each person. Peyewik has told me how much the Original People have been through already. I can feel their suffering, which sadly, will allow the Rage to come to them easily. But someone would have to teach them how to use it in battle, how to fight."

Trib nodded. She had already thought of that.

"Tribulation, you cannot..." Jongren's voice wavered.

"I have no choice," she said.

"You have a choice! You said you did not want to ever use the Rage again. Why inflict this horror on the People, who have only ever raised their voices in song and prayer?"

"I don't want this!" Trib said, whirling on Jongren. "I liked it when you said I could learn to sing instead of summoning a Rage. I liked it when Peyewik told me I was a friend, and Kwineechka told me I might find a new place here with...the People. I want that, not this, not more raging and fighting. But I have no choice. If the People want to fight for their home, I owe it to them to help in any way I can."

"You feel this way because you love them," Jongren said. "Can't you understand? It is all the more reason not to do this to them. This is why your mother refused the Rage. Because she believed in love such as you are feeling, not Aoifa's vengeful, Raging Goddess."

"Look at what that love did to her, to my family," Trib said. "They're dead because she wouldn't fight."

Jongren looked away from her, and she knew she had hurt him again, though this time she hadn't been trying.

"I ain't going to let that happen again," she said quietly.

"Does Kwineechka want you to do this?" Jongren asked. "You deny your relationship with him, but I have seen how you care for him since the first time I saw you with him. Instead of stories you would have him use his voice to summon a Rage that threatens his very soul?"

She tried not to think about Kwineechka, about how he had suffered when a Rage started coming to her, and how she had said she would stay with him until Aoifa's voice no longer bothered him.

"He'll go with the Away People," she said. "Far from here and beyond Aoifa's reach. He won't need me anymore, and he'll never have to summon a Rage."

"But the others? And yourself? It will destroy you. It will make you like Aoifa and the Scath."

"The Rage has already done its damage to me. I'm willing to sacrifice what's left of my damaged soul to help the People. They will only have to use it once, to defeat Aoifa. It won't destroy them the way it has me. If you're so against it, you should go with the Away People, run away like you did before..."

Jongren recoiled as if she had hit him. "This is wrong, and I pray you don't do it. But I would rather die than ever leave you again. If you are staying here to fight, so am I."

Trib was struck dumb by this. Even when she found her voice, she could not speak to Jongren. She turned to Peyewik instead.

"You think this is wrong?" she asked, not bothering to ask for a translation. "You think I shouldn't teach the People the Rage?"

Peyewik glanced at Kinteka and Morrigan, both victims of different kinds of rage. Then he looked back at Trib and spoke.

"Only you and Manito know the truth that is in your heart," Morrigan translated. "You must listen to that truth. I cannot tell you what to do."

"Dess damn it, I don't even know what that means," Trib said. "What about you?" she asked the priestess. "I can't do this without you."

"Peyewik speaks the truth," Morrigan replied. "Only you and the Goddess know what is in your heart, and you must listen to that, nothing else. If your heart tells you to do this, I will help you."

CHAPTER FORTY-FOUR

Kwineechka

Kwineechka came awake with the feeling of cold fingers trailing on his skin. It was still night and he was alone. Crow Woman wasn't there. But neither was Trib. The sleeping skin beside him was empty. She had left him alone, and Crow Woman had come for him in his dreams.

Then he heard footsteps and saw a dark shape emerging from the shadows, moving towards him.

"Where have you been?" he said, sitting up suddenly.

Trib jumped, her long knife flashing in the moonlight.

"Kwineechka," she exhaled, "don't scare me like that."

She lowered the weapon and went to kneel beside him. He could see her hair, dark and loose on her shoulders. He touched it and felt the dampness. The fabric of her shirt was also soaked through.

"You have been bathing?" he asked, surprised.

"Aye," Trib replied. "Someone got me into the habit."

"It is nighttime," he said. "And it is cold." He pulled a sleeping skin across her wet shoulders.

"Well, I can't do it during the day with you always at my side, can I? Unless you want to see more of me than you bargained for. What would your ma think of that?" She laughed softly.

The cold touch on Kwineechka's skin and the echo of Crow Woman's song had left him as soon as Trib appeared. As he listened to her laugh, he felt a sudden urge to reach out and touch her face, to feel the heat that would rush into her cheeks when he did so. He had thought it the strangest thing when he first saw it, the way her face would suddenly turn red. He had thought she was ill. Now he understood that it meant she was feeling something like shame or anger or excitement.

He didn't touch her. Instead he said, "You must marry me."

Trib laughed again.

"Why would I do a damn fool thing like that?"

"My mother...the People...they would understand if we were married."

"They would understand that you're marrying a pale-skinned, fire-haired monster like me because I'm the only thing that keeps an even greater monster from stealing your sanity and soul?" she asked.

"We are leaving tomorrow," he said. "A journey with many people. It will be hard for us to..." He gestured between their bodies and towards the pile of sleeping skins.

"You mean, if we were to marry, you'd be allowed to come with me while I bathe?" Trib said. Her tone was teasing, but Kwineechka heard a hint of anxiety behind it.

"Would you expect to do more than just bathe and sleep?" she asked.

Kwineechka lowered his head. He had not been thinking of that, only of the relief she gave him from the torment of Crow Woman.

"You heard her," Trib realized. "Just now, while I was away."

"Yes."

She took hold of his hand, her grip warm and strong.

"I'm sorry I left you," she said. "And I'm sorry I let Aoifa do this to you." Her voice shook slightly. "I told you you'd always have a place with me. And you do. I'll do whatever it takes to keep you safe."

"You will marry me?" he asked.

"If it will help you sleep better to hear me say it, then yes, I will marry you. Though I doubt it will keep your aunties from having fits over us."

Kwineechka stared at her through the darkness, remembering when she had seemed to him like the pale-skinned, fire-haired monster she described. She didn't seem like that anymore, and it wasn't just because she could silence Crow Woman. She had changed. She had become something he wanted to be near, like a warm fire that kept the chill at bay. She was no longer the person she had been, and he believed her when she said she would stay with him and protect him.

He nodded, reassured.

"You can go to sleep now," she said. "I ain't going anywhere. She won't bother you again tonight."

Kwineechka lay down. Trib did not lie down with him, but kept one hand on his shoulder and the other on her long knife. He drifted back to sleep with her keeping watch over him and his nightmares at bay.

He was awakened by a flutter of black feathers and a whisper of Crow Woman's song. He opened his eyes, reaching for Trib. But there was no one. Just the forest, empty in the morning light. She was gone.

The flutter of feathers grew stronger, until it beat inside his head and his throat, threatening to choke him. Crow Woman's song grew louder, and he began to hear words.

Trying to ignore them, he rose shakily to his feet, telling himself that Trib couldn't be far, that she would come back soon. She had promised. He stumbled towards the village, expecting to see her at any moment. He found everything in chaos as the Away People said their farewells to the Original People. The men of both villages hung back, stony-eyed, still angry after the conflict over food, but there were tears and embraces among the women.

He searched the crowd desperately, locating Trib near the cooking fires. She was speaking intently with her father, and he felt a surge of relief. That was why she had left him, to speak to her father. Surely she would come back to him now. Just then she turned towards him, and her eyes were hard, her body tense. Her features softened when she saw him, but it was too late. He knew what was happening. She was getting ready to fight.

"Why?" was all he could say.

"I told you I would do whatever I could to keep you safe from Aoifa," she said.

"You said you would marry me."

She shook her head. "You only want to marry me so the People won't think badly of you. But if you go away from here, away from Aoifa, she'll lose power over you. You won't need me."

"I need you now," he said. His voice sounded distant in his own ears, muffled by Crow Woman's feathers. The words of her song were growing louder. Soon he would no longer be able to ignore their meaning.

"I have to stay and teach Okahoki and the Original People how to fight," she said.

"You cannot." Kwineechka looked to Jongren for agreement, knowing he wouldn't want his daughter to do this. Jongren kept his eyes fixed on the ground and said nothing.

Kwineechka felt someone touching his face and realized he had closed his eyes. He opened them, expecting again to see Crow Woman. Trib stood before him, but her hands were cold like stone and Crow Woman's voice was louder than ever.

"Do not touch me." Kwineechka staggered backwards.

He saw pain in Trib's eyes as she tried to reach him again, and he liked it. He was overcome with a desire to cause her more pain. Before he knew what he was doing, he clenched his fist and struck her with all his strength. Once, then again. He felt the ache in his hand, bruised against the bones of her face.

Trib was on the ground, blood trickling from her nose and mouth.

Without thinking, he lifted his foot to kick her.

"Enough of this, my son."

Kwineechka's mother's voice, soft and close to his ear, slipped in under Crow Woman's harsh song.

"Come away now," his mother said. "It is time to go."

As the People made their final farewells to friends and family, she led him by the hand to his place in line, right behind Chief Mikwin. He followed her blindly as the People left the place that had been their home and their ancestors' home since the Story of the People began. Crow Woman's song was loud and clear now, distorting that story into one of violence, fear, and abandonment. Kwineechka tried to look back once but could see nothing through the darkness of feathers that blocked his vision.

CHAPTER FORTY-FIVE

Trib

Twenty Natives and a dozen Puritanics eyed each other from opposite sides of a clearing. Trib, the Reverend, Jongren, and Okahoki stood between them, negotiating the coming conflict.

"Jongren and I have been training Okahoki's people in basic combat for four days," Trib said. "And Okahoki agrees with us that it's time to start practicing with actual bodies. That's where your men come in, Reverend."

"We will help where we may," the Reverend replied. "I have advised my men not to hurt the Natives."

Trib glanced at Okahoki and saw the fierce glint in his eye as he stared at the Reverend. He had agreed to the original alliance with the Pure Men in the hopes of preventing further bloodshed and conflict, but that had been before he decided to stay and fight Aoifa to the death. When Trib had told him that she would stay and show his people how to fight the New Murians, the first thing he had said was, "The men who destroyed my village will fight with us?"

"I ain't thrilled about it either," Trib had replied. The idea of fighting alongside her life-long enemies had been nearly inconceivable to her when Jongren reminded her of the alliance. But Jongren had been able to convince her of the logic of it.

"There's no arguing with the strategic benefits of it," Trib had told the chief. "Aoifa thinks you're still in conflict with the Puritanics.

It adds to the element of surprise, which is the main thing we have going for us. Plus the more people we got fighting on our side, the greater our chances of survival."

Okahoki had nodded at this and said no more. Most of those who had stayed behind to fight with him were Original People who had lost homes and loved ones to the Reverend's raids. They would do as their chief ordered, but as Trib watched the chief out of the corner of her eye, she realized she had no idea whether his goals had anything to do with survival.

"I can't guarantee Okahoki has advised his men the same way," Trib told the Reverend.

The Reverend laughed. "Surely you don't think four days of training could turn these primitives into a threat to my men who have been fighting for years?"

"No," Trib replied. "But burning their homes and killing their friends and family might."

Jongren stepped in before the Reverend could respond. "We should get started. Reverend, tell your men we'll begin practicing one-on-one with weapons and choose your first volunteer."

The Reverend went to talk to his men and Jongren said, "You're going to have to be civil to them or this could end badly before we even see a New Murian."

"I reckon not ripping their guts out like I've been trained my whole life to do is damned civil of me," Trib replied.

Jongren turned to face her fully, a troubled look on his face. "Tribulation, I know it has been hard for you since Kwineechka left. If your judgment is at all affected..."

"It ain't," Trib said forcefully. "That's over and done. I made my choice, and I'm going to see this through, even if it kills me. Which it most likely will. So there's no point thinking about anything else."

She was relieved when the Reverend returned, preventing Jongren from saying any more.

"This is Josiah," the Reverend introduced a short, dark-haired young man carrying a sword. "He'll fight first."

At a signal from Okahoki, one of the Natives came forward to meet the young man.

"You're mocking me," Josiah said, stiffening.

"Kinteka is one of our best fighters," Okahoki said through Jongren. "She will fight you."

"Josiah cannot fight a woman," the Reverend said. "It's beneath him."

"He fights women all the time," Trib pointed out. "That's why we're here, ain't it?"

"That's different. The New Murians have the Rage."

"Exactly," Trib replied. "Kinteka will be up against a much stronger opponent when she faces the New Murians. Best get her used to that from the beginning."

"It's on your head if she gets hurt," Josiah shrugged.

Trib stifled her anger over the man's arrogance and gave Kinteka a nod of encouragement. The round-faced young woman didn't look nervous at all, but Trib had to force herself to relax as Jongren called for the sparring to begin. Kinteka was turning out to be one of her best trainees, but Puritanics weren't to be trusted.

Kinteka raised her weapon, a stone-headed ax, and went for Josiah just as she'd been taught, managing to dodge the first defensive sweep of his blade. She didn't get close enough to land a blow, but Trib was pleased with her anyway.

Once Josiah realized that she wasn't completely unskilled, he put a little more effort into fighting her. He disarmed her and got an arm around her throat fairly quickly. He was in the middle of shouting his victory when Kinteka stepped back, shifted her weight, and threw Josiah off balance. He went down, and Kinteka pulled a knife from her boot and held it to his throat.

Trib was joined by the other Natives in cheering loudly and laughing as Nishingi and his brother did a victory dance in Kinteka's honor.

Kinteka was smiling as she stood and offered a hand to Josiah. When he refused sulkily, the Reverend surprised Trib by calling out, "Lose with grace, man! You were over-confident, and the girl was smart enough to use it against you. Give credit where credit is due."

At the end of the day, after the last sparring session, the Reverend turned to Okahoki and said, "Your men did well today. I apologize for underestimating them. I don't know how well they will stand up against the Rage, but you can at least rest assured that they are getting good training."

It took Trib a moment to realize that the Puritanic had paid her a compliment, and then she didn't know what to say to him.

"Er...be back here at first thing tomorrow. We've got a lot of work to do."

"Of course," the Reverend said and wished her a good night. He rounded up his men and headed back to the encampment they'd set up in the woods near the training field.

Watching them go, Trib saw Josiah throw a bitter look at Kinteka and resolved to keep an eye on him. Compliments or no, Puritanics still weren't to be trusted.

"Good thing they didn't set up camp too close to the village," she said to Jongren.

"To avoid awkwardness with Okahoki and the Original People?" Jongren asked. "I thought they did well together today, all things considered."

"Aye, that," Trib said. "Also because they stink." She wrinkled her nose at the pungent odor that lingered even after they had gone.

"The Reverend wasn't lying. Okahoki's men did well today," Jongren said.

"Nishingi and Nikismus could be good fighters if they stopped thinking of this as a game," Trib replied, watching the brothers laughing and joking as they headed back to the village.

"Goddess knows we need the laughter though."

"Aye," Trib agreed. "Thank you," she added.

"For what?"

"You think this is wrong, but you ain't said a word against it since...the others left. And you've been a help to me, translating for the People and running interference with the Puritanics."

"Wherever you go and whatever you do, I'm with you," Jongren replied. "But Trib, you know we're going to have to tell the Reverend about the Rage Initiations."

"I don't see what for. If he knows, he'll want his men initiated too."

"Would that be such a bad thing? We'll never be stronger than Aoifa, but as you pointed out, the one thing we have going for us is the element of surprise. Aoifa doesn't know Morrigan is still alive and therefore can have no notion of her teaching the Natives the Rage."

"Aye," Trib said. "Let the Reverend be surprised along with her."

"Tribulation," Jongren said slowly. "Aoifa would never expect the Puritanics to use her own greatest weapon against her."

Trib knew he was right, but the thought of it made her sick to her stomach.

"I can't allow it." It was hard enough knowing that the Natives would be using the Rage against her former comrades. She couldn't bear the thought of arming Puritanics with the one thing that had kept her people alive and free of their control for so many years.

"Very well," Jongren said. "But it will not go well when the Reverend discovers you've kept this from him."

CHAPTER FORTY-SIX

Kwineechka

Kwineechka hunched under his wet cloak and listened to the roar of the swollen river, wishing it could drown out the sound of Crow Woman's song in his head. It could not, and he had no choice but to listen to it, feeling it draining him of his will and all hope of ever escaping her.

Trib had justified her decision to stay behind and fight by saying that Crow Woman would lose her hold over him as the Away People moved farther away from her. But her song had only grown louder in the eight days since the Away People had left their home.

"I have crossed this river many times on hunts," Kwineechka heard one of the hunters say, his voice raised to be heard above the roar. "I have never seen it flooded like this."

"Can we cross?" Shikiwe asked.

Kwineechka's mother had asked him to accompany her and some of the hunters to assess the river while the rest of the People set up camp for the night.

"Not until the rain stops and the flood waters go down," the hunter replied.

It had been raining for three days straight. It was unseasonably cold as well. The People had continued to travel through the terrible weather, but now it appeared as though they could go no farther.

"When will that be?" Shikiwe asked.

244

"It depends on when the rain stops," the hunter replied. "We will have to wait at least two days beyond that before crossing."

"I will tell Chief Mikwin," Shikiwe said, reminding Kwineechka of all the responsibility she had taken on since the People had decided to leave the village. It was unusual for a woman to take on such a leadership role, but the chief seemed unable to manage without her.

"You will come with me," Shikiwe used the tone of authority she had adopted over the past few days. It bothered Kwineechka, but the People seemed to find it reassuring and were glad to follow her instructions when it came to setting up camp, distributing food stores, and dealing with the difficulties and discomforts of their journey.

Kwineechka tried to avoid her attention by following a few paces behind as she and the hunters returned to the camp, but she stopped and waited for him to catch up, letting the others go on ahead.

"You still cannot hear the ancestors?" she asked, taking hold of his arm. "It would do the People much good to hear a story."

Kwineechka shook his head. "I still cannot hear them."

Shikiwe looked as though she wanted to say more, but they had arrived at the chief's lean-to. She reported the state of the river, and the chief responded by waving vaguely and saying, "So be it."

Shikiwe stood for a moment, waiting for him to say more, but he just went back to smoking his pipe.

"Should we wait until the flooding goes down, or change our route?" she prompted him.

"I must be allowed to smoke my pipe in peace," Chief Mikwin replied.

"The People are cold and tired. They need to know what your plan is."

"I am your chief!" Mikwin declared. "And I am telling you to leave me in peace."

He stood up and left the lean-to, walking out into the rain with his pipe still in his mouth. One of the hunters tried to stop him, but the chief shook him off and headed into the woods.

"Chief Mikwin has never had to lead in times of real trouble," Shikiwe said, watching him go. She turned to the closest hunter. "Tell the People that we will stay in here until the flooding goes down. Can you hunt for food in this weather?"

The hunter shook his head and Shikiwe said, "Then I will begin rationing the stores we brought along."

The hunters left and Kwineechka tried to slip away with them, but Shikiwe stopped him.

"I know what is wrong with you."

Kwineechka suddenly felt ill at the thought that she might know what Crow Woman had done to him.

"It is Flame Hair," Shikiwe said. "She put a spell on you."

"It is not Flame Hair," Kwineechka said.

"You should not have spent some much time with her and among her people."

Kwineechka did not argue with this, but Shikiwe wasn't finished. "You have been foolish. You let yourself be drawn in by her spell. She made you think think you care for her."

Kwineechka shook his head, but Shikiwe didn't let him speak.

"Your foolishness has done the People great harm for we are now far from home without the guidance of the ancestors. We become more lost with each passing day, and it is your fault."

Crow Woman's song threatened to drown his mother out as Kwineechka was overwhelmed with shame.

"I know how to fix this," Shikiwe said then.

Kwineechka looked at her warily. "How?"

"Go to your tent and rest. I will come see you when I have finished with the rations and all the other work that needs to be done. I will tell you then."

Kwineechka made his way to his tent, aware along the way of the People watching him, blaming him for their bad luck because he had lost their connection to the wisdom and guidance of the ancestors. Even though his mother hadn't gotten it completely right, she was right about that part. It *was* his fault.

"How long since you have slept?" Kwineechka looked up to see Peyewik standing in front of him.

"When I sleep, I see Crow Woman, I am with her again. So I try not to sleep."

"Make a tea from these herbs and drink them tonight. They will help you sleep without dreams." Peyewik handed him a small pouch. "Remember what I told you. Only you can release the shadow that clings to your spirit."

"It is too late," Kwineechka said. "She took the story from me. I can never get it back. She will torture me forever, and I will never be able to tell another story."

"So long as you believe so, it is true."

"I am sorry, Little Brother. Thank you for the herbs, but you can't help me. No one can."

Kwineechka continued on to his tent, climbed inside and lay there until he heard someone approaching some time later.

"My son, come out and speak to me."

Reluctantly he crawled out into the damp evening and found that his mother was not alone.

"You remember Hinutet," Shikiwe introduced the young woman standing beside her. "You played together as children."

Not wishing to appear rude, Kwineechka gave the girl a weak smile and said, "I remember," though all he wanted was for both women to leave him alone.

After an awkward silence Hinutet said, "My mother is waiting for me. I should go. I am glad you are with us, Kwineechka. So long as the People have their Storyteller, they cannot forget who they are or where they came from. They can never be lost." She smiled and walked away.

Kwineechla was sickened by her words and looked up to see his mother watching him intently.

"Hinutet will make a very good wife," she said.

"For someone, yes..."

"*You* must marry her. She will cure you of the spell Flame Hair put on you. You will forget all about that fire-haired demon. You will remember your people and your place among them and the stories will come back to you."

Kwineechka opened his mouth to argue but was interrupted by a sudden scream. He looked towards the sound and saw Hinutet standing alone before the bedraggled form of a wolf.

There were more screams and cries as the People became aware of what was happening. The hunters tried to help her, but every time they got too close, the wolf snarled and snapped at the girl.

Then a small figure stepped between Hinutet and the wolf. It was Peyewik.

"He'll be killed!" Shikiwe gasped.

Kwineechka forgot to breathe as he watched.

Peyewik appeared perfectly at ease, his body relaxd as though he was speaking with an old friend. He made no sound, but after a time the wolf stopped growling and the fur on its neck no longer stood up. The wolf dipped its shaggy head once, turned, and padded away into the rain.

Shikiwe and a number of the women ran to Hinutet's side as she collapsed to the ground. The hunters followed after the wolf to make sure it wouldn't come back.

Ignoring everyone Kwineechka went straight to the boy. "All of these terrible things are happening because of me, because I have angered the ancestors."

"No," Peyewik replied. "The wolf came here because he was hungry. The river is swollen because it has been raining. Remember, I can talk to the spirits. I know none of this is because of you." He smiled impishly. "You aren't nearly that important."

Kwineechka shook his head, wishing he could believe the boy.

CHAPTER FORTY-SEVEN

Trib

Trib and Jongren stood in one of the abandoned houses of the Away People, studying an assortment of stone-headed hammers and axes that had been laid out on one of the sleeping platforms.

"It doesn't feel right sending them into battle without proper weapons," Trib said.

"The People have been using these tools to kill as well as build for a long time," Jongren pointed out.

"Aye, but I can still wish for a few blades, maybe a gun or two, to match the New Murian weaponry."

"The Reverend might have a few guns stashed away."

"Reckon he won't share them with us," Trib snorted.

"You misjudge the Reverend," Jongren replied. "He is not the antagonist…"

He was interrupted by someone shouting Trib's name.

"What now?" Trib said, pushing open the door flap to see what was happening.

The Reverend was storming across the village with a number of his men in tow.

"What was that you were saying about the Reverend?" Trib made a face at Jongren before stepping outside to meet the Puritanics.

One of them was bloody and leaning on a crutch. Trib recognized him as Josiah, the man Kinteka had beaten on the training field the day before.

"I didn't think Kinteka beat him that badly," Trib commented to Jongren, who had followed her outside. She crossed her arms and planted her feet as the Reverend came to a stop in front of her, spit flying out of his mouth as he yelled.

"What was your plan?!" he shouted. "To teach them all the Rage and then turn on us?"

"What in Dess's Name are you talking about?"

"You've been teaching the Natives the Rage behind my back!"

"I haven't."

"You lie!" the Reverend declared.

"No one has been taught the Rage," Trib said, speaking very slowly and carefully, trying to keep her temper in check until she better understood what was happening.

"Then what happened to my man?" The Reverend waved towards Josiah, who was leaning on his crutch and looking pathetic.

"Kinteka beat him in a fair fight yesterday," Trib replied. "You said so yourself."

"She used the Rage on me!" Josiah cried.

"That ain't possible!"

"I've seen the Rage before," he insisted. "She shrieked and attacked me with an ungodly strength."

"I saw her beat you on the practice field yesterday!" Trib said. "She didn't use the Rage!"

"Not on the practice field," Josiah replied. "This morning, in the woods."

"You're lying. Kinteka wouldn't do that. She couldn't!"

The Reverend took an angry step toward her, but Jongren intervened.

"Kinteka herself is coming. We should hear her version of events."

The Reverend surprised Trib by backing off and saying, "You are right, Jonathan. All sides of the story should be heard."

Kinteka wasn't alone. Morrigan walked with her, leaning on a staff that, as a result of Aoifa's beating, she would probably have to use for the rest of her life. Nishingi and Nikismus followed close behind. They drew near, and Trib saw an ugly bruise on Kinteka's face. Nishingi and Nikismus carried weapons and stared at Josiah. Trib had never seen them look so serious and intimidating. Nishingi started toward Josiah but stopped at a word from Kinteka.

"By Dess, what happened?"

"We would have come to you sooner," Morrigan said, "but her injuries needed tending."

"Tell us," Trib said through clenched teeth.

Kinteka spoke, and Jongren translated. "She went to sing her prayers and bathe early this morning. She was coming back when this man waylaid her." Kinteka pointed at Josiah.

"He made it clear he wanted to lie with her. She refused and tried to walk away. Then he tried to force her. She fought back, but he was stronger..."

"You did not mention this," the Reverend interrupted, speaking to Josiah. "Tell me this is a lie."

"It is true," Josiah said. "But..."

"You forced her?" the Reverend asked, his voice low and dangerous.

"I did not!"

"Only because she fought you off," Trib snarled, flickers of red showing in the corners of her vision. Suddenly all she could think of was Aoifa touching Kwineechka without permission.

"She used the Rage on me!" Josiah insisted.

"You lie to cover your deeds!" Trib shouted.

"No, Tribulation," Morrigan said quietly. "He speaks the truth. Kinteka used the Rage."

252

"You initiated her?" Trib asked, confused.

"I did not. Kinteka does not know how she did it either. She was very scared when the Puritanic attacked her. She thought of her sister, and suddenly her fear turned to anger. She said it felt like fire in her veins and she became strong enough to fight him off."

It sounded like the Rage to Trib. "But how?" she demanded.

"I believe the Rage can come to anyone under duress," Morrigan said, "though they cannot summon it at will unless they are initiated." She turned to the Reverend. "I swear by the Goddess that I did not teach anyone how to summon the Rage."

"Whether you did or not," the Reverend replied, "I see she did not use the power without good reason." He turned to Josiah with a dangerous glint in his eye.

"Aye," Trib agreed. "What do you have to say for yourself?"

"I don't need to defend myself to you," Josiah spat.

Before Trib knew what was happening, the Reverend had Josiah by the throat. "Then defend yourself to me and to your Lord!" He let go so Josiah could speak.

"She humiliated me yesterday," Josiah said in a pleading voice. "It wasn't right."

"But what you attempted to do to her was?" the Reverend asked.

"You told us these primitives were no more than animals!"

"I did not say they were animals. I said they were like animals in their awareness of God. Josiah, you know as well as any Puritanic here that rape is a sin."

"You preached that we are spiritually superior. It was not rape. I was teaching her a lesson, as her spiritual better..."

Jongren was translating for the Natives. When Nishingi understood what Josiah had just said, he gave a furious yell and dropped into a fighting stance. His brother followed suit. They were outnumbered three to one by the Puritanics, but they didn't seem to care.

Trib couldn't blame them. She was relishing the thought of helping them when the Reverend turned to Kinteka.

"It is my fault if my men did not understand my sermon," he said, a stricken look on his face. "It is true that in accordance with the Puritanic dogma I preached, that we were your spiritual betters, with a responsibility to bring you to our God with respect and care. But..." The Reverend's voice cracked with emotion. "Josiah's actions have proven that we are no one's betters. He has committed an abomination, and we are all responsible."

Trib's thoughts of revenge foundered in confusion. The Reverend's regret seemed genuine. Nishingi and Nakismus, however, remained unmoved. Nakismus raised his ax in challenge.

"Reverend Wilson," one of the Puritanics spoke up. "What Josiah did was wrong, and we're sorry for what happened to the girl, but we will fight back if we are attacked!"

Just then Okahoki arrived, carrying an ax. Behind him came many of the Original People, also carrying weapons. The same weapons Trib had been inventorying earlier. They moved to stand with Nishingi and Nikismus against the Puritanics. The tables had turned, and now it was the Reverend and his men who were outnumbered.

"Dess damn it!" Trib cried. "They're going to kill each other before Aoifa gets anywhere near them."

CHAPTER FORTY-EIGHT

Kwineechka

Kwineechka was sitting outside his tent, sharing breakfast with his mother and father, when two hunters entered the camp carrying a large, hide-wrapped bundle on their shoulders.

"The rain has stopped and already the hunters have found us more food," Shikiwe said. "Manito is smiling on us! Soon we will be able to continue on our way and leave Snakebrother far behind."

Kwineechka wasn't so confident. Although Peyewik's herbs had enabled him to sleep dreamlessly and awaken rested for the first time since leaving the village, Crow Woman's song had started again the moment he opened his eyes.

"It is not food," Kwineechka said as the hunters came towards Shikiwe, their faces grim.

"If that is not a deer, then what is it?" she asked as the hunters placed their burden on the ground before her.

Kwineechka's father, Nitis, knelt down and pulled away the wrappings to reveal the cold, gray face of Chief Mikwin.

Shikiwe cried out, drawing the attention of the People nearby.

"We left before dawn to hunt," one of the hunters said. "We were following the river when we found him."

"Manito is punishing us," Shikiwe said, and began to weep.

There was outcry of dismay from the People as they recognized their chief's body. Kwineechka was paralyzed by horror and the song

255

in his head. Then, suddenly, Crow Woman's voice stopped, replaced by the sound of a different song.

It was Peyewik, singing Chief Mikwin's spirit across the River of Death. Shikiwe joined him, her voice weak from crying, and eventually the rest of the People joined in as well.

⚌

Later in the day, after the songs had been sung and Chief Mikwin had been buried, Shikiwe found Kwineechka standing beside the river. He had gone there to escape the accusatory looks and whisperings of the People.

Shikiwe stood beside him, looking down into the angry waters. Though the rain had stopped, it was still flooded and dangerous. The People could not safely cross for another day or so.

"Some of the People are blaming you for all of this," she said. "First the bad weather and the river, then the wolf attack. Now our chief is dead, and we have had to bury him far from the land of our fathers. What will happen next?"

"I do not know..."

"Our hearts are breaking. We need a story to remind us of the trials the People have faced in the past and how we survived by keeping faith in Manito. Speak to us with the voices of our ancestors and reassure us that we are not lost and alone, that Manito is still with us."

"You know I cannot," Kwineechka said, close to tears.

"What I know is that ever since you were chosen as the Storyteller of the People, it has been a great burden to you."

"No. It was an honor."

"You were never comfortable with the ancestors taking over your voice and body."

Kwineechka wanted to tell her how much he had prayed to Manito to have the ancestors back, to hear them again instead of Crow Woman, but he couldn't say this to her.

"Marrying Hinutet will free you of Flame Hair and the Pale Ones once and for all. Then you will be able to tell stories again."

"I do not want to marry Hinutet," he said, remembering that he had already asked someone to be his wife. At the time it had seemed like a matter of convenience, so that the People would not think badly of him for spending so much time with Trib. Now he realized two things. That the People would've thought badly of him for spending time with her, married or not; and that it hadn't entirely been a matter of convenience. He had loved her before she betrayed him.

"It does not matter what you want," Shikiwe said harshly. "You have shamed yourself and the People by your involvement with Flame Hair and the Pale Ones. They are Snakebrother's creatures and you attached yourself to them. You became infatuated with Flame Hair, and this is why the ancestors have forsaken you. So you must marry Hinutet, to prove to them that you are free of the Pale Ones."

"It would not be right..."

"You must do this," Shikiwe interrupted him. "You must be able to tell the stories. If you are not the Storyteller of the People, you are nothing, and we do not need you."

She left him then, and Kwineechka stood where he was, knowing she was right. He was nothing if he wasn't the Storyteller of the People.

As he stared down into the water, he wondered if Chief Mikwin had chosen to be taken by the river because he no longer recognized himself or his place in the world, and so had chosen to leave it.

CHAPTER FORTY-NINE

Trib

"We cannot let them kill each other!" Jongren cried.

Trib stared helplessly as Okahoki and the Original People advanced on the Puritanics. The Puritanics raised their weapons in readiness. The Natives outnumbered the Puritanics, but the Puritanics were armed with swords, and Trib counted at least four pistols among them. The Natives carried only their stone tools. The Puritanics also had more extensive combat experience, though Trib could see the fury and grief in the People's faces. They were tired of being abused and ready to fight to the end. It would be a bloody confrontation.

Okahoki swung his ax into the air.

"In the name of God, stop!" someone cried, and all heads turned towards the Reverend as he pushed his way past his men to stand before Okahoki. He was carrying no weapons.

"You'll translate for me?" he asked Jongren quickly, then turned to Okahoki. "I beg you to hear what I have to say. Josiah has profaned his faith and shamed his brethren. He has committed an atrocity against this young woman and against your people. One of many, you must agree, that we have committed against you."

Okahoki stared at the Reverend without speaking. He had lowered his ax to shoulder height, but did not lower it the rest of the way.

"I do not deny this," the Reverend continued. "I stand before you, before my brethren, and before my God, to ask for forgiveness. I see now that those who are weak try to build themselves up by oppressing those with even less power. This is what Josiah did, and I see for the first time that this is what I have done. I begin to understand why the New Murians unleashed the Rage against us all those years ago. Kinteka had no choice today. What Josiah would have done to her, if she had not used it, is unthinkable. My atonement is this: I will send my men back to the north where we came from, never to harass you again. And I offer you my life in recompense. It is my ignorance and lack of understanding that led my men to abuse you."

There were distraught murmurs from the Puritanics.

Speaking through Jongren, Okahoki said, "What do your men think of this? Who is to say they will not ignore your orders and attack us again the first chance they get?"

"We follow the command of our reverend as the command of God," one of the Puritanics spoke up. "We do not believe God wishes us to harm others unnecessarily. We know one of our own has blasphemed."

The rest of the Puritanics, with the exception of Josiah, nodded or made sounds of agreement.

Okahoki replied, his gaze never leaving the Reverend's face.

"I do not want your life. I care only for my people, which is why I say this. You will live, and your men will stay. You will be our allies against the Fighting Women, as we originally planned."

The Reverend bowed his head. "We will fight and die for you if that is your wish."

"Your men agree?" Okahoki asked.

"Any who do not wish to stay and fight are free to go," the Reverend replied.

None of his men moved.

Finally, Okahoki lowered his weapon all the way.

"Praise God," the Reverend said. "I thank you for your mercy."

But Okahoki wasn't finished. "If one more of my people is hurt by a Puritanic, I will kill every last one of you myself."

The Reverend held out his hand. Okhoki switched his ax to his other hand and grasped the Reverend's forearm briefly.

"Thank the Goddess," Morrigan murmured.

"I got something to tell you," Trib said to the Reverend. "Morrigan is set to begin training the Natives in summoning the Rage today."

She waited, holding her breath, to see if this would shatter the tentative peace.

"So you did lie to me," the Reverend said.

"Actually, no. I just didn't tell you."

The Reverend nodded. "In light of what has transpired here today, I cannot blame you. It is a horrifying notion to think what some of us would have done with the Rage in our misguided states."

"So what do we do now?" Trib asked.

"Teach the Natives the Rage," the Reverend said. "We will fight beside them without it."

Trib was stunned.

"I turn Josiah over to you to punish as you see fit," the Reverend said to Okahoki.

"No!" Josiah threw himself at the Reverend's feet. "You can't give me to these barbarians! They will do ungodly things to me. "

"You are the barbarian," the Reverend said in a low voice. "It is your actions that are ungodly."

Josiah staggered to his feet and tried to run, but his injuries slowed him down.

"You continue to shame me," the Reverend said as two Puritanics caught Josiah by the arms and turned him over to Nishingi and Nikismus.

"What will Okahoki do with him?" Trib asked.

"He has asked Kinteka what Josiah's punishment should be," Jongren said. "Nishingi and Nikismus are offering suggestions on her behalf."

"I don't blame them," Trib replied, thinking once more of Crow Woman and Kwineechka.

"I would rather hear them telling jokes," Jongren replied. "They have finally found something they cannot laugh at."

CHAPTER FIFTY

Kwineechka

That night, as the People ate supper, Kwineechka watched Hinutet serve stew to her family. She was kind and gentle and smiled
often. She was graceful and gracious and also very pretty. His
mother had been right that she would make a very good wife. She
was the opposite of Trib, who was rude, angry, dirty, sodd-looking,
clumsy, and violent. She would have made the worst wife.

And yet she was the one Kwineechka had asked.

Kwineechka reminded himself that he had been desperate to keep
Crow Woman at bay. He still didn't understand why Trib's presence had
been able to do that, but it had been such a relief to him that he couldn't
imagine being parted from her. He told himself this was the only reason
he had been foolish enough to propose to her. True to her upbringing
among followers of Snakebrother, she had betrayed him, leaving him to
Crow Woman's violations without a second thought. It was her nature.

Later, as he fell asleep, his last thought before slipping into dreams
was to wonder if Hinutet was as beautiful a dancer as Trib had been.

He dreamed he was still locked in the windowless room with
Crow Woman. She laughed at him and taunted him. She told him
that escaping had been the dream and that he would never truly get
away from her. She had claimed his spirit for herself, and she would
never let go. She would have her way with him as many times as she
wanted and then she would have her way with the People...

262

Kwineechka woke, shivering in the darkness. He could not close his eyes again for fear that he would return to Crow Woman's room. When he heard the dawn birds start singing, he got up and went to the tent where Hinutet's family slept. He sat and waited until the sky began to lighten and he heard movement inside the tent. Hinutet's father emerged, on his way to relieve himself in the forest. He saw Kwineechka and stopped.

"Please send your daughter out to me," Kwineechka requested politely.

"Why?" her father asked, rubbing sleep from his eyes.

"I want to marry her. Today."

It was a great honor to be asked to marry the Storyteller of the People so Hinutet and her parents both agreed, unperturbed by the urgency of his request. In the absence of a chief, Muhkrentharne performed the marriage ceremony. Kwineechka felt immediately better, as though the ceremony had cleansed him of the past few months, and none of it had ever happened. Crow Woman's song was only the tiniest echo in the back of his mind, and he was sure that it would fade away completely soon.

Shikiwe was beside herself with joy.

"They were meant for each other since they were children!" she told everyone. Then she turned to Kwineechka. "Now you must celebrate your marriage by telling a story."

This time Kwineechka did not resist. He stood before the People and saw his new wife among them, smiling up at him. He returned her smile and then opened himself to the story, confident that the ancestors would come. And they did. He felt himself being filled with their presence and welcomed them, glad of their return. He opened his mouth to let them speak through him...

But something was wrong. Instead of returning to the past, to relive the ancestors experiences, Kwineechka found himself in Crow Woman's prison again, reliving her violation and the theft of the story. To his horror, he realized the People were there with him. He was not speaking with the voices of the ancestors, but with Crow Woman's voice, and she told everything that she had done to him and everything that she would do to the People once she found them. Kwineechka fought her with all his strength. He thought he heard Peyewik calling to him, trying to help. This time there was nothing the boy could do. Crow Woman couldn't be stopped until her version of the story was over. When it ended and Crow Woman's voice at last fell silent, Kwineechka opened his eyes and saw the People staring at him. He saw the disgust and betrayal in their faces and the shame was unbearable. He turned and ran from them.

He didn't know where he was going, but he felt drawn towards her. He realized he could finally be free of his suffering if he just turned himself over to her, let her do with him what she wanted. All other thoughts fell away, and Kwineechka heard only Crow Woman's voice as he ran on and on through the night.

CHAPTER FIFTY-ONE

Trib

Trib and Morrigan stood outside the makeshift house where the priestess conducted the Rage Initiations. It had been removed a fair distance from the village because of the disturbing sounds that sometimes arose during the process.

"The final initiation was completed last night," Morrigan reported. "Ten of the People chose to undergo them, including Kinteka and the brothers, Nishingi and Nikismus."

Trib's heart sank as she remembered how hard it had been to get the brothers to take anything seriously when she first met them. She hadn't seen them smile once since Kinteka had been attacked by the Puritanic.

"Okahoki?" she asked.

Morrigan shook her head and leaned against the side of the hut.

"You aren't well," Trib said. The priestess was pale and shakey. The circles under her eyes were so dark she looked as though she had been beaten again.

"Guiding people to relive their worst memories and then teaching them how to harness the destructive power of those memories takes a toll." Morrigan gave her a wan smile. "Most priestesses could not have done so many so fast. My ability to feel what others feel makes me very good at it. It was why Aoifa chose me as her apprentice."

Trib had never thought of the effect that Rage Initiations might have on the priestess who carried them out. Now she realized that Morrigan had suffered through the horrors of her intiates as though they were her own, and she had done it ten times over. Trib felt queasy.

"I'm sorry," she said quietly. "I didn't realize. You should have told me."

Morrigan shook her head. "After the first initiation she had me do, I knew for sure that something was wrong, that Aoifa no longer worshipped the same Goddess I did. She was exploiting people's pain, twisting it to her own ends."

"If the initiations are so wrong, why did you do them for the People?"

Morrigan was silent for a moment, her eyes closed. When she opened them she looked weary, as though she had aged ten years overnight.

"I have seen the worst memories and deepest pain of the Natives who wished to be initiated," Morrigan said. "All of it was caused by us."

"But it was the Puritanics who attacked..."

"Tribulation, why were the Puritanics here? Why do they live the way they live? Because the New Murians harry them endlessly, and they are forced to live lives of violence and distrust. We are equally responsible."

Trib suddenly saw how this was true. "We've drawn the People into it as well, to the point where they had no choice but to fight back or be destroyed. Kwineechka was right from the start. We brought Snakebrother to the People, and he is winning. What does the Goddess have to say about all this?"

"That there is more of the story to be told."

"Ain't that always true?" Trib asked. "The thing we never know is what's going to happen next."

Morrigan smiled. "Did you ever think you should have become a priestess instead of a warrior?"

Trib laughed. "No way in hell." After a pause she said, "You going to be all right?"

"I'll live long enough to see this battle happen," Morrigan replied, reminding Trib that she had known it was a losing cause from the beginning.

"How long do you think we have before Aoifa finds us?" she asked.

"Aoifa's anger is a force of nature," Morrigan replied. "I can feel it drawing near, like the approach of a storm."

"Do you think the People are ready?"

"I've given them the Rage, you've taught them how to use it. The rest is in the Goddess's hands."

A twig cracked nearby and Trib held up a hand, listening. There was another crack, and rustling.

"There's someone in the forest," Trib said, pulling her sword off her back.

"One of the People?"

Trib smiled grimly. "I wouldn't have been able to hear one of the People coming. She's found us..."

"Tribulation Sarahdaughter!" a voice cried out. "Turn around and fight, you honorless coward!"

Trib watched two New Murians emerge from the trees, swords drawn.

"Master Jezebel," she said. She recognized the other New Murian, a young apprentice, no more than 13 years old, but couldn't remember the girl's name.

"Traitor," Jezebel greeted her in return. "Both of you," she said, pointing her sword at Morrigan as well.

"Don't reckon you'd want to hear my side of the story?" Trib asked, slowly moving to stand in front of the priestess.

"You've betrayed Aoifa, the Scath, your fellow warriors, and all of New Murias," Jezebel said. "What more is there to tell?"

"You reckon I should hang, no questions asked?"

Jezebel shook her head. "No time for that. Aoifa'll be just as pleased if I bring her your head and tell her I caught you trying to teach those primitives the Rage. It won't help them, of course. The Goddess gave us the Rage, to use against our enemies. It won't work for them. I don't even know if it will work for you anymore, though I'm willing to find out."

"Jezebel, we ain't supposed to engage," the apprentice said nervously. "The Scath's orders were just to find the primitives' village and report back."

"We found the village," Jezebel replied without taking her eyes off Trib. "You know how? Because that pretty-eyed Native of yours told Aoifa all about it."

Trib felt the earth tilt beneath her feet. "What did you say?"

"Aye," Jezebel sneered. "Aoifa's been having her way with him for days now. He's told her everything she needs to know. Now summon your Rage, traitor. If you can."

The veil of red instantly started closing over Trib's eyes, but she shook her head to clear it away.

"I ain't going to fight you," she said through gritted teeth. She had no desire to hurt Jezebel. The person she wanted to kill was Aoifa, and she intended to try immediately.

Jezebel let out the blood curdling shriek of her Rage summons and threw herself at Trib. Trib heard a second Rage summons and assumed it was the apprentice. She managed to deflect Jezebel's first frenzied assault but knew she couldn't defend herself against two Rages without summoning her own.

Jezebel was tearing in for her second attack when she suddenly stopped and pitched forward. She landed face down and didn't move again. The back of her head was caved in. Kinteka stood over her, her face red, her eyes bulging. She held a bloody ax in her hand. It was her Rage summons Trib had heard.

Kinteka turned towards the young apprentice, who was now crying in fear. Too late Trib realized the girl hadn't even been Initiated yet. She couldn't summon a Rage to defend herself.

"Kinteka, stop!" Trib shouted, but it had no effect. The apprentice was cut down as she backed away from Kinteka, begging for her life.

"No!" Trib cried, starting towards the girl.

Morrigan stopped her. "Kinteka is still in the throes of her Rage!" Kinteka spun back towards Trib with her bloody ax raised. Trib watched her come, unwilling to summon her own Rage. All she could think of was what Morrigan had said about causing the Native's deepest pain. She wasn't in the least surprised that Kinteka was identifying her as the enemy.

Morrigan had begun to speak to Kinteka, her voice quiet and soothing, and so low Trib couldn't tell what language she was using. Kinteka lowered her weapon as the Rage drained out of her. Eventually the Rage left her completely, and she dropped to her knees, exhausted.

Morrigan knelt down beside her and put an arm around her shoulders.

"She'll need some time before she regains enough strength to walk back to the village," Trib said.

"I'll stay with her and see to the apprentice. You go now."

Trib looked surprised.

"Go," Morrigan said again. "Find your storyteller. I will tell everyone to get ready, that Aoifa is coming."

Trib didn't need to be told a third time. She turned and started running in the direction of the New Murian fort and Kwineechka.

CHAPTER FIFTY-TWO

Kwineechka

Kwineechka felt no pain. He felt no grief, he felt no shame, and he felt no hope.

"You are home now," Crow Woman sang and he knew she was telling the truth. "You belong here with me, nowhere else."

Crow Woman's song was all he had. He didn't want to hear anything else. He felt her hands on his body, but he didn't care. His body didn't matter to him anymore.

"You belong with me. You will never leave," Crow Woman sang.

Kwineechka tried to remember where he'd belonged before her, but it all felt meaningless.

"Tell me where your village is..."

He had no reason not to, so he told her. He told her where the village was and how many people remained in it. He told her that Trib was going to teach them to fight so that they could defend themselves against Crow Woman.

She laughed and kept singing.

After a time Kwineechka became aware of a noise that wasn't Crow Woman's voice. At first it was only a mild annoyance, and he waited for it to go away. The noise grew louder. It was another voice. He thought he recognized it.

"Ignore it," Crow Woman sang. "She means nothing to you. Think only of me."

Kwineechka started to obey, but then he felt someone touching his face.

"Kwineechka!" the familiar voice rang out. "Wake up!"

For a moment, Crow Woman's voice left him. Kwineechka's eyes came into focus, and he knew where he was. He was trapped in Crow Woman's prison again. And he knew the person standing in front of him.

"Trib!" he gasped.

Then her hands were torn away from his face.

"Do not listen to her," Crow Woman sang. "She is a bad dream, and I will not let her trouble you any longer. Stay with me. You have nowhere else to go, and no one else cares about you."

He felt the warm darkness closing around him. His sight failed. Trib's voice faded, and he didn't think of her again.

"Storyteller of the People."

It was a new voice, strong and clear.

"I used to go by that name," Kwineechka replied. "No longer."

He became vaguely aware of the sounds of struggle around him.

"You were chosen by the ancestors to be the Storyteller of the People. You cannot stop being the Storyteller until you die and even then your voice will remain part of every story told."

"I allowed the Story of the People to be taken from me," Kwineechka said. "I am not worthy of the title of Storyteller. I am nothing."

"No story can be taken from you."

"Who are you to know this?" he asked.

Suddenly his sight was fully restored to him, but instead of Crow Woman's prison, he saw a multitude of shadowy figures surrounding him. The voice spoke again, and he knew it was not one voice but many speaking as one.

"You know who we are."

Kwineechka knew, deep in his blood, bones, and being.

"You are the ancestors," he said.

He could still hear Crow Woman's song. It still pulled at him and filled him with a sense of hopelessness.

"Free yourself," the ancestors said.

"I cannot. She took the story. She controls it now. Me, the story, and the People. I am not strong enough to defeat her."

"You have the power of the Storyteller."

"But the stories are all yours. I only let you speak through me."

"That is not the power of the Storyteller. It does not belong to us. It is yours and has always been yours. Use it now."

"How?" Kwineechka cried.

"Release the past, release Crow Woman. She has no power over you except what you give her. Tell your own story. Tell the story of now. We will lend our strength and help you, but we cannot tell it for you."

"Kwineechka!"

He heard Trib's voice again. Then he opened his mouth and started singing a new story. A story in which he was free and Crow Woman had no power over him. A story in which the shame of what she had done to him was hers alone, not his. And a story in which he still belonged among the People as their Storyteller. The ancestors joined him, and Crow Woman's song died away completely.

Kwineechka brought his story to an end, and when all was silent once more he blinked his eyes and looked around. The ancestors were gone. He stood in Crow Woman's prison. Crow Woman was a crumpled heap on the floor. Trib, lost to her Rage, was overcoming the last of Crow Woman's guards.

"Trib," he said calmly, "you can stop fighting now."

She dropped to her knees as the Rage left her.

"We are leaving now," Kwineechka told her. He helped her to stand.

"There will be guards outside, more warriors," she said.

"They won't bother us," Kwineechka replied, the power of the story still echoing in his voice. He didn't know how long it would last, but he knew that for the moment it would go however he chose to tell it.

He heard Crow Woman's voice behind them, small and broken. There was no power in it even when she laughed and said, "Run now, but you told me where your village is. I will come for you."

"Let me kill her," Trib said, turning back. "Or we'll never be free."

Kwineechka held her tight. "We have always been free. She has no power over us."

Trib let him lead her out of Crow Woman's prison.

CHAPTER FIFTY-THREE

Trib

"How long do you think we have until she attacks the village?" Trib asked as she and Kwineechka moved away from the fortress under the cover of darkness.

"At least a day," he replied. "She is weakened after I broke her spell. We will have time to warn the People."

"What did you do back there?" she asked. "How did you break her siren?"

"I released the shadow that clung to my spirit," he said. "I stopped believing her story."

Trib couldn't see his face, but she heard the smile in his voice. She wanted to ask him more about it, but so many questions were crowding into her head, and she was exhausted after travelling all day to get to the fort and then using the Rage. She couldn't seem to organize her thoughts into coherent speech.

They walked in silence until the eastern sky began to lighten. Then a single thought floated to the surface of Trib's chaotic mind.

"I'm sorry," she said.

Kwineechka turned to look at her as he walked. His face was blurry in the faint light, but her heart skipped a beat at the sight of it. She realized how much she had missed him, so much that it caused her physical pain.

"Why are you sorry?"

"I promised to stay close to you. I promised I wouldn't let Aoifa touch you again."

She looked away, overwhelmed by regret at the thought of what he must have undergone as Aoifa's prisoner.

Kwineechka stopped walking and took hold of her arm so that she had to stop too.

"You could not protect me from her, and I should not have asked you to. Even if you stayed by my side forever, she still would have had power over me until I learned how to free myself."

Trib pulled away, instantly missing the warmth of his fingers on her arm. She continued walking. He fell in step beside her, easily, as if there was nowhere else he wanted to be.

"I betrayed you when I stayed to teach the People to fight," she said.

"I understand why you did this. You wanted to help the People."

"Yes, but I didn't want to hurt you. I..."

"You what?"

"Nothing," she said.

They continued walking as the morning progressed, sometimes in silence, sometimes talking of the things that had happened since they'd last seen each other. Trib told him about training the Original People and the Puritanics to fight together.

"I would not have believed it possible after what the Pure Men did to the village of the Original People," Kwineechka said.

"Aye, they nearly killed each other at first."

Kwineechka was quiet after she told him about the incident between Josiah and Kinteka, though he seemed impressed when she told him how the Reverend had responded.

"They are men after all, not just monsters."

"For now they are united against a common enemy," Trib said. "We can only hope this alliance holds until Aoifa attacks."

"And Kinteka? She is all right?"

"She seems well enough," Trib said, thinking of the deaths of the two New Murians the day before. "She took to both combat training and the Rage well. It's Nishingi who seems most upset."

Kwineechka smiled. "He has wanted to marry her since we were boys." His smile faded. "I think he will not get the chance now."

Trib knew this was true. Many would die in the coming battle.

She realized they were drawing close to the village of the Away People and knew she wouldn't have another chance to speak with him alone.

"I need to tell you something," she said, her heart suddenly pounding.

Kwineechka stopped and waited.

"I tried to put you out of my mind," she said slowly, keeping her eyes carefully on the ground. "I thought I would never see you again. But when Jezebel told me Aoifa had you..." Her voice trailed off and she kicked fiercely at a pinecone.

"I reckon I care for you like I've never cared for anything or anyone," she said finally. "Didn't know I was capable of such a thing, but it's the truth."

Kwineechka remained silent until she looked up at him.

"Say something," she said miserably. "Please."

He stared at her. The expression on his face was so unhappy that she turned away in humiliation, her heart sinking.

"Tribulation," he said and the next thing she knew she was in his arms. Her first instinct was to fight the embrace—she had never really been held before, except in situations where it wasn't a good thing. Some other instinct took over almost immediately, and she relaxed against him, wrapping her arms around his waist and resting her face against his chest, holding him as tightly as he held her. For a moment, it felt like the most natural thing in the world, like she had been waiting her whole life to find herself in this place. The only other time she had felt anything like this was when she was dancing—like everything fit, and she knew where she belonged.

Then he stepped back and she saw that he still looked unhappy.

"I am married," he said.

It was as though he had hit her again, the moment after impact before the pain set in.

"Oh," she said, moving a few steps away, trying to put distance between them before it started to hurt. "To who?" she asked vaguely.

"Hinutet of the Away People," he replied.

"Oh," she said again, feeling dizzy.

She leaned forward and put her hands on her knees. "Of course," she muttered. "I'm a fool..."

"You do not understand..." Kwineechka took a step towards her, but just then a terrible cry arose from the direction of the village.

Without another word, Trib straightened up and ran towards the sound, pulling her sword from her back as she went. Her mind was blank except for one horrifying thought—that Aoifa had arrived sooner than expected.

Aoifa had not arrived in the village of the Away People, but the scene that greeted Trib was almost as bad as if she had. She heard Kwineechka arrive behind her and then heard him retch at the sight of so much blood. For a moment Trib's mind was a confusion of destroyed bodies—her mother, her sisters, Cuss, Heresy, Morrigan...Then she returned to the present and identified the body on the ground as that of Josiah, the Puritanic who had attacked Kinteka.

Kinteka stood over him, soaked in his blood. To Trib's horror, as she looked at Kinteka, she realized the young woman was not in the thrall of a Rage. She had killed without it, just as Trib had killed the Puritanic boy.

"No," she moaned.

Kinteka sank to the ground, her face in her bloody hands. The People stood around her, silent and still, unable to make sense of the atrocity they had just witnessed.

No one knew what to do until Nishingi rushed forward and gathered Kinteka in his arms. He lifted her to her feet and led her away from the carnage. As he passed Trib she heard him saying something over and over again, crooning as if to a child.

"What is he saying?" she asked Kwineechka, her voice barely more than a whisper.

"He is saying she should have let him do it."

Okahoki stepped forward to stand beside the body. He spoke to the People who had gathered and then began to sing. Slowly, the Original People came out of their stupor and began to sing with him.

"They are singing his spirit across the River of Death," Trib said. "I recognize the song."

"Yes, and he has sent someone to get the leader of the Pure Men, so that they may bury him according to their custom."

Trib saw her father among the singing people and went to him. He put his arm around her shoulders, and she let him. She didn't know the words to the song so she stood and prayed to the Goddess or Manito or whoever would listen, and asked that the angry spirit of Josiah would not linger around Kinteka.

The Reverend came alone to gather Josiah. As he pulled the body away from the village on a litter of pine branches, Jongren spoke to him.

"Will your men seek recompense?"

The Reverend shook his head. "We knew he would end this way, though I had not expected the girl to do it with her own hands." He looked at Trib and nodded. "I will pray for her."

When the Reverend was gone, Trib said, "I need to see her."

Jongren walked with her to Kinteka's house. As Trib pushed through the door, she saw a blood-stained dress on the ground and stopped.

"What is it?" Jongren asked.

"The dress Kinteka embroidered. Her sister made one too, and she let me wear it to dance in. Before I turned her into a killer."

"Trib, don't..." Jongren started to say but Trib moved past him.

She found Kinteka asleep, wearing a clean robe. Morrigan sat beside her on the sleeping platform, washing blood out of her hair. Nishingi sat beside her on the ground, his knees pulled up to his chest. His brother stood near the door, his arms crossed, his face hard.

"You used the siren on her?" Trib asked, crossing the hut to stand beside the sleeping platform.

"To make her sleep," Morrigan replied.

"Can you use it to make her forget?" Trib asked hopefully, suddenly remembering what the Scath had told her about Aoifa using her spells to make her forget the day her family was murdered.

Morrigan shook her head. "She will remember."

As Trib stood looking down at Kinteka, she heard the singing continue outside.

"Josiah is gone," she turned to Jongren. "Why are they still singing?"

"They are singing for Kinteka now."

She thought of how she had felt after killing the Puritanic boy and knew that Kinteka now knew the same horror.

"And for all of us," Jongren added.

As Trib listened to the People's song, she realized that Josiah's death was only the first of many to come. She dropped down on one knee. "What have I done?" she whispered.

Someone knelt down beside her and she thought it was Jongren until she looked up and saw Kwineechka. She hadn't realized he was in the hut. He pulled her to her feet again. Jongren murmured something about getting some rest, and Trib remembered that she hadn't slept in two days. Jongren said he would find her later, and then Kwineechka was pulling her outside and leading her to another hut.

"This is my father's house," he said. "You can rest here."

Trib climbed onto the nearest platform covered with animal skins, curled up into a ball, and started sobbing like a child. Not long ago she had been ashamed to cry in front of the storyteller, to let him see her weakness, but now she had no choice. It felt as though grief was all that was left of her, and she could show him nothing else.

He sat down and put his arms around her.

"How can you stand to touch me," she said thickly. "I'm a monster."

"You are not."

"I've hurt so many people."

"If you were a monster, you would not care that you've hurt people. You would be like Crow Woman. But you are not."

"I'm Snakebrother, just like you said..."

"No, you are one of the strongest people I've ever known. And it is your heart that makes you strong, not your sword. This is not the work of Snakebrother."

He did not let go as she cried herself to sleep.

❊

When Trib woke again, she could see stars through the smoke hole in the roof. She sat up with a start. "Aoifa!" she said. "She's coming. We have to be ready."

"We are," Kwineechka replied, startling Trib with the nearness of his voice.

"Okahoki and the Reverend are good leaders. Crow Woman will be here at dawn, and the People are ready. All you can do now is sleep. Jongren will wake you in a few hours. You will need your strength for tomorrow."

He reached for her, and she jumped at his touch.

"You're married," she said.

"Yes," he replied. "But I love you. My wife is far away, with the Away People, and Crow Woman will be here at dawn. "

She let him pull her back down into the bed. In the weak light of the stars she looked into his golden eyes and said, "I understand now."

"What do you understand?"

"That you can't take anything that has a spirit. You can only share it."

"Yes," he said, and she felt the smile on his lips when he kissed her.

CHAPTER FIFTY-FOUR

Trib

Kwineechka was awakened by Jongren's voice calling from outside the hut.

"Tribulation, it is time."

"I'm coming," she called back softly and Kwineechka realized she was already awake and dressed, sitting on the edge of the sleeping platform he'd shared with her. He saw the glint of her long knife resting across her knees. She stood up and strapped it onto her back.

"I'm going with you," he said.

"No. Someone needs to lead the women, children, and elders to safety after we're…" Her voice trailed away and she had to take a deep breath before finishing. "…if Aoifa wins. You can take them to Jongren's cave."

"They will not go," Kwineechka replied. "The People have been divided too much already. They will not be separated from any more loved ones."

"They'll be killed. Or worse. Aoifa will spare no one."

"I know," Kwineechka said. "The People know."

"Please don't come with me. I've lost too many people I love. I couldn't stand to lose you again."

"I have to," he said. "I am the Storyteller of the People."

"But what if you're killed? Then there will be no Storyteller."

"If I am killed, another Storyteller will be born, and I will come to him as an ancestor and tell him how it happened, and it will be the Story of the People, not Crow Woman's story of fear and loss."

"Tribulation!" Jongren called again. "We have to go. Scouts are reporting that Aoifa is close."

Trib stepped away from him. "Aye, then, but stay close to me. I will protect you as long as I can. Now let's go. My father is waiting."

⁂

The sky was just beginning to lighten when Kwineechka found himself standing on sandy ground in the middle of a large clearing surrounded by thick pine trees. All around him were the Pure Men and the People who were waiting to fight Crow Woman. Behind them, hidden among the trees, were their families.

"Storyteller," Chief Okahoki extended his arm in greeting. "We are glad to have you with us on this last day."

Kwineechka took his arm. "I am glad to be with you," he replied.

"I miss our brothers and sisters of the Away People," Okahoki said. "But I will die easier knowing that they are safe somewhere, that some of the People will live on."

Kwineechka thought about his friends and family who were so far away now. He was glad to be home, even if he was about to die, but he would have liked to explain to them what had happened, and why he had run away. And he would've liked to say goodbye. He thought of Hinutet and felt sorry for making her a widow before she had the chance to be a real wife.

Kwineechka saw his childhood friends, Nishingi and Nikismus, among the fighters. Their once good-natured faces were hardened by grief and anger as they stared into the darkness of the trees, waiting for their enemy to appear. Kwineechka did not see Kinteka, but knew she would be nearby, staying close to her loved ones until the end.

A figure emerged on the far side of the field. Some of the waiting fighters twitched and raised their weapons, but Trib called out that it was just the Pure Man scout.

"The New Murians are coming!" he said breathlessly. "Not far behind. They are more than we expected, three times our number…"

"That ain't possible," Trib said. "She doesn't have that many warriors, even if she turned every apprentice she had into a warrior."

"It's not as though the odds were ever going to be in our favor," the Reverend pointed out.

"Aye," Trib agreed, "but it gives me a bad feeling."

After that no one spoke or moved as they waited for Crow Woman to arrive. Time seemed to stretch and slow. Kwineechka could hear his own breath, harsh and loud in his ears. Each inhale and exhale seemed to last a lifetime. And then he heard it, a distant rustling that grew until it sounded like a hoard of demons crashing through the underbrush towards the clearing.

The first of Crow Woman's fighters emerged from the trees.

"God damn her," the Reverend said, and Kwineechka heard murmurs of dismay from the other Pure Men.

Crow Woman's front line was made up of men carrying long-knives, their faces blank and staring.

"She used her spell-song on them?" he asked.

"Aye," Trib replied. "They're the brethren and kin of the Reverend and his men."

"Tribulation, we cannot fight them," the Reverend said.

"They'll do whatever she tells them. Hack you to pieces if she says so."

"We cannot," the Reverend said again, and Kwineechka heard the pain in his voice.

Trib heard it too. She nodded her understanding, but then said, "Do you expect the rest of us not to hurt them as well? Because I ain't going to ask the People to stand by while these manservants…Sorry, I mean these sirened men…attack them."

Kwineechka realized that the alliance between the People and the Pure Men was once again tenuous, at the worst possible moment.

"We will not kill them," Okahoki spoke up, and Jongren translated.

"If they attack you?" the Reverend asked.

"We will stop them, but we will not kill them."

"God bless you," the Reverend said. "I can ask for no more."

Just then Crow Woman stepped into the clearing, followed by the hulking figure of her sister, Bear Woman, and all of her Fighting Women. They were all armed with long-knives and some with guns. None of them seemed overly concerned about the coming battle. Some of them even laughed when they saw their opponents.

Crow Woman moved out in front of the sirened Pure Man and sneered as she surveyed the field.

"Is this all there is? A few mangy Puritanics and some primitives carrying sticks and stones?"

Her voice was hoarse and broken, and Kwineechka knew she was still weak from his defeat of her two days earlier. She looked aged and shrunken. He was no longer afraid of her, but her weakened appearance did not reassure him. She was like a wounded animal, made even more deadly by her pain, and she was still dangerous to the People.

It was Jongren who stepped forward to meet her.

"Aoifa, let these People go in peace."

Crow Woman stared at him coldly. "I remember you. You were Sarah's man, Tribulation's father. It is your fault they died, you know?"

Jongren flinched, and Kwineechka suddenly remembered the first time he'd met Jongren. He'd only been a child, and Jongren had been mad with grief over the deaths of his family. He remembered that some of the children of the People had been scared of him, but he had only felt sorry for how sad the strange man had been.

Some of this sadness returned as Jongren stood before Crow Woman, but there was no trace of the madness left in him.

"Sarah and my children died because you had your sister kill them," he said. "Please, let there be no more innocent blood spilled. Stop this now. Go back to your fort and leave the People in peace."

"I am not interested in peace and mercy," Crow Woman said, speaking loudly so that all could hear. "If they will not submit to the will of the Goddess, then they will suffer the consequences."

"It is not the will of the Goddess, Aoifa. It is your will and yours alone." Kwineechka turned to see Morrigan step forward.

"The traitor!" Crow Woman said. "Twice now I've thought you dead and had been deceived. But no matter. You won't escape a third time."

She laughed. "As for the rest of you, don't you know you are already beaten? Your storyteller told me everything, how half of your people fled in fear, leaving you to die here alone. You aren't even worthy opponents for my warriors. It's an insult to ask them to fight you. These untrained manservants will be able to take you by themselves."

She turned to her sister.

"Take the warriors back to the fort. I will order the manservants to fight. We will let them finish each other off."

"I reckon that ain't the best idea," Bear Woman replied. "The manservants would be outnumbered, and they don't have the Rage."

"Outnumbered?" Crow Woman said, taken aback. "There are only a handful of the primitives, and the Puritanics won't kill their own."

"Turn around," Bear Women growled.

Everyone turned then and found the Away People standing behind them. The Original People who had been hiding stepped out to join them and all at once the People were reunited.

Kwineechka saw his mother and ran to her.

"Where did you come from?" he asked. "How is this possible?"

Shikiwe put her arms around him and said, "My son, I am sorry. Forgive me."

"Then the warriors stay, and the primitives die together!" Crow Woman shouted.

"Mother, you must go back and hide!" Kwineechka said.

Shikiwe shook her head. "Peyewik told us what Crow Woman did to you, how she took the Story of the People. We realized how fear had been driving us further and further from our loved ones and ourselves. Peyewik told us it was time to come home, and we knew he was right. We have returned and the People will not be divided again, even if we are to die today."

"Summon your Rages!" Crow Woman cried then. "Kill them all!"

CHAPTER FIFTY-FIVE

Trib

Trib raised her sword and waited for the New Murian warriors to attack.

"Lower your weapons!" It was the Scath. She wasn't ordering her opponents to surrender, but commanding her own troops. The New Murians looked confused.

"Do not interfere, Sister!" Aoifa shrieked.

"I demand one-to-one combat," the Scath said.

Aoifa started to protest, but the Scath cut her off. "I've never asked ye for anything. I've carried out yer bidding even when it destroyed my honor. Grant me this now."

Aoifa narrowed her eyes at her sister. "State your terms."

"Me and Tribulation. We finish what was started years ago. No Rages."

Trib stepped forward.

"Trib, no!" Jongren cried.

Trib turned to him. "It's all right, Da," she said. She spoke the name naturally, without a thought, and knew she had said it before. She had called him "Da" when she was a child. She remembered suddenly, along with the scratchy feel of his beard on her face and the tobacco smell of his shirt. She turned to him and saw that he was crying.

"She's taken my entire family from me," he said. "I let her take you too."

"She won't, Da. I promise you."

She moved to stand before the Scath. "If I win?"

"Then I'm dead. And my sister promises to let the primitives go in peace."

"Never!" Aoifa hissed.

"YOU WILL DO THIS!" the Scath roared.

Aoifa looked coldly furious, but she said, "Very well."

"If I lose?" Trib asked.

"The battle continues. Most likely all yer people die."

"Most likely," Trib agreed. "Then I'll do my damnedest to make sure it doesn't come to that."

"Aye," the Scath nodded, drawing her sword. "I'd expect nothing less from a warrior of mine."

"I ain't yours anymore," Trib began circling her opponent warily.

"No, ye ain't," the Scath agreed, and launched her first attack.

The last time Trib had fought the Scath, the old warrior's experience and anger had dominated. Trib had survived only by her mercy. It was different this time. Trib had grown and taken on care and responsibility for others. There was no room for hesitation or self doubt. She put her entire being into the fight, and the Scath was too old and too slow to keep up.

Trib forced her into submission quickly, disarming her and forcing her to her knees.

"I ain't going to kill you," she said.

"Ye have to or my sister takes everything. Ye want to offer me mercy, fight me to the death. There's no honor left in this life. I can't stand what Aoifa and I have become. Do it as a last favor to the woman who raised ye."

Trib let the Scath stand and pick her sword. "Keep fighting," she said.

The Scath gave her one last nod of approval then put all her strength into a final strike. There was tremendous force behind it and, if it had found its mark, Trib knew she would've died instantly.

Instead, she dodged out of the way and slipped in behind the Scath's guard.

The Scath fell, a blood stain spreading across her chest.

Trib dropped her sword and knelt beside the old warrior, surprised to feel hot tears running down her face.

"I'm sorry," she said.

The Scath clutched at her arm. "Don't be. Ye did good."

Trib looked up at the New Murian warriors, all of them staring in shock at their dying leader.

"Don't just stand there!" Aoifa shrieked at them suddenly. "Kill them! Kill them all!"

"You promised!" Trib shouted.

"My sister just told you I have no honor," Aoifa sneered. "I only care about power. To have power, I must win. KILL THEM!" she ordered again.

The New Murians were still confused, but they began moving towards the Natives and Puritanics.

"STOP!" roared The Scath, staggering to her feet with Trib's help. "I am still the head warrior of New Murias, and this is my final order. Ye will not fight these people. They do not deserve our Rage."

"Traitor!" Aoifa screamed. "Don't listen to her. She's a dead woman. If these people were innocent, the Goddess would not allow you to use the Rage against them."

The Scath looked sad beyond measure at her sister's words. "Dess forgive us," she said. "Aye, I'm a dead woman," she continued, "but I tell ye the truth. The Rage can be used by anyone, against anyone. It ain't the Goddess giving ye permission to kill anyone who displeases ye. It's my sister taking advantage of ye and I've helped her do it for too long. It's time to become women of true honor. Never use the Rage against an innocent again. Never follow my sister's orders again."

"You can't disobey me!" Aoifa cried. "You are mine!"

She was wrong. The Scath collapsed to the ground then, but lived long enough to see her warriors obey her dying command. The New Murians lowered their weapons and stood still, uncertain of what to do next.

Trib looked down into the battle-scarred face of the woman who had killed her mother and sisters, and wept. Trib knew that they were more alike than different. The old warrior had done terrible things, but many of them had been out of love for her sister and the New Murians, to protect her family and her people. She hadn't known any other way to do this and her fate could easily have been Trib's own.

Then Trib realized that along with her grief was a growing sense of elation. The battle had been avoided after all. The People would not have to fight and die. She was looking around for Kwineechka when she heard it. The familiar sound of Aoifa's singing.

Her elation was instantly replaced with dread. Aoifa was using her siren on someone. She looked around to see who it was and realized with horror that Natives, Puritanics, and New Murians alike were raising their weapons against each other. Then she felt the siren taking hold of her own body and mind.

This time the siren was different from her past experiences of it. It wasn't soft and soothing, intended to quiet her into inaction. Instead, images and sensations came to her unbidden, of her mother and sisters' bodies, of her friends dying in the marsh, of Peyewik being drowned, of Kwineechka being molested, of Kinteka going mad...It was an unending barrage, and Trib felt the Rage rising in her like never before, a fury so hot and strong it threatened to destroy her from the inside unless she took action.

Without a thought, she stood up and raised her weapon. All around her, New Murians, Puritanics, and Natives were doing the same. A sickening realization swept over her. Everyone around her had hurt her at one time. She had no reason to spare any of them from her hatred and anger. Trib struggled against this impulse, and against Aoifa's siren, but it was too strong. She watched powerlessly from deep within herself as her body lunged for the nearest enemy. It happened to be a New Murain, and she heard the woman's responding shriek of fury. The last thing she knew before the Rage-siren took over completely was the feeling of hot blood splattered across her face.

CHAPTER FIFTY-SIX

Kwineechka

Kwineechka watched helplessly as Crow Woman's spell song overtook everyone. He was the only one who remained unaffected. He had finally managed to overcome her, only to be forced to watch as she made everyone he cared about fight to a bloody end. Every way he turned people were fighting. Fighting Women, Pure Men, the People, and the vacant eyed men Crow Woman had brought with her. Even the women, children, and elders of the People were fighting. It was a horrific scene, and Kwineechka was sorry that it was what he would carry with him across the River of Death. For it was only time before someone turned on him. He was sorry it was how they would all die, enthralled against their will by Crow Woman's anger and spite. He put his hands over his face, despairing.

"Storyteller."

Kwineechka looked around to see Peyewik and Morrigan standing with him. They had both managed to resist Crow Woman's spell as well. As he looked at them, he knew neither one of them had called to him.

"We must stop this," Peyewik said.

"But how?" Kwineechka asked hopelessly.

"Storyteller," he heard again and recognized the multitude of voices.

"Please!" he cried. "I do not know how to stop this."

"It is time, Storyteller," the ancestors said. "You learned how to take your story back from Crow Woman to save yourself. Now you must use this strength and power to save the People."

"It's not enough!" Kwineechka said. "She is feeding off the fear and anger of every person here. She is too powerful."

"Peyewik and Morrigan will help you."

"How?" he asked.

"I feel the rage and grief of every person here as if it were my own," Morrigan said. "I also feel their hope and their love. It's buried deep, but it's there. She can't take that from them."

Then Peyewik spoke. I feel the spirit animals of every person here," he said. "Even the men whose spirits have been trapped by Crow Woman. I can feel their longing to be free. They may look different and speak different languages and pray to different gods. But they each have a spirit, just like the trees and the animals and each other. You too know everyone here, Storyteller, but in a different way."

And Kwineechka realized it was true. He didn't feel their feelings, or sense their spirits, but he heard the stories of the People, the individual stories that joined together to become The Story of the People. More than that, he could hear the stories of the Pure Men and the Fighting Women. It didn't matter what language the story was being told in. He heard and understood them all. And he heard Crow Woman's song reaching deeply into everyone, summoning their worst hurts and fears, accessing the well of grief and anger surrounding every loss they'd ever experienced, and turning these into the main events of their lives. Their stories became about nothing but grief, violence, and revenge, unmitigated by love or compassion of any kind.

"You know what needs to be done. We will help you," the ancestors said.

"And we will help you too," Peyewik said.

Kwineechka was scared, but he knew what he had to do. He began to sing. He felt the ancestors join him, just as they had in the past, but this time they did not take over. Instead they sang with him, allowing his song and story to join and harmonize with all the stories of all the People who had gone before. Kwineechka felt himself transported to a new place, a place where the past and present coexisted. As he sang from this place he felt Peyewik join him. Or rather he heard Peyewik join him, the boy's voice adding a harmony that was the sound of summoning every spirit, all at once. The way he had summoned the thunder spirit, he now called to all spirits, and Kwineechka knew that he was also calling to Manito. Then a new voice joined them, adding a harmony that sounded and felt like nothing Kwineechka had ever experienced before. It was Morrigan, using her powers of empathy to connect deeper than Crow Woman's spell could go, diving beneath the anger and violence to the vulnerability of every living person present. She sang of their pain but instead of inciting them to violence, her song was about the underlying sadness and loss they all felt. Loss of friends, family, home, religion...Her song went deep enough that the differences disappeared. The differences between the Fighting Women and the Pure Men, and then, as she sang on, the differences between the People and the Pale Ones as well. For a while, Kwineechka could shift his attention and hear the songs and loves and griefs and joys of everyone on the battle field. Then he realized he could extend his awareness further...And then, suddenly, the harmonies matched and the song was huge and sublimely complete. It wasn't just a sound—it was a vibration that went beyond sensory perception and resonated with everything and Kwineechka lost himself to it entirely.

CHAPTER FIFTY-SEVEN

Trib

I t was pain that brought Trib back to herself. There was nothing but fire and blood, and then she became aware of the tiniest pulse of discomfort, somewhere in her body. She could still hear someone singing, but it was no longer Aoifa's voice. Her vision began to clear and she remembered where she was. She wondered if she had been wounded. She watched the people around her struggling against each other, heard them yelling and choking and crying. As she watched, she realized that the pain she felt didn't come from a physical wound. As the fear and fury of her friends and enemies washed over and through her, she realized the pain came from her heart.

The singing grew louder and she recognized Kwineechka's voice, gasping as she felt his pain just as clearly as she heard the notes of his song. Then his voice changed, became the voices of many, singing as one, and the pain became nearly unbearable. She felt the pain of everyone present as if it were her own.

The fighting around her began to die down, and she understood that everyone heard what she heard and felt what she felt. It was impossible to sustain Rage and violence in the presence of such sensations. It was as though she could hear the hearts and minds of every person on the battlefield. Her father, Peyewik, Kwineechka, the Reverend, Okahoki, and every other New Murian, Native, or Puritanic present. There were unique melodies, different words and images for each person, but the feelings and impulses beneath them all told the same story. Love, fear, and longing created a universal harmony that took Trib's breath away.

The song resolved into a single voice again. It was not Kwineechka, as she had expected, but she knew the voice. She had heard it before, in a dream where the Goddess had spoken to her and to Peyewik.

Then the song ended. The sound stopped, but she could feel the vibration of it still humming through her body. Everyone around her stood with looks of rapt and reverent attention on their faces. Weapons had fallen on the ground, Aoifa's siren to battle long forgotten.

Trib looked around, searching for the Storyteller. Instead she found Aoifa, sitting hunched and weeping over her sister's body.

Trib found herself walking towards the priestess, with no idea what she would do when she got to her.

"You should kill me for what I've done," Aoifa said as she drew close. Her eyes were red and swollen in her pale face. In breaking her final siren, Kwineechka had broken all of Aoifa's spells. She was no longer flawlessly beautiful, but looked as scarred and aged as her dead sister.

"I ain't going to kill you," Trib replied, surprising herself.

"My power is gone, but if you let me live I will try to get it back, and I will hurt more people."

"You don't have to do that."

"It has become my nature," Aoifa replied. "I no longer have a choice."

Trib thought again of the dream in which she had heard the Goddess speak.

"The choice is yours," the Goddess had said. "Love or fear. You decide."

Trib realized she had repeated the words out loud. When Aoifa did not respond, Trib left her to go in search of her father.

All over the battlefield people were slowly returning to themselves. Their expressions were a mixture of fatigue, confusion, and awe. Many were injured and needed help. She found Jongren talking to the Reverend.

"What happens next?" she asked them both. "You reckon this peace will hold?"

"It will on my account," the Reverend replied. "Now that Aoifa's siren has been broken once and for all, many of my brethren will be returning to their senses, some for the first time in many years. They will be wondering what happened, where their families are. My men and I will seek them out and offer assistance."

"I imagine the People will want nothing more than to rebuild their homes and go back to living in peace," Jongren said.

Trib's heart sank as she thought of Kinteka and the lasting effects the Rage might have on her. "Will they ever be able to go back?" she said.

"Manito knows," Jongren said sadly. "As for the New Murians..."

Trib looked around the battlefield at the warriors, milling about in a daze.

"They are used to following orders," Jongren pointed out. "They're lost without a leader."

Trib realized that New Murian warriors and civilians alike had lost their leaders. The Scath was dead and Aoifa was broken. The future of the settlement was nothing if not uncertain. Before she could think more about it, she saw Kwineechka walking towards her. His golden eyes still had the faraway look he got when he told stories, but they refocused as he looked at her. He was no longer lost in the story, just as she was no longer lost in her Rage. There were many things to do, many questions to answer, but all of it could wait. Trib smiled at Kwineechka and when he smiled back at her, it was the most beautiful thing she had ever seen. "Kwineechka!" a woman cried, stepping in front of him. She threw her arms around him and from the look he gave her over the woman's shoulder, Trib knew who she was. It was Hinutet, his wife.